WOUNDED

HEARTS

Margaret,
Happy reading!
Jayne Rylon

JAYNE RYLON

eBook ISBN: 978-1-941785-27-0
Print ISBN: 978-1-941785-73-7

Ebook Cover Art By Angela Waters
Print Book Cover Art By Jayne Rylon
Interior Print Book Design By Jayne Rylon

Sign Up For The Naughty News!
Contests, sneak peeks, appearance info, and more.
www.jaynerylon.com/newsletter

Shop
Autographed books, reading-themed apparel,
notebooks, totes, and more.
www.jaynerylon.com/shop

Contact Jayne
Email: contact@jaynerylon.com
Website: www.jaynerylon.com
Facebook: Facebook.com/JayneRylon
Twitter: @JayneRylon

OTHER BOOKS BY JAYNE RYLON

Touch of Amber
Long Time Coming

COMPASS BROTHERS
Northern Exposure
Southern Comfort
Eastern Ambitions
Western Ties

COMPASS GIRLS
Winter's Thaw
Hope Springs
Summer Fling
Falling Softly

PLAY DOCTOR
Dream Machine
Healing Touch

STANDALONES
4-Ever Theirs
Nice & Naughty
Where There's Smoke
Report For Booty

RACING FOR LOVE
Driven
Shifting Gears

RED LIGHT
Through My Window
Star

DEDICATION

For Machelle Walton—down an arm, no less of an amazing person. Your daughter rocks. ☺

Also, huge thanks to Christina, the AmputeeOT, for her educational YouTube videos and encouragement while writing this book.

CHAPTER ONE

Ellie's knee bounced furiously, jiggling the beaded fringe on her slinky red party dress. She stared at the casino's neon *EXIT* sign. Could she slip out the door before her well-intentioned friends stopped her and hauled her back to their girls' night out?

Lights flashed, bells dinged and people shouted as they tried to one-up the music pumping through the speakers in the ceiling. Laughter and hoots echoed around her. Machines chimed over and over as the ladies she'd come with fed the penny slots at the casino that had opened up about an hour from their midwestern city.

Each pulse of color or barrage of sound jolted Ellie, making her flinch. It reminded her of the trips she'd endured while involuntarily taking Sex Offender—a libido-enhancing drug so powerful it had threatened society. True, almost no one but law enforcement agents knew that since they had successfully destroyed the narcotic before it was perfected and distributed by her ex-boss, who'd experimented with the formula on her. The uncomfortable intensity of her senses had made the world around her seem overwhelming. Like now. She shivered, certain she didn't wish to recall any more of

1

those memories. Pretty much ever, but definitely not here—in public. Not tonight.

There were far too many witnesses. She'd never hear the end of it if she broke down now, after months of therapy and supposed progress. Nightmares would give her plenty of time to relive her imprisonment and the horrific things that had been forced on her while she'd been the captive of a mad scientist. She chafed her arms.

"Doing okay?" Lily asked as quietly as she could, given the cacophony of stimulation encompassing them. Perceptive as always, the woman used her people-reading skills gained as a Domme too often for comfort. Lying would be futile.

"I'm trying." A weak smile accompanied Ellie's admission. Heart racing, palms sweating, she barely restrained herself from looking over her shoulder for the thousandth time in the past five minutes.

"Want some fresh air?" Shari, another of her friends, asked. "I know I can smoke in here, but it feels weird to do it inside these days. I could use a cigarette if you want to come outside with me."

Jambrea—one of two nurses in their group—opened her mouth. Lacey looked ready to back her up by reciting the Surgeon General's warning.

With a slice of her hand through the air, Shari cut them off. "Not a word. I know. It's not good for me. Tonight, I don't care. We're having fun."

New mom and tiniest of their group—though possibly the toughest, despite being a reformed socialite—Izzy didn't stop there. "I guess I'll have to text Ben and Ryan and see what they have to say about that."

Completely distracted from her mounting terror, Ellie laughed. Her brother, Ryan, clearly had a crush on Shari—smoker or not. A bad habit or two or twenty wasn't going to deter him. Where that left him or his roommate—Ben—who also seemed interested in the usually quiet resort manager, she couldn't say.

Hell, for that matter, Ellie thought Ben and Ryan had something going on with each other after the time they'd also spent as prisoners in Morselli's lair, trying to rescue her and Ben's family from Morselli and his crony, the Scientist. Since then, they'd shared an apartment. Ben's eight-year-old niece lived with them. He'd saved the girl, although he'd been too late to do the same for his own sister. None of them emerged unscathed from that disaster. Maybe it was simply a matter of bonding in a time of crisis that kept the two guys together.

Ellie hated that she'd been the reason her brother had gotten ensnared in the mess. And he wasn't the only man who'd gotten hurt trying to rescue her…

Suddenly it was hard to breathe again.

"Let's go." She yanked on Shari's elbow. They headed for the outdoors together.

Ellie ignored the concerned glances the rest of their friends exchanged. It was a skill she'd perfected in the past year or so. She dodged cocktail waitresses in skimpy outfits and fishnets that highlighted their awesome legs, drunk guys who had her shuddering as she recalled the men who'd abused her, and a throng of people near the entrance that made it hard for her to gulp clean, crisp air into her lungs.

When she pushed the glass door open, it banged into the side of the building hard enough to make her surrender a nervous laugh. "Oops."

"You're okay." Shari knew better than to touch Ellie, though she looked like she might offer a hug or a pat on the back.

"Am I?" Tears welled in Ellie's eyes. She stared up at the night sky—admiring the twinkling stars out here, away from the city, in her glassy vision—willing the moisture to recede. All that effort on her makeup would *not* go to waste. Besides, she'd done enough crying to last her a dozen lifetimes.

"You're getting there." Shari grimaced as she fired up her lighter. She lit her cancer stick then lifted it toward her friend in a mock salute before taking a long drag and letting it out slowly. "We all have issues."

Ellie snorted. "You've got a vice. So what? I'm fucked up. Completely fucked up, and I don't know if I'm ever going to be even halfway normal again."

"This isn't a contest or anything. You've survived more shit than I can imagine. I just want you to know that you're not alone in your struggles. I miss my brother. Always will. Don't say anything to Jambi about this, please. But I have nightmares about him dying alone and unloved. Nothing I do will ever fix that. And it's worse when I wonder if I'll end up just like him."

Ellie's mouth hung open as she looked—*really* looked—at Shari for the first time. Maybe ever. Sadness lingered in her pretty brown eyes even as she worried about their mutual friend.

Jambrea had loved Shari's brother once, before fate had ripped them apart, reality intervening in what could have been an epic pairing. Still, Ellie knew it didn't have to be that way for Shari. What incestuous friendships they'd all forged!

Connected through the infamous Men in Blue and their cases, they'd become a family of sorts.

Before Ellie could bring up her brother and his handsome roommate, Shari did it for her. "Then there's Ryan and Ben. I wish I were half as brave as you and could do something about the spark I feel between us..."

Could the woman's cigarette be more than a bad habit?

It was a crutch. They dealt with the shit on their plate however they could.

This time it was Ellie reaching out, enfolding Shari in a light embrace.

"Honestly, you've come so far. You should be anything but ashamed," her friend murmured, squeezing Ellie back. "I'm proud of you. So is everyone else. The girls here tonight and the Men in Blue. Ryan, of course. And Ben too. You have so many people who care about you and are cheering you on. It's only going to keep getting better. I promise."

Ellie sighed as she thought about the one man in their circle of acquaintances that Shari hadn't dared to mention. Her extra-sore spot.

Lucas.

If only *he* were impressed with her. The ex-military Special Forces fighter had shown nothing but derision toward her since he'd lost the lower half of his right leg. She couldn't blame him. Indirectly, she'd been responsible for his injury. He'd come to her rescue, before he'd even known her, and been critically wounded in the attempt that had saved her life.

Because of her, his leg had been crushed. Amputated eventually. He'd sacrificed everything important to him—his career, his aspirations. Even part of his body.

Ever since then, he'd wanted nothing to do with her.

So, of course, he was the one man she wanted. Desperately. The only one who could replace her night terrors with something pleasurable. Steamy dreams of him had been intermixed with nightmares for months now. A waste of time, since he wouldn't even let her near him long enough to help him with his recovery, never mind jumping his bones.

As if the sadness replacing Ellie's panic had shown on her face, Shari linked their fingers. She snuffed the butt of her cigarette then squeezed Ellie's hand. The fact that she could tolerate even that much skin-to-skin contact with another person did speak volumes about her slow healing.

"Come on, let's get back in there." Shari smiled at her. "Grab a couple of those free drinks if you need to loosen up. We need to win some of this place's cash!"

"That would be nice." Ellie hadn't worked since the disaster, as she thought of it. The Men in Blue had generously assembled a charitable fundraising campaign for her treatment and living expenses while she rehabilitated. Lately, she found herself antsy to return to productive society.

Except, being a lab tech didn't hold the same appeal as it once had, knowing the dangers and the evil purposes her work could be put to. Probably, it was time to consider a change of career.

But not tonight.

Ellie found herself grinning as they made their way to the group of gorgeous women, all so different and yet so tightly knit, huddled around a bank of one-armed bandits. Jambrea was statuesque, kind. Lily and Izzy, half sisters, ultra-petite yet fierce. Lacey had a girl-next-door vibe that masked her true spark. They were each amazing in their own way.

Maybe she could be too.

"Shari?" Ellie said just out of hearing of the gang.

"Yeah?"

"Thanks." She grinned. "I hope you remember this little chat when I get around to lecturing you about my brother and pursuing the chemistry between you."

"Not you too." Shari shook her head.

"Yep. For sure." Ellie winked then trotted over to the digital cashier and loaded up her freshly minted reward membership card with some of the cash she'd hoarded from her birthday presents. She wouldn't mind if they made these Saturday night outings a regular thing.

Next time she could host them for a dinner party, if she could keep her shit together that long.

***

A while later, the rest of the women were huddled around Ellie's stool at the slots. They cheered as she made it into the bonus game on her fancy machine for the fourth time in as many spins. Already up about five hundred dollars on the original forty she'd plunked down to start, she figured she could keep riding her hot streak.

The rainbow hues of the whirling wheel didn't bother her now as excitement flowed through her, helped along by the slight buzz she had from the free drinks that kept coming around. Sure, they were watered down, but she hadn't had alcohol since before her confinement. Hadn't trusted herself to enter any altered state since then. Well, of course, that didn't count the antianxiety medicine she'd been popping left and right for months.

When the blur slowed and she could start to make out the digits, her eyes grew wide. The grand prize logo ticked upward as if in slow motion. And when it stopped, directly in line with the gleaming gold *JACKPOT* marker, she simply sat and stared.

The rest of her friends went wild. Screaming, jumping up and down, and high-fiving each other, they were still careful not to grab Ellie and shake her, as they did each other. Instead of roaring, or cheering, or crying—Ellie scrubbed her eyes and looked again.

It couldn't be.

Could it?

"Holy fucking shit!" Lacey whooped as she twirled around in a circle. "I admit I'm kinda drunk, but I'm pretty sure you just won forty-seven thousand dollars!"

Tingling rose up Ellie's wrists and into her arms as she blinked at the display.

It didn't take long before a crowd began to form around them.

A spotlight shone down on her and a voice boomed across the casino's sound system, "Congratulations to our first big winner!"

Then things went from slow motion to fast forward in an instant. A man in a black suit came up behind her, startling her. She gasped then put her trembling hands over her open mouth.

Lily stepped between the guy and her, giving her time to adjust to his presence and focus on exactly where they were—and were not—and what was going down.

Behind the bulky dude, who was almost certainly a security guard of some sort, a man wearing the standard casino uniform and a bronze nameplate rushed to her side. When her friends saw that she was okay, they let him pass. He infringed on her personal space, causing her to gulp.

"Lucky lady!" the man shouted with a gleaming smile that was too perfect to be entirely God-given.

Ellie reached out and grabbed Shari's hand as she stood. Her friend grinned and stayed close by her side as she and the rest of their group were herded to the edge of the slots. The phony man's lips were moving, but Ellie couldn't make out what he was saying.

Everything seemed garbled, as if she were watching it play out from underwater.

"I'm sorry. W-what?"

"I said it'll be just a few minutes." He practically bounced, as though he'd hit the big one. "We need the machine operators to certify everything was functioning properly when the win went through."

His offhanded shrug made her eyes narrow.

Beside Ellie, Jambrea practically growled, "We all saw it. She won that money."

Things might get ugly if they tried to deny it.

Ellie giggled internally at the idea of her five feminine friends kicking some serious ass. They would, too, if they thought one of their gang was mistreated. It felt nice to be considered one of them. Even better than winning nearly fifty grand. Almost.

She did a double take, verifying the slot machine—which now beeped and buzzed and jangled like it was a rocket about to launch into space—still claimed she'd hit the jackpot.

It did.

A hint of pain whipped through her as she nibbled the inside of her cheek. It seemed to take forever for another handful of men in suits to reach them, then put the guts of her slot machine on display as they hovered over some screen and a readout only they knew how to interpret.

Ellie looked up, noticing the cameras everywhere. It was like they were putting on a show for the surveillance crew. Or maybe this was some TV prank and someone was about to jump out and tell them they'd been fooled.

Instead, the trio of bean counters began to gesture excitedly. One turned and flashed them a thumbs-up.

Ho-ly shit.

Blackness infringed on her vision, making it sort of tunnel in on the neon-green numbers scrolling past on the slot machine—$47,292.

"Woo-hooo!" she whooped, spinning to face her friends.

They beamed at her, and Shari even had a single tear tracking down her cheek. Her friend sniffled then said, "If anyone deserves something good, it's you."

"We all do." Ellie pumped her fist in the air. "Next ladies' night is on me."

They cracked up as the casino personnel whisked them off the casino floor to a well-lit, marble-tiled space. In front of them was a teller's window.

Ellie tried to focus as they put form after form on a clipboard and had her filling out just about every detail of her life. They might have asked for her bra size somewhere in that mountain of crap. Her eyes crossed before she'd made it even halfway through.

When she handed them to the cute young teller, he winked at her. Refusing to make eye contact, she glanced over her shoulder at her friends, who were leaning up against various walls, talking excitedly on their phones. All of the Men in Blue must know about their escapades by now.

What would Ryan say when he found out she'd gotten so damn lucky?

Or Lucas. Would he even crack a hint of a smile at the news?

"All right. Here you go." The teller slid a canvas, zippered bag through the opening of his window. He had to shove it a little to smoosh it through, like she did when squashing her ass into her skinny jeans at the wrong time of the month. Or after she'd baked too many cupcakes when she couldn't sleep.

Unable to help herself, she peeked inside.

"Wow. That's a crap ton of cash." She whistled.

"Almost fifty large, yep." The teller grinned back.

"I mean, I guess I thought you'd write me a check or something." Ellie shrugged.

"Oh, sorry. The slip says you opted for cash. We can change it out, but I'll need you to complete a new set of forms and—"

"No. This is fine. Good. Great, really." She shook her head, feeling the need to get out of there and back to her somewhat regular life. Anxiety built within her, as did a sense of impending doom. Out of place and surrounded by chaos, she had taken as much as she could for one night.

"I'd like it this way myself. Maybe just roll around naked in it tonight or something before you take it to...the *bank*...in the morning." The guy stared dreamily at her, as if he imagined what she'd look like covered only in green bills. Sure, he was attractive and friendly, but all she could think of was escaping before he could try to slip his number in with her spoils.

Only one man could interest her. Worse, most of the rest of them scared her. How could she ever truly trust again?

With Lucas, it was easy. He'd been there for her, come to her aid, never let her down. Even when it had cost him dearly. The rest of the Men in Blue too.

Though they were all attached these days. Everyone else...well, they were a bet she wasn't willing to take.

***

On the ride home, she rested her forehead against the car window, letting the coolness seep into her skin. Sometimes she swore she could still feel the incessant burning of Sex Offender lighting her nervous system on fire. Tonight, though, she breathed deeply, fingering the sack of cash in her lap while the glittering lights of civilization drew nearer.

For the first time in a while, she was happy.

More because she'd overcome her fears than because of the cosmic reward she'd been handed for her bravery. Still, that didn't hurt either. Maybe she could see how many credits she'd need to get a revamped degree. Start a new career. Get back on her feet all the way.

Lost in thought, she didn't realize they'd already gotten so close to home until they pulled up in front of her house.

"Want me to walk you in?" Shari asked quietly.

"Nah, I'm okay. Promise." Ellie desperately wanted it to be true. So she darted from the car before they could make any more offers she'd be tempted to accept. "I need to grab the mail anyway. Go ahead, I'm fine."

Grinning, Ellie waved at the ladies in the car then jogged across the street to pick up her bills. Nothing besides that and junk would be waiting in her box. At least she could get rid of a few of them now.

Once she had those in hand, she skipped up the sidewalk to her modest house. The cute cottage had been the ideal starter home. At least before she'd become afraid of spending nights alone.

A shiver ran up her spine and she slowed as she neared. She looked over her shoulder, dismissing the tendril of fear that overcame her as the taillights of Jambrea's car disappeared around a corner.

She paused and drew in a deep breath, and then another.

Knowing she would hate herself later for overreacting, yet still unwilling to be anything but prepared, Ellie circled around to her side yard and knelt by the oversized watering can she'd left there.

Peeking over her other shoulder, she quickly retrieved the sack she'd stashed in it—one of many emergency kits she'd littered around her home. Swapping it for the bag she carried, the one with the bricks of hundred-dollar bills, she pretended to tend to something nearby before heading inside.

Just in case.

Ellie rolled her eyes at herself.

With no one to witness her foolishness, she satisfied her own rituals. Hey, at least this time she didn't false alarm and enlist the Men in Blue to check out the entire interior of her home, as she had more than once in the past year. She debated calling Ryan, just to hear his voice for a second, but it was past Julie's bedtime and she didn't want to risk waking the girl up.

There was Lucas... Not that he'd pick up, since he hadn't the past 3,517 times she'd tried to contact him.

She squeezed her eyes shut then planted one foot on her bottom step.

Geared up, Ellie began to climb her front stairs.

Before she could open the lock on the front door, it burst outward, knocking her off-balance.

13

Without even giving her time to scream, a black-gloved hand shot out and wrapped around her waist. A matching grip covered her mouth. Then she was dragged inside.

No, this couldn't be happening.

Not again.

Instead of freezing, her entire being went into survival mode.

She stomped on her attacker's instep, like the Men in Blue had shown her. Her hands dipped into her sack and withdrew a bottle of pepper spray. Aiming it point-blank, she depressed the button on top, blasting the man with a stream of violent chemicals.

Ellie might have made it outside again if there weren't two other men waiting to charge her while their associate writhed on the floor, clutching his face, which now dripped snot and tears.

This time they were more careful, smashing her wrist against the doorframe until she dropped her weapon. They also attempted to snatch the bag from her grip, taking the rest of her supplies too. But she fought harder and they backed off temporarily, knowing she was trapped.

"You won't be needing that anymore," one guy rumbled, making her shiver. "Thanks for being our mule. Should we give her a cut, boys?"

"I can think of other ways to repay the lady," another one cackled as he ran his hand along her exposed thigh.

Ellie tried to ignore the slimy coating his molestation released in her gut, but she couldn't. Not again. She wouldn't survive if she couldn't get out of there.

Quick.

CHAPTER TWO

Lucas kicked back in his leather recliner. It had been his favorite chair until his prosthesis had torn the footrest. Every time he looked at the ragged slash in the damn thing now, it only reminded him of the endless ways in which his life had been altered. He massaged his stump, especially the knee, which ached after the long run he'd pushed himself through earlier.

It'd been nearly seven months since his amputation. He'd never worked harder to get back to normal, whatever the hell that was these days. Though he'd trained like a madman when his life had depended on his physical and mental abilities, he was more cut than ever. Endless gym time had guaranteed it. His gaze wandered down his ripped, freshly tattooed chest and the muscles of his abdomen, which were pretty damn defined, even while he slouched, completely relaxed.

Or as close to it as he ever got.

He picked up a controller and turned on his gaming console, ready to slay some aliens and save the human race again. Like he did most nights, until he nodded off in this piece-of-shit chair, which now sported a dent the size and shape of his ass. He couldn't believe how much he sat. Before, he'd been active, only getting horizontal to hook up with a fine woman or grab a few hours' rest before heading to the next assignment. Now he spent most of his time outside of his rehab efforts here, hoping to settle his mind enough to doze off. Sometimes, it was the only way he could sleep at all.

Lucas figured he'd give his other leg to be back out there, making a difference in the world. Except he knew if he tried, he'd only put others at risk. Endangering his team was something he would never do. Despite all his efforts and therapy, he'd never be as agile, as stealthy or—probably most important—as mentally unhindered as he'd been before his injury. Blending in and hiding his identity on covert ops would be impossible with such an easy tell for his enemies to discover. The military probably assumed they'd done him a favor by medically discharging him with full salary and benefits for the rest of his life.

He scrubbed his hand over his face.

Then again, he wouldn't take his leg back if it meant the evil he'd witnessed the day it had been crushed went unchecked. Often, he dreamt of that closing gate and his last-ditch effort to keep it from trapping victims—Ellie included—inside a ghastly prison, by using his body as a doorstop. They'd gotten her out of the Scientist's clutches. Not in time to avoid being wounded, at least as badly as he had been, but in time to keep her—and dozens of other innocents like her—alive.

Both of them had survived, if in one hell of a state. His partner, Steve, hadn't been as lucky.

Breath wheezed out of Lucas as he remembered the look on Ellie's drugged face when their friend Lily had hauled her from the cloud of Sex Offender that had turned her fellow prisoners into monsters who attacked her. During the tenure of his career, it was

16

the single most disgusting thing he'd ever witnessed. Insane with chemically induced lust of her own, she had somehow struggled against the potent concoction.

The pure fight she'd shown in escaping the hellhole they'd yanked her out of had made it impossible for him to quit, even as his leg had screamed in agony. She'd clearly been assaulted. Repeatedly. Her moans and cries had been like an audible interpretation of his own debilitating pain as Jeremy had helped him hobble on his destroyed leg to relative safety. The sound of her terror was burned into his memory.

His fingers clamped on the arm of the chair, threatening to make more holes in the upholstery.

Recollections like that made him feel sick for wanting her. How could she ever welcome the kind of primal advances that had taken center stage in the thoughts he'd had of her since then? Why would she, or any sane woman, want a man like him now?

"Fuck." He pounded his fist on his thigh, welcoming the *thud* that distracted him from his downward-spiraling thoughts.

Staring at the ceiling, he drew in a ragged breath and groaned.

After a solid five minutes spent wrestling the urge to blank out his overactive mind on the pain pills prescribed to him, his phone buzzed on the side table nearby.

Please don't be Ellie.

Tonight he might not have the strength to ignore it, letting her go to voice mail, then listening to her messages at night when he was wide-awake. His fingers curled inward. Frequent calls from her were hard to resist. Even tougher than the siren song of his narcotics, which he'd been trying to wean himself off entirely. Late-night rings like these meant she probably slept as shittily as he did. Her attempts to contact him had slowed recently, coming fewer and farther between. While he'd tried to be happy about that, the fact was he missed seeing her light up his screen. That barest of contacts had the power to make him smile. At least for a moment, until he remembered the shit-ton of reasons they couldn't be together.

The good thing about having a detachable foot was that he could actually shove it up his own ass if he kept acting like an idiot.

Lucas couldn't help himself—he snatched the vibrating phone, hoping for a glimpse of her name or the profile picture he'd set for her contact. It was a formal shot of them, all dressed up, that had been taken at Lily and JRad's wedding. She'd looked more gorgeous than usual that day. Hell, they'd even danced together once as he deluded himself into believing his leg might still get better, despite the advice of his doctors who'd encouraged him to amputate immediately.

Turned out wearing a prosthesis was actually better than hanging on to a mangled meat foot when it came to living an active lifestyle. He'd been screwed even then, but at least his denial had been strong enough that he enjoyed one last happy occasion with his friends. And Ellie.

It always came back to her.

"Son of a bitch!" he roared at himself. Especially since it wasn't even her calling.

Instead, the face that flashed on-screen belonged to Jeremy Radisson, though the label said "JRad", since his friends on the force used that nickname for the geeky cyberdetective with an impressive Dominant streak.

A wave of mingled relief and disappointment washed through Lucas. Anxiety too. It was always kind of awkward talking to one of the guys who could understand exactly what he had lost—camaraderie, purpose, honor—along with his leg. Still, part of him was glad to have someone to talk to in the darkness.

Speaking of, why the hell was the dude calling so close to midnight? It must be important. Lucas swiped his thumb across the phone to answer.

Before he even had a chance to say hello, Jeremy was talking in a hurried, hushed rumble.

"Hey, Lucas," JRad greeted him with a cautious edge to his tone. This couldn't be good.

"What's up?" The guy never buzzed him this late. None of their mutual friends did anymore either, though they all worked fucked-up shifts. Ah, the life of a peacekeeper.

It was like they didn't want to interrupt his beauty sleep in case that would make his fucking leg grow back. In the military, especially his covert branch, he hadn't been used to people tiptoeing around him. He found he didn't like it much either, now that he was disabled.

"Wish I could say this was a social call. Sorry." It felt oddly good that the first ten minutes of their discussion wasn't something along the lines of "how are you feeling today, buddy".

Oh fine, just missing a foot, an ankle and most of my shin—that's all. Could be worse—could've had my dick chopped off. Ha-ha...

In other words, the same old bullshit he'd been reciting for months now.

They dove into the important stuff without fucking around with feelings and shit. Finally, something like his regular modus operandi. Years of late-night summons, life-or-death emergencies and running on adrenaline had made his recent couch-potato act all the more unnerving.

"The rest of the Men in Blue and I are on a case. Getting close to cracking it." JRad's urgency penetrated Lucas's gloomy thoughts.

"You need help with something?" Sometimes they made use of his government connections or picked his brain, which was essentially a database on immoral dealings and the inner workings of criminal organizations, after nearly two decades combating them.

"Yeah, if you don't mind."

"Of course not. How can I help?" Lucas sat straighter, leaning forward in his ruined seat.

"It's the girls—"

"Ah shit. Some pussy assignment? I thought you actually needed me for important shit." He deflated, sinking into the cushions again.

"They're the most valuable things in our lives," JRad was quick to correct him. "You know we wouldn't trust their safety to just anyone."

"Be honest, you're trying to make me feel useful here." He stopped short of rolling his eyes. Badass soldiers, even retired ones, did *not* roll their eyes. "What's next? A crossing-guard vest? Jesus, JRad. Fuck off."

"Hey, wait. Don't hang up. Shit. We need you." A ragged breath from JRad convinced Lucas not to punch the End button just yet. "We're stuck on this case. There's no way we can bail now. Not even one of us could sneak out without blowing our cover. Sending in anyone else from the station would risk spooking Ellie."

"Ellie?" Lucas could have decked himself for repeating her name. Letting the other guy know he was as obsessed as ever with the beautiful young woman wouldn't be in his best interest. Not tonight or anytime in the future when the guys and their ladies decided for the millionth time to try and play matchmaker with a hopeless pairing.

"Yeah."

"What's she got to do with this?" Fuck it, why hide it when it was obvious to everyone, anyway, exactly how much he wanted her? Felt responsible for her somehow. It was pretty common in their line of work, actually, to get attached to certain people they had a hand in helping.

Wasn't smart, though.

"I guess Lily, Jambrea, Izzy, Lacey and Shari convinced her to go out to that new casino north of the city with them tonight."

"Now I know you're screwing with me." Lucas took the phone from his ear for a second to glare at JRad's picture. What kind of game was he playing? Ellie could hardly stand a stroll in a garden, never mind the chaos of a casino. She spooked as easily as a soft, pretty bunny. Not that he blamed her in the least.

Besides, most people wouldn't notice because of the tough mask she wore. But he was a trained observer. So were the rest of the Men in Blue. The tic of her sculpted jaw or the rapid blink of her mesmerizing blue eyes, which caused thick lashes to flutter onto the pale, creamy skin of her cheeks—all of it screamed how scared shitless she was of the world around her.

Lucas figured she was the bravest woman he'd ever met for not falling apart with that bucketload of terror coursing through her veins constantly. The

21

adrenaline aftereffects alone had to be exhausting to her system.

"I'm not shitting you." JRad huffed at that. "I didn't think they'd con her into doing it either, but they did. She's getting better lately, Lucas. Healing. Not so raw as she used to be. Which you'd know if you hadn't cut her out of your life, dickhead."

"Stick to the facts." He'd had enough lectures from her five female cohorts. Additional shit from JRad was entirely unnecessary.

"Look, they went out tonight. Sexy as hell. The six of them dressed up, sending us enough naughty selfies to torture us while we're stuck in this damn apartment, spying on druggies."

JRad's clear sexual frustration had Lucas grinning. Too bad, so sad. The man would eventually go home to his feisty, sometimes-submissive-but-only-for-him Mistress Lily soon enough.

"At least Matt and Clint can suck each other off in the bathroom. Mason and Tyler too. It's just you and Razor who are screwed, huh?" Lucas shrugged, though no one could see him and despite the fact that he knew they wouldn't. Not on the clock. They took their jobs as seriously as he had once.

"Anyway, the girls headed over there after dinner at some fancy place downtown. Ten minutes ago our phones started lighting up at once. Scared the shit out of us," JRad confessed. Each of their ladies had fought through some hard times and survived her own personal threats. It had their guys on edge still.

"They're okay?" Hopefully they hadn't been in a car wreck or something like that. Lucas swallowed hard, preparing himself for bad news.

"Actually, yes."

"Then what the hell?" He scratched his head.

"Turns out Ellie must have taken her lucky rabbit's foot along." JRad paused, as if he'd realized the absurdity of that mental image for Lucas.

Instead of getting pissed or being offended, he laughed. "Huh. Wonder if some bunny's got *my* damn foot in its pocket."

"Er—"

"Anyway, she's up for the night? Beating the house? Are they partying to celebrate? Need a designated driver or something?" He steered them back to their discussion. Good for Ellie. He knew money was tight. Had contributed as much as he could manage as an anonymous donor to the fund he'd set up for her recovery, before handing it off to the Men in Blue to administer so she wouldn't get suspicious.

"We're not talking about a couple hundred bucks here, Lucas." JRad sighed. "She won almost fifty grand on the fucking penny slots. Cash. They're driving home with it right now."

"Are you *shitting* me?" Call him cynical, but that seemed nearly impossible. In his world, that usually meant something was up. "That place isn't going to be in business long if they're handing out sacks of money like that. Why wouldn't they have written her a check?"

"Lily says the claim form wasn't clear and they didn't feel like wading through the paperwork again to switch the payment type. Six smoking-hot women and a huge chunk of cash. You know every man in that place noticed them and they're going to talk. Shit, it's probably plastered all over social media by now. TV will be next. That's a fuck ton of temptation. Maybe you could stay with Ellie tonight and escort her to make a deposit once the bank opens in the morning?"

JRad cursed under his breath. "I know that's not ideal for either of you, considering the circumstances..."

"Don't worry about my end of things. It's fine. She shouldn't be alone with that much money on hand. People have done stupid things for less. Sleeping in my car, or her backyard, isn't a problem either. I'll just go over and let her know I'm out there, keeping an eye on her place."

Lucas might have been avoiding Ellie, but only for their own good. He cared for her. A lot. If she was in danger, he would be there, regardless of their twisted personal relationship. He went to stand as if he still had two complete legs, nearly toppling. His cell tumbled from his grip in the process.

Sometimes he acted purely on instinct, forgetting his altered body completely. Like when the power went out and he still flipped the light switch when he entered a room. Unlearning ingrained actions was tough. He fished around until he reclaimed his phone, cursing violently the entire time. When he glanced at it, the screen was jumbled. Harsh static scratched from the speakers. "Sorry, dropped the damn phone."

"Lucas?" JRad hesitated.

"Yeah?"

"You haven't been drinking tonight, have you? Or taking your medicine? You don't sound like it, but we'll find someone else if you have. Maybe Ben and Ryan, though you're definitely better qualified for the job. I don't want you going if you—"

"Stone-cold sober, my friend." His shoulders hunched as he realized that probably was a pretty rare occurrence lately. He didn't feel it was necessary to admit he'd run out of whiskey yesterday. Or that he hadn't had the energy to put his leg back on to hit up the liquor store after he'd come home from his marathon run earlier and cleaned out his sweaty liner. Only the smidge of resurging pride that JRad had considered him over Ellie's brother *and* the guy's partner pulled him from his funk.

"And you're comfortable driving, even at night? Razor says I'm a dumbass and you don't need a ride, but I figured I should offer anyway. We could send a patrol car over to pick you up if you want."

"I'm missing some of my leg, not my eyeballs," he sneered. A man could only take so many blows. "I'm not *completely* incompetent, you know?"

"Shit, sorry," JRad muttered. "Especially for making things any more awkward between you and Ellie. Maybe this will be a good opportunity—"

"Let me worry about her. You go back to fighting crime and keeping the city safe, okay?" Lucas tried to act like everything was cool when his guts were churning at least as much as the time he'd been forced to eat partially spoiled fish to blend in while infiltrating terrorist camps in the Middle East.

"Good idea," JRad replied, even as there was some commotion in the background.

"Hey, you think I've got time for a quick shower before heading out? How far are they from Ellie's place?" Lucas didn't give a shit about the sweat drying on his skin. If it had been anyone else he'd encounter, he'd have gone as is. He admitted, if only to himself, that he didn't want Ellie to see him at anything less than his best. Hard enough, given his current condition.

"Sure. I've got Lily texting me every few minutes. Their ETA is about twenty-five minutes from now. Probably only takes you, what...less than ten minutes to get to Ellie's neighborhood, I'd guess." JRad couldn't help but tease him like the guys always did about his house out in the woods. "Would be faster if there were a real road up by your place. She doesn't live too far away as the crow flies."

Three point six two miles.

Not that Lucas would admit to his friend that he knew that. Worse, he'd wished himself capable of his old habit of traipsing through the forest to relieve stress once he realized she'd been so damn close all that time. Creepy, sure, but he'd thought about how often he could have peeked from the branches he'd loved camouflaging himself in when on leave. He would have enjoyed watching the warm glow of her lights, knowing she was safe and happy inside, at least if he'd known she existed back then.

People like her were why he'd risked his life for so long.

Her cute house on the developed part of the mountain suited her with its earth-tone paint job and small, neat yard surrounded by beds of wild flowers.

"Hey, Lucas. We've got some action here. I better get off the phone." JRad spoke in an urgent hush that had Lucas's heart rate accelerating even though he wasn't on the job. JRad might have said more, but the crispy sound snapping from Lucas's phone obscured whatever he'd said.

"Okay. Go. Don't worry. I've got this covered."

"Thank you." He hung up without saying goodbye.

When the phone went dark, it didn't seem to want to turn on again. Lucas jabbed all the buttons and swiped his finger across the screen. Nothing. Damn. He'd have to stop by the mall after the bank tomorrow to grab a replacement. Thank God for insurance.

He scrubbed his hands over his face then prepared himself to move. He glared at the wheelchair across the room. It didn't do him much good since his house had lots of stairs. A few here and there between the different living areas, plus the full flight to the upstairs bedroom He'd appreciated the unique flow of the house a lot more before he had to navigate its uneven surfaces one-legged.

Usually, he found it most expedient to traverse the rooms in an animalistic combination of hopping, crawling and scrambling that would humiliate him if anyone could see it. With a grunt, he pushed out of his chair to standing, balancing on his good foot.

Then he bent and put one palm on the coffee table and hopped. That got him halfway across the living room. Using the back of the sofa as a guide, he made it to the stairs to his bedroom. Lucas put his knee on the highest tread he could reach from the ground then planted his good foot beside it. Gripping the railing, he pulled himself upright then planted his knee once more.

It only took three repetitions before he'd made it to the top of the staircase. Much faster than relying on crutches. Probably safer too, since he wasn't swinging all over the place with his center of gravity high up, threatening to pitch him to the hardwood floors below. Wouldn't win him any beauty pageants, though.

Once upstairs, he grabbed the door handle and then hopped a few times until he could use the bed for leverage. Finally, he made it to the bathroom. It probably wasn't wise to be so far from his prosthesis. Wearing it at night bothered him, though. Sometimes he just wanted to feel normal instead of carrying around a million extra things just to do something as simple as walk.

Lucas stripped off his jogging shorts then plopped onto the bench in his shower.

He reached forward to turn the water on and cursed when he realized he'd left the sprayer slightly out of reach. Levering himself up with a grip on the soap dish embedded in the tile wall, he snagged it then made sure he had his body wash and shampoo in place before settling in again.

What used to take him three minutes, tops, was now an ordeal, exactly like every other task he encountered. Even adapting his daily routine to his new body took more effort than he had expended in an entire week before.

Cursing, Lucas finished rinsing soap from his body then climbed from the shower, careful not to bust his ass...again. He hated to admit it, but he'd knocked himself unconscious not long after his surgery, when he slipped on the tile floor and tried to catch himself with a foot that was only a figment of his imagination.

Good thing he was hardheaded.

With a glance at the clock, Lucas realized he was later than he'd planned. If he didn't hurry, Ellie would be home alone with her prize money. Unlike going out with wet hair, there were some things he couldn't rush. He took the time to thoroughly dry his stump. Otherwise he'd have to worry about his skin getting irritated or developing sores that could keep him from being able to wear his prosthesis.

Nothing would be worse than having to rely on people if he was unable to be self-sufficient.

Hell, even getting dressed was a pain in the ass. He hopped to his dresser then tugged on a faded navy T-shirt with a black-and-gray drawing of a bald eagle, then a pair of boxer briefs. Tossing his jeans around his neck, he grabbed his liner off the drying rack, his prosthesis and a backpack with supplies.

Weighed down with more shit than he'd have needed for a weeklong excursion in the wild before his accident, Lucas sank onto his bed. Still feeling like he was doing everything backwards, he put his jeans on his prosthesis first, shoving until they pooled around the mechanical ankle. Then he turned the gel sleeve, called a liner, inside out and pressed the end against his residual limb.

Rolling it up his leg reminded him of all the times he'd watched super-sexy women putting on stockings. This kind of thigh-high was far less attractive to him, though. For a moment, he wondered if he'd ever let himself get laid again. At least with his clothes off and the lights on. Didn't seem likely at this point.

The liner had a plastic strap attached to it. Lucas selected a few stump socks from the collection in his backpack then fed the strap through the slit in the side of them until he had rolled on a couple of varying ply cotton. Then, finally, he put his leg in the socket of his prosthesis, aligning the strap on his liner with the proximal lock. Standing and stomping a few times caused the plastic to ratchet down and bind his artificial foot to his real remaining leg.

Only then was he able to put his good foot into his jeans and pull them up over his legs.

Never again would he take putting his pants on for granted.

What a pain in the ass.

Sure, he could have made it easier by wearing shorts, but he liked that he could obscure his leg this way. After more work on diminishing his limp, he thought—maybe, someday—people wouldn't be able to tell at all.

Lucas was grateful that he'd been in good shape before his accident. Nimbleness and a fantastic sense of equilibrium came naturally to him. With his prosthesis, he was probably more able-bodied than the majority of adults, though he often got frustrated with the diminished capacity from his own personal peak performance.

He strapped on his watch, grimacing at how damn long that had taken, snatched his backpack off the bed, withdrew his gun from the top drawer of his dresser, loaded it and tucked it in the back pocket of his jeans, then jogged down the stairs and to the car. If his stump throbbed in protest, he ignored it.

***

Behind the wheel of his Volvo S60, Lucas revved the special-edition 450 hp engine a few times. Maybe now that he was less concerned with being inconspicuous, he could have his friend Rebel at the Hot Rods garage in Middletown help him find and fix up something more fun.

Lucas thought about that, and how the guy had helped his friend Dave overcome a critical injury of his own, as he drove to Ellie's place. Anything to keep his mind off of the disaster that would await him when he got there and actually had to work this situation out with her.

He figured one of two things were likely to happen. Either she'd boot him out on his ass or they'd end up making out against her entryway wall. Option two sounded far more appealing until he considered what the next steps would be and where that would leave them after his responsibilities there were over.

The last thing he wanted to do was hurt her.

Despite his better judgment, his lips had begun to curl as he imagined what the night might have in store and how much better it could be than getting drunk and zapping pixelated bad guys on his big screen.

Just before turning onto her street, he spotted an oncoming car that looked familiar. A short toot of their horn had him smiling and lifting four fingers from the wheel in a hello aimed at his friends' ladies. Shit, he had hoped to be outside waiting so that Ellie didn't have to face him alone if that wasn't what she wanted. Or freak out when someone knocked at the door so damn late.

A couple of other vehicles lined the narrow street, including a black pickup with dark-tinted windows and no identifiable markings. His senses went on high alert. That seemed like exactly the kind of vehicle he might have driven himself on prior missions.

Stop making shit up.

It was hard to merge into a world of regular people after living hypersuspicious of his surroundings for so long. Lucas sighed and shook his head. The vehicle probably belonged to a teenager who thought it looked cool, or maybe someone messing around with selling weed on the side of their mostly average suburban life.

He rolled to a stop across the street from Ellie's house. There weren't any lights on. In the shadows of the side yard, he saw her ass and long, willowy legs framed by daisies. A much nicer sight than one of those painted wooden yard-art thingies of an old lady's bum. What the hell was she doing messing around with the watering can at this time of night?

Distracted by her perfect body, he nearly missed it when she strode for the front door. He started to get out of the car, slightly delayed by his foot getting caught on the gas pedal. Shit, he wanted to catch her before she went inside.

As he opened his mouth to shout to her, something stopped him.

Her front door flew open and an arm encased in a black-leather jacket reached out, wrapping around Ellie's face. Another banded around her slender waist. It happened in the blink of an eye.

Whoever had been waiting for Ellie snatched her out of view in an instant. If he hadn't been staring at her, he would have missed the grab entirely.

"Fuck!" he hissed, then crouched down, in case anyone was watching the street.

Why hadn't he rushed straight over? Why had he wasted time taking a shower as if she was going to let him within a square mile of her delectable body or give a shit if he smelled as bad as he'd treated her lately? His vanity had put her in danger.

Now it was up to him to get her out of it.

Lucas slipped his phone from his pocket to call for backup. And was met with the same dead screen as before. No help there.

Could a one-legged ex-superspy still kick ass? They were about to find out.

"Fuck. Fuck. Fuck."

CHAPTER THREE

Ellie ignored the fragment of her that was scared shitless. The steely grip around her jaw and abdomen hurt. Distinct and familiar, the pain of her teeth cutting into the inside of her upper lip could easily have slammed her into memories of her time in captivity, when men had touched a hell of a lot more than her face. More brutally too. Instead, she focused on the part of her that was pissed off. This was not about to happen to her again. Lax in her attacker's hold, she let them think she might go down without a fight.

As if.

Mentally, she reviewed every single lesson on self-defense she'd learned from the Men in Blue. Especially the ones Lucas had taught her. He fought dirty, and she liked that.

Stay calm, think and keep looking for opportunity, she recited in her mind.

She allowed herself to be manhandled by the goon who'd grabbed her, getting a feel for his size while she listened carefully to see how many assailants there were in total. One chance might be all she had to escape and she wanted to make the most of it whenever it arose. Forcing herself to swallow back bile and concentrate, Ellie went limp.

"That was easier than I thought," said a bastard, laughing.

"You're gonna be a good girl and let us have what we came for, right?" the man holding her asked with a disgusting artificial sweetness to his tone.

The only thing she was about to give him was her knee to his nuts the moment he provided a glimmer of an opening.

Someone tried to rip the bag from her hand.

She clung to it, knowing it was her best chance at escaping this clusterfuck in one piece. Mostly. Already her mind tried to spiral into darkness, but she focused on her purpose and what she needed to do to break free.

Ellie crossed her arms over her chest, tucking the bag close to her body, as if she were protecting herself from their leers, which she swore she could feel raking her.

Playing along was the hardest thing she'd ever done. In Morselli's dungeon, she'd fought until Sex Offender stole her will. Never willingly had she betrayed herself.

"Mmphf." Ellie tried to talk. The guy behind her had his hand over her mouth. She bit him lightly, not enough to hurt through the leather of his gloves. Enough to signal that she was trying to communicate.

"Back off," he instructed his crony who'd pawed at the bag in her clutches. "Let's see what she has to say first. Wouldn't mind a better look at her. She's pretty fine."

Ellie accepted the twisted compliment. At least knowing he found her attractive put another tool in her belt.

When he suddenly released her, she stumbled. Still, she remained on her feet through a display of sheer willpower.

They'd dragged her to the rear of the house, her kitchen, where they weren't visible in any of the windows facing the road. From here, a back door led to her yard, which butted up to a forested state preserve. A small guest room opened off to the side. If she could lock herself in there, even for a minute, she could go out the window somehow. Maybe.

It was a shitty plan. The only ray of hope she could generate at this point.

"Please." She didn't have to fake the tremble in her voice, though she didn't plan to buckle under the terror swirling around her. Living in fear for so many months had taught her to function despite debilitating panic. "I don't have anything you want."

"Oh, come on. You can do better than that, honey." The man laughed. "We know what you walked out of that casino with."

"I—I *need* that money." She formulated a strategy as best she could, given the circumstances. It was risky. Her time in the Scientist's laboratory had taught her the lengths some men would go to in order to violate someone. It was the only thing she could think to bank on in that moment. "I've been out of work for a while. I'm begging you, don't do this."

She didn't expect them to walk away without the sack in their hands.

However, Ellie did plan to distract them as long as possible, until she could come up with a way to escape. Because she didn't believe for one second they'd be satisfied with taking her cash and leaving her here to identify them to the cops. Although they were wearing ski masks, she'd already heard and seen enough to be a risk. No, the instant she surrendered her loot, she was in trouble.

So she stalled while working up the courage to make them a deal they couldn't refuse. She'd go through with it if she had to. It wouldn't be the worst thing she'd done to survive.

"Everyone's got problems. Do you know how big ours would be if we left here empty-handed?" a third man, whom she hadn't see while pinned to her captor's chest, asked. "What do you think you have that could make us cross our boss?"

The way he licked his lips made her sure they were thinking along the same lines. Nasty ones.

"No way, Dino," another of the burglars, apparently the dumbest one in the bunch, objected. She couldn't believe he'd used the other guy's name. "I'm not trading nothing for that cash. Are you fucking nuts?"

Ellie tried not to grin. They were playing a game she couldn't afford to lose. The other two men would never let the loser in the bunch tell them what to do. Of that she was sure. She shivered as she realized she might get what she was hinting at.

Turning back now would be impossible. So she forged ahead, doing her best to make them as vulnerable as possible, though it was nowhere near as exposed as she was about to be.

"I've been told my blow jobs are worth a lot of trouble." She shrugged one shoulder, drawing the three attackers' gazes to her chest, which looked pretty spectacular in the dress her friends had urged her to haul out of the way, way back of her closet for their special occasion. "I just need enough of the stash to pay off some bills. I'll take care of you. You tell your boss I blew some dough on the way home. Don't hurt me and I'll pretend like I never saw you. Deal?"

One of the guys was practically stripping her with their stares. The third, the one who'd grabbed her, didn't seem convinced.

She forced a giggle. "It will sort of be true. Except it'll be you I blow. What do you say?"

Please let this work! What was she getting herself into? Was she digging this hole deeper?

Would they use her body then kill her anyway?

No. She would find a way out of this. The first rule was *stay alive*. Her time in Morselli's dungeon was proof of that.

"Why not have some fun with her first?" The guy nearest her thrust his hips toward her, grinding against her hip so that she could feel his puny boner stabbing her. Either the power he wielded over her, their mission to steal her winnings, or both, did it for him. She'd bet he was one of those guys who liked to hurt women while they fucked. And she didn't mean the consensual kind of pain her friends in the BDSM lifestyle enjoyed, either.

Immediately, she quit wriggling as a flash of memory surfaced.

Ellie saw herself buried under a pile of stoned victims who pawed at her, practically tearing her apart in their urgent need to fuck. Then the vision shifted and she recalled blurred snippets of herself doing the same to a man who'd paid to sleep with a drugged aggressor instead.

She shuddered.

Fortunately, her revulsion only seemed to enhance her captors' interest.

"Fine, fuck. But don't take all damn night when it's your turn," the tall guy snarled at his companions. "And I'm going first."

Ellie shrieked when he lunged for her, wrapping his hand around her upper arm like a vise. The bruising force of his grip nearly made her drop her bag.

"Change your mind?" He laughed at her fleeting display of fear. "Too bad. No taking it back now."

"No, no. I'm game if you are. I just... Can we go in there? For privacy?" She jerked her chin toward the spare bedroom.

"Good idea." He stared at her boobs while he talked. "I don't need these two jacking off while they watch you suck my cock."

Ellie tried not to roll her eyes. Under different circumstances she'd like the idea of men secure enough to masturbate together, maybe give each other a hand. Not today. Not like this.

So she played into her assailant's phobias and his immoral streak, which was wider than the enormous gap she'd had between her front teeth in the BB—before braces—years. Alluding to any number of dirty deeds, she steeled herself and leaned into his harsh hold before whispering, "That way they won't know if I let you do...*more*...with me."

She yelped as he dragged her into the spare bedroom then kicked the door closed behind them. He flung her to the floor where she skidded on the hardwood, banging her knees hard enough to make lights flash behind her scrunched lids.

Nothing she hadn't endured before.

He'd have to do far worse than that to break her.

Ellie tuned her mind to the sound of imaginary ocean waves. She loved the sea and had used its lulling rhythms to help her endure the horrible realities she'd survived in the past. In her vision, she was swimming in warm, salty surf instead of kneeling at the boots of a disgusting pig who planned to violate her.

His fingers wrapped around her neck and yanked her closer so that her face mashed against his musty crotch. Reflexes took over and she gagged.

"We haven't even gotten to the fun part yet." He chuckled at her discomfort. "Don't you dare wimp out on me now."

Ellie mumbled, "Sorry."

In her heart, she'd come to associate the word with "fuck you". Even if it was only in her mind, she'd conditioned herself to say one thing and mean another entirely. Tricks like those had preserved her sanity— at least the portion she'd managed to salvage—when she was an unwilling sex slave.

The guy didn't waste time. He jammed his hand in her bodice and popped her tits out of the top so that they sat on her strapless bra and the crumpled fabric of her dress like it was a ruby shelf. He pinched her nipples. Hard.

Ellie reared back then tried to make her roar of outrage sound more like a groan.

The glint in his obsidian eyes made it clear he wasn't fooled and didn't care.

Hell, he might have enjoyed it more that way.

Committed to distracting him, Ellie reached up and slid his zipper open. She held her breath then nuzzled his hard-on as he shoved his briefs down low enough to reveal his bare cock and shriveled balls hanging below.

Swallowing hard, she parted her lips then grazed them along his length.

With a groan, he shut his eyes.

Perfect.

Ellie continued to distract him as she started to slide the zipper of her sack open.

Suddenly she wished she'd grabbed the pistol stashed a little deeper in her flowerbed, instead of this lame pepper spray and stun gun. It would have been more effective, but completely irreversible. Deep down she knew she'd have trouble pulling the trigger, even in these circumstances. Killing someone wasn't something she was sure she could live with.

Memories of the men and women as blameless as she was, who'd died around her that day the Men in Blue rescued her, still haunted Ellie. In fact, she saw their faces flashing in front of her as she made the man she was servicing grunt and groan, not so different than the sounds she'd heard that day.

From the other room the burglars jeered, mimicking their partner and making crude jokes.

As if they'd be any different when it got to their turns. Not that it ever would.

Snapping out of her dazed recollections, Ellie shook her head, opening her eyes only for a moment. Something glinted in the light streaming from the window. She caught the shimmer in her peripheral vision—the barrel of a gun and righteous fury beaming from warm eyes she would recognize anywhere.

Lucas! Holy shit, had it really been him? She didn't dare risk another glance.

"No time for second thoughts, bitch." The guy grunted and reached for her hair, wrapping it around his fist. "Ignore those assholes out there and really get to work here. Quit stalling."

Then Ellie didn't have to wonder about the insanity developing around her anymore. That rich, smoky voice she'd heard endlessly in her dreams lately commanded, "Get down!"

So she hit the floor. Immediately. She dropped, ignoring the wrench of her neck as her hair slithered from her confused attacker's grip. Ellie covered her head with her arms, acting on blind faith.

Lucas had been her savior once, and here he was again precisely when she needed him most. She couldn't help but wonder how much he'd seen and what he would think of her for the acts she'd been about to perform to stay alive.

Especially considering it wasn't the first time either.

While the guy beside her scrambled to pull up his jeans, several things happened at once. Ellie snagged the bag she'd dropped, finished unzipping it and withdrew the stun gun inside. She flicked the power switch and Tased the fucker who'd planned to violate her, zapping him right in his sweaty balls.

His scream was lost in the chaos as another one of the robbers barged into the room—gun drawn, pointed directly at her heart—and shouted, "What the fuck was that?"

Lucas blew him away before she could even flinch from the guy's reappearance.

Next he used the butt of his gun to smash out the remaining glass from her window. Then he shouted at her, waking her from her slow-motion daze. "Come on, Ellie! Run! Now!"

Heart racing, she abandoned the pouch she'd clung to like a lifeline and launched to her feet. Her heels slipped in the splatter of blood, which pooled around the man who gurgled behind her. The third man stood in the doorway, nearly as shocked as she was, as she dove toward Lucas and the darkness that surrounded him.

Quick to avert his gun, he let her pass through the opening—less than gracefully, her belly sliding across the jagged glass—before whipping his weapon toward the last of their intruders still standing.

When she finished tumbling to the bushes below then bouncing to her feet, the man held his hands up though his eyes darted to the bag she'd abandoned. Of course, all he really cared about was the money.

Except it wasn't in there. The only thing left in it was her pepper spray and the case for the Taser. It wouldn't take him long to figure that out.

They needed to get the hell out of there before he realized she'd deceived them.

Lucas began to walk backward, talking to the burglar as calmly as if they were watching this nightmare transpire on TV instead of right before them. Though his gait was slightly uneven, it was steady. "We're leaving now. Keep the light on so I can see you standing right fucking there. Wait ten minutes. Then take what you came for. Make up some lie. Tell your boss there was an accident and she didn't make it. Whatever you need to do. Figure it out. Or you'll end up just like your friend there. I'll make sure of it."

"Who the *fuck* are you?" the man asked, though he had to know Lucas wasn't about to answer.

This side of him—cold, calculating, utterly capable—would make any sane person crap their pants.

Thankfully, she was a tad bit nuts.

Ellie could have kissed him for saving her ass. Again.

"Lucas..." she whispered so the intruder wouldn't pick up on her white knight's name. Should she tell him the money wasn't really there?

"Not now, E."

His pet name for her had Ellie ready to burst into tears when everything that came before hadn't so much as dampened her eyes. Relief, longing and lingering terror mixed into a potent cocktail, making her drunk on him.

Here he was, every bit as wounded as she was, and not letting it stop him from being a complete badass.

Hell, he'd shot someone for her. Killed for her.

There was no way that guy was getting up after being hit so accurately in his chest.

Oh yeah, Lucas had also lost a limb for her.

She owed him her life, twice over.

When they'd retreated far enough that the grass of her lawn transitioned to the moss of the forest floor, Lucas began to relax. He also glanced down to make sure his footing was secure. Shit, this had to be difficult for him.

Before she could worry too much about it, a stream of curses came from within her house. "Where'd it go? Fuck!"

At nearly the same time, an engine gunned down her street at a roar that spoke of reinforcements instead of the sedate grannies who were her neighbors. They didn't stick around to see whose side the newcomers were coming to aid.

"I'm not expecting help. Let's get out of here." Lucas grabbed her hand, spared half a glance at her bared breasts then clenched his jaw. Neither of them was willing to risk delaying to protect her modesty. At least not until they put some distance between themselves and danger.

He took off at an uneven jog, his foot catching awkwardly on a tangle of roots. She held his hand—the one without the gun—tight and helped lever him back to balance. Together, they scrambled over some logs.

"How'd you know—?"

"Later." He grimaced. "If I slow you down, I want you to go on ahead of me. I may not win any races like this, but I can still hide if I have to. Especially at night. They'll never find me."

Lucas shook his fingers free of hers for a moment. Her vision had adjusted enough that she could make out him fishing in his jeans before he drew out a wicked-looking pocketknife. One of those utility kinds that had about a thousand attachments and could probably launch a rocket to the moon in the right hands. Hands like his.

In the wrong hands...she shivered.

"What's this for?" Stabbing someone seemed extreme. She'd like to think she could if her life depended on it, but she didn't want to have to test that theory. Besides, she was no match for a muscled man with experience and her free-blow-job shtick was only going to work so many times before word got around.

"There's a compass in the handle." He glanced at her as he guided them deeper into the woods. "If we get separated, head northeast. If you walk as fast as you can in those shoes, you should come out somewhere near my house in about...two to three hours, maybe."

"I'm not going anywhere without you." She tried to take stock of everything that was happening. At lightning speed. Where the hell had her simple girls' night out gone? And how could he assume she'd be selfish enough to leave him to fend for himself when he was in this mess because of her?

"It'd be harder to conceal us both. You have to trust me, E."

"I do." It was the honest truth.

"Good. It's not what I want, either. You will if you have to." He cursed as he stumbled again, his prosthesis throwing him off-balance on the rocky terrain. "No matter what, don't use your phone. Remember what happened last year when Jambi called the guys from that hotel room?"

How could she forget?

Ellie and Lucas had been helping Matt, Clint and Jambrea out. But Jambrea had gotten a glimpse of necrotizing flesh on Lucas's foot and reached out to experts at the hospital for assistance. The lunatics chasing Jambrea had tracked them within minutes of that call, making them all scatter and run. It had been the day Lucas had finally quit fighting and allowed the doctors to amputate his leg. The day he had stopped talking to her.

"In fact, go ahead and take the battery out now." Lucas cleared his throat before pausing their flight. Ducking into the branches of a particularly thick pine tree, he shoved her behind him as he scanned the area around them and cocked his head, listening intently.

When Lucas spoke next, it was quieter and more strained. "Then pull your dress up. Please."

She couldn't help her cringe, though not because she'd forgotten her body was on display. That hardly fazed her anymore.

While she did as he asked, she wondered, "Why? Are you disgusted by what I did to survive?"

They both knew she wasn't only talking about tonight. It'd been something she wondered for months now. Was her time in Morselli's dungeon contributing to why he didn't want her around?

"No, but I might be tempted to go back there and kill someone else if I keep seeing the proof of their filthy hands on you." He spat on the ground without glancing at her.

Ellie glanced at the maroon fingermarks that would likely bruise her breasts by morning. "Oh."

She yanked up her sweetheart neckline and finished tucking herself into place. Then she stripped her battery from her phone, slipped it into the pocket of her dress and spun on her heel, which sank into the muddy ground. With Lucas wearing his prosthesis and her in these stupid shoes, they weren't going to be moving very fast. She wanted to put as much distance as possible between her and her house while they could. Even if it meant marching into pitch-black woods.

"Let's get the hell out of here then."

"Good idea, E."

CHAPTER FOUR

After thirty minutes, Ellie was fairly sure no one was going to jump out from behind a tree and shoot them. Lucas seemed to concur, since he'd jammed his gun in the waistband of his pants so that he could use both hands to steady himself as they plunged deeper into the forest. That seemed like a pretty decent way to shoot off his fine ass, but she figured he knew what he was doing since he had ninja-level fighting skills.

He'd also slowed his pace from Olympic-record-setting to I'm-about-to-miss-a-bus-and-the-next-one-isn't-for-an-hour. Maybe that had more to do with his leg than his assessment of their safety level, though. His limp was definitely pronounced, compared to when they'd started out.

The moon was bright out here in the middle of nowhere. She could see his muscles rippling beneath his clothes. Focusing on that helped her keep going while her feet screamed in agony. Sweat poured down Lucas's temples and his jaw was clamped so tight she was afraid he might crack a tooth.

"Psst." Her hiss sounded as loud as his gunshot had earlier, ringing in her ears after their long, silent march.

His head whipped around. The intensity of his stare would have frightened her if she hadn't known—

all the way to her soul—that he would never be a threat to her. At least not physically.

Her heart was another matter. The damn thing wanted him, even though he'd turned her down eleventy-bazillion times already.

"Need a break?" he asked.

She didn't, but she thought he might. So she lied, "If it's not going to put us in a terrible position, yes."

"I think we can afford a couple minutes."

He slowed then used his T-shirt-covered biceps to scrub his forehead. They'd been following a stream uphill, against the flow. She guessed it was leading them to the lake behind his house.

It probably would have been a beautiful hike if she could see more than ten feet in front of her, or if she'd been dressed appropriately, or if maniacs weren't hunting them. Preferably all of the above.

He scoped out the area, ushering her to a fallen tree nestled in a mound of bushes. When they sat, huddled close together, each facing in opposite directions so they didn't have their backs to anything, he sighed. Even that tiny admission of relief was monumental for Lucas.

Ellie tried to relate. "I would love to kick off my shoes for a second, but I'm afraid I'll never get them back on if I do."

How much worse must it be for him?

He grunted. "I hear that. Unfortunately, I do need to take this thing off to make a quick adjustment."

Lucas knocked his prosthesis against the tree trunk twice in rapid succession.

"Take my gun while I do. I won't be any good to you until my leg is back on. I'll be fast. You remember how to shoot, right?" He'd taken her to the range a few times right after she'd been released from the dungeon, empowering her and teaching her to fend for herself.

"I practice once a week." She nodded, though she was sure he knew that from their mutual friends. Unless he forbade them to talk about her too.

The thought tweaked something inside her. Could he hate her that much? It didn't seem like it when he took such good care of her. Then again, he was a noble bastard. Maybe he'd do the same for any damsel in distress.

"I wasn't sure since you had a Taser and pepper spray on you, but not your Glock." He double-checked the safety then carefully handed her his weapon.

"Foolish me." She rolled her eyes at herself then watched intently as he began to doff his prosthesis. Every few seconds her gaze swung out to their surroundings, making sure it was still clear. "I guess I just thought the worst had already happened. Besides, the idea of taking someone's life—"

"It's a serious choice. Never easy." He paused as he rummaged through his backpack. The bob of his Adam's apple was clear, even in the dim light.

"Shit. I'm sorry, Lucas."

She stared into his eyes, which seemed a little glazed. Over what he'd done tonight? Or countless times before? She couldn't quite tell. But neither must be pleasant for him to think about.

"If I'd grabbed my gun instead of my wimpier survival kit, maybe you wouldn't have had to..."

"My hands are already plenty dirty. Stained with blood." This time he didn't shy away from her inquisitive glance. "I'd rather you stay innocent."

A laugh bubbled from her chest. It frightened her that it sounded kind of hysterical. "We both know I'm anything but pure."

Lucas's stare morphed into a glare. "Don't you *dare* do that to yourself."

"What? Tell the fucking truth?" She flung her hair over her shoulder with the hand not holding his gun.

For a while, he was silent. He withdrew his fist from his backpack, clutching a ball of cotton.

Without a moment's pause, he unsnapped his jeans, yanked the zipper down, hooked his thumbs in the waistband then stripped them down to his ankles.

Ellie nearly drooled at the sight of his thick thighs and the bold swirls of his tattoos that ran down each leg. That was even before she dared to glance at the bulge in his boxer briefs.

She wished it weren't so damn dark.

Unselfconscious about his nudity, he sat there for a moment as if gathering courage to unveil his leg to her. As if that could make him any less incredible.

Ellie refused to look away for even a moment. She quit trying to hide how attractive she found him. If that's what he needed to feel more secure, she could easily give it to him.

As she watched, he pressed a button on the side of his prosthesis. Holding it steady, he pulled his thigh back while keeping the socket in place. A strap slipped through the lock, allowing his residual limb to slide free.

Clever.

She'd never seen the inner workings of his leg since he hadn't willingly let her within a mile of him after the surgery.

Still enveloped in his jeans, his foot made a dull *thud* as it landed on the leaf-covered ground.

Ellie would have been lying if she didn't admit that seeing his leg end short didn't take her by surprise. Maybe because he still seemed so extremely normal that with his clothes and shoes it was easy to imagine he hadn't changed. Now the difference was evident.

He flexed his knee a few times, rubbing the front of it while the few inches of his shin remaining below that swung up and back. It must be sore as hell if that was where all his weight was resting as he tromped through the forest.

Beneath the fiberglass he had several layers of fabric on. A few that looked like socks. Then something gray that seemed thicker, almost like neoprene or some kind of fabric-backed gel. He unfurled the ball of white cotton in his hand and selected one from the middle, a medium weight compared to thinner and thicker versions in his stash.

Curious, she watched as he rolled it over his residual limb, lining up a slit in the side so that the strap—which looked sort of like a giant zip tie—could poke through.

"This is kind of genius." She reached out, her fingers skimming the device.

"It's called a proximal lock. The strap is glued to my liner and then slides into the prosthesis, keeping my foot attached to my leg," he said, though he jerked away from her touch.

So she let her hand drop.

For the span of several irregular heartbeats, they simply stared at each other. Each of their insecurities laid bare. Raw and not entirely healed.

"Neither one of us is the way we were made anymore," he finally murmured, as if it'd taken him that long to rein in his temper after her earlier revelations about herself. "I'm working on being okay with that for myself. But I want you to know that I never thought, for one instant, that what was done to you made you any less of a woman. In fact, I admire you more for having persevered. Triumphed."

"Then I suppose we understand each other perfectly." Ellie smiled tightly up at Lucas, though his short-cropped hair, chocolate eyes and lightly stubbled jaw wavered in her liquidy gaze.

She wished they were safely inside his cabin. If they had been, she might have chanced leaning forward and lifting her lips to his. Just one taste. That was all she hoped for.

Okay, that was a big, fat lie.

But she'd settle for it if she had to.

Lucas broke their eye contact, going back to the task at hand.

"Can I ask what you're doing?"

Genuine curiosity about this man and the new aspects of his life flooded her. She wanted to know everything about him and how she could help. *If* she could. Damn it, she'd been trying to do exactly that for months. Except he hadn't wanted her assistance.

Or maybe he'd been worried about her pity. Though he shouldn't have.

She'd never treat him like a victim. She knew enough about whispers and sidelong glances to want to deck anyone who treated her like that. If that was what he expected from her, he'd be waiting a long damn time.

"Uh, yeah, I guess." He glanced at her from the corner of his eye, as if making sure he wasn't freaking her out or something.

"Come on, Lucas. Give me some credit here. I'd rather be educated than ignorant. I'm not going to be grossed out or something." She flailed her arm before remembering that she held his gun.

He ducked and held his hands up. "Whoa. No need for violence."

She snapped to attention, keeping the weapon safely pointed away from them. Horrified, she looked back in time to find the crazy bastard grinning. The full wattage of his smile was enough to light up the entire state preserve, all seventy-five square miles of it. It nearly knocked her off the log they shared and onto her ass.

In her skimpy dress, that would have given him quite a view, and probably resulted in her shooting something at the same damn time.

"Shit. Shit. Shit. Sorry." This time she really did mean it.

As if her gaff had loosened his inhibitions, he gave her what she'd asked for. Information.

"My stump. Er, my leg, or whatever you want to call this here"—he waved to his residual limb—"is still changing. Less now than right at first. Hell, it shrunk so much in the beginning I could probably fit two of these stumps in the first test socket they made for me."

"Is that normal?" she wondered.

"Yeah." He nodded. "I had to wear a shrinker to keep the swelling down and stuff. Anyway, now it's more stable. Even still, the volume of my stump changes throughout the day. Always will. Probably four or five times, when I'm just doing normal crap, I've got to take this outside shell off and add or subtract stump socks to adjust the fit on my prosthesis. Otherwise it's really uncomfortable and it can start to impact my skin integrity and make sores. Nothing's worse than that for an amputee because it means I might not be able to wear my leg until it heals or risk infection. Then I'm stuck."

Ellie hadn't realized how complicated being an amputee was. There were probably a million other things she hadn't thought of either. Yet, here Lucas was, just seven months postsurgery, back on his feet and looking stronger than ever. Determined. Capable. And sexy as sin.

Seriously, she didn't remember him having such defined arms before and his chest filled out his shirt to absolute perfection. Ogling him as he concentrated on refitting his leg—threading the strap into the lock and stomping until it clicked and ratcheted into place—she felt like a perv.

So she distracted herself with a lame attempt at humor. "Guess it's a good thing I'm not an amputee then, because I'm pretty sure I have blisters the size of Lily's whip collection going on after taking a stroll in these puppies. They're really more for looking good than for walking."

Her nervous laughter cut short when his gaze snapped to hers. "Fuck, Ellie. Why didn't you mention it? Are you okay?"

"Considering everything else that's happened tonight, it doesn't rate." She shook her head at his concern, though she'd be lying if she said she didn't appreciate knowing he cared.

"Let me see," he ordered.

"It's nothing, Lucas." She shook her head. "We should get going again if you're good."

"I'm not moving until I take a look." Stubborn was this man's middle name. It might be his first and last name too.

When she would have kept arguing, he cut her off. "I'm sorry, E. But we've still got a long way to go. Another two hours at our pace, probably. If we don't take care of this now, it's only going to get worse. Like

I am now...I don't know if I could carry you. Let's fix the problem before it turns into something we can't handle."

Well, when he made it sound logical, how could she resist? Damn him.

***

Lucas felt tension melt from him as Ellie toed off her shoes then tucked her feet up beside her, into his lap. Impressive how she did that while still holding his gun, balancing on the log and managing not to flash him in the process, despite the ruined-though-still-phenomenal dress hugging her curves exactly right.

Fuck, he was never going to get the picture of her wearing it out of his mind.

Plenty to jerk off to later, he supposed.

He figured he was going to have to make the rest of this hike with a boner...until he glanced down and saw the mangled skin of her feet. A bloody mess, they looked nearly black in the darkness.

"Son of a bitch! Ellie!" He let his voice rise to a whisper-shout.

The instant she attempted to withdraw, he shackled her ankles with his fingers. Unthinking, he gripped her tight and refused to let her draw away now that he realized she needed medical attention.

The soft smile that had curled her lips despite their situation vanished. She froze, every muscle locked down tight. Her eyes went blank and her pupils dilated. The rise and fall of her perfect breasts sped up as she fought to draw in a breath.

Lucas had triggered her.

Immediately, he let go.

"E," he crooned, trying to bring her back from a land of nightmares. "It's me, Lucas. I didn't mean to frighten you. You're safe, I promise."

So, that part might be a lie. But at least she was free of the demons he knew she was seeing around her. If his simple hold had terrified her, what would happen if he did what his libido had been urging since he'd gotten to know her? If he unleashed the full blast of his attraction for her, he'd probably terrify her so bad she might never recover.

Afraid to touch her, he let his hand hover a hairsbreadth from her arm while his other reclaimed his weapon and put it safely aside. Despite the need inside him to destroy the people who'd done this to her, he kept his voice calm and reassuring as he rambled soothing nonsense.

It worked.

Ellie blinked up at him a few times and then flushed.

Far more embarrassed than she'd been earlier, with her entire chest displayed to the world, she pressed her palms over her face and peeked at him from between splayed fingers. "Shit."

"It's okay."

"That happens sometimes. It's getting better. I just, I can't help it when something reminds me. I know you would never—"

"Don't worry, E." He rummaged in his amputee survival kit for the first aid supplies he needed, while giving her time to recover. When she sniffled, he couldn't keep his gaze averted any longer.

What he really wanted was to hug her tight.

Maybe a hell of a lot more than that.

And that was exactly why he should stay far away. No way was she ready for that.

Not with him or anyone else.

"Is it okay if I touch your feet?" he asked quietly. "I have some 2nd Skin in here. It's pretty awesome stuff. It'll give you instant relief. It's an occlusive bandage. Keeps out water and air too. It'll stop your shoes from rubbing on these spots for the rest of our trek."

Ellie cleared her throat then said, "I'm good now. Please. Do it. That sounds awesome."

Lucas started carefully, brushing his thumb across her ankle. Even swollen from the abuse they'd put it through, it was delicate. Fine-boned.

When she seemed to relax further, tolerating his caress, he stroked the top of her foot.

A sigh rushed from her before she surrendered a soft laugh that had his heart flip-flopping in his chest. "Keep that up and I'm going to beg you for a massage when we get to your house."

That only brought to mind images of her naked, lying on his bed as he smeared warm, scented oils over her shapely back. Candlelight would glisten off her lubricated skin.

He cleared his throat.

Focusing on fixing her up, he opened a bottle of water then apologized in advance, "This is probably going to sting."

She nodded, biting her lower lip. "Go."

He splashed the damaged skin of her feet until the blood and other fluids were washed away. Then he uncapped a tube of antibiotic ointment and smeared some on the patch of bandage. Who knew what kind of germs had embedded themselves in her open wounds?

He aligned the material with the worst of her sores then pressed it into place.

Ellie's pretty painted toes curled and she groaned.

"Sorry." He promised, "It'll be better in a minute."

Quickly, he finished applying similar patches to the rest of her blisters.

While he worked, she talked. He suspected she was distracting herself, so he kept their conversation going, even when he might otherwise have clammed up.

"You obviously didn't walk all the way to my house." It wasn't a question.

"Nope." He figured she could tell this was a strain on him too.

"So, I assume your car was on the street in front of my house, unless your superpowers include flying. Won't they know where we're going?" She peeked up at him, taking her focus off what he was doing to her.

"My plates are untraceable. Nothing identifying inside either." He shrugged as though everyone existed that way. Like a ghost.

"Given the night we've already had, I *really* hate to tell you this..." Ellie winced.

"Go ahead. This is by far *not* the worst situation I've ever been in." He flashed her a wry smile.

"Me either." Her lips formed a thin line.

Lucas hated seeing her worried. Almost more than he hated how her toughness had prevented her from telling him she'd torn up her feet, which he had finished bandaging, but kept in his lap. "So, what's up?"

He acted on instinct, reaching out to cup her hand in his.

It surprised the hell out of him when she winged her gaze to his, pretty blue eyes flashing despite the darkness surrounding them. It wasn't fear he read there this time. More like astonishment and delight, to be honest.

"You know I won a crap ton of money tonight, right?" She winced.

"Yep. The Men in Blue sent me to your place to make sure you were safe overnight. Guess I fucked up that assignment."

"Are you shitting me?" She stared at him with wide eyes, her fingers clamping on his when he tried to withdraw his hand. "You saved my life. Again."

"If I'd gotten there sooner..."

"I'm thankful you didn't get there any later. You showed up exactly when and where I needed you. Thank you."

He cleared his throat and looked away for a moment. "Anytime."

"Let's hope I don't need this kind of assistance often." She snorted. And then she recovered, as if she remembered what she'd wanted to say. "Ah crap. Lucas, I left the money at my house. That last douche bag probably stole it anyway. Not that I care about any amount of cash more than my life, but I hate to see scum win. When will the nice guys start coming out on top?"

Lucas wasn't bothered at all by her admission. Instead, he grinned.

"You have good instincts, E." His praise seemed to warm her. Good thing since her arms and legs had to be cooling down now that they'd stopped moving. "Don't doubt your decisions."

He interrupted himself when he realized she was probably freezing her ass off.

"Want me to take some of your chill away before we get going again?" He held his arms open to her.

Without hesitation, she went into them.

59

He lifted her into his lap and wrapped her in his heat and admiration. Though he was rarely cold, he could never be frosty with her this near. She fired his internal furnace in more ways than one.

Ellie rested her cheek on his shoulder, cuddling entirely too perfectly into his hold.

Shifting her so that she wouldn't feel his hardening cock, he nuzzled the top of her head. As he'd expected, she was practically a popsicle. Fine tremors ran through her as he rubbed his hands up and down her back and legs.

In his dreams, he'd pretend it was desire, not necessity, that caused her reaction.

The early morning temperature had dipped far below comfortable. Hell, even at the peak of summer she'd need more than that beaded red scrap to keep warm overnight.

When she could talk without her teeth chattering, she continued their discussion. "Thanks. I thought I was being paranoid when I came up to the house. Something seemed off. I guess I should have listened to my gut."

"Never a bad thing. But you were smart enough to stash the winnings and grab your safety kit before going in. Even if I hadn't been there, I'm betting you'd have slipped away. I just don't want to think about what you might have had to do to distract those fuckers long enough to make your move." He nearly growled that last part.

"Hey, how do you know I hid the money and stuff?" Her brow rose. "Were you outside?"

Busted.

"Uh. Yeah. I saw you." Lucas groaned. "I was kind of checking you out."

Why the hell was she grinning up at him like that?

60

It only made him a pig, like most every other man she'd dealt with in her life.

"And because of that, I didn't act fast enough. I didn't see those guys waiting inside for you." He stared into her eyes, which were shockingly blue, even in the starlight. "I'm sorry, E."

She leaned in closer to him. "You're human too, Lucas. I know you thought you were invincible for so long maybe you've forgotten—"

"I'm pretty sure the universe made that clear to me last year." He glared at his leg, which throbbed from the abuse he'd put it through today.

"Hey, we all have flaws. Make mistakes. Like the *fifty-thousand-dollar* doozy I made tonight." She shook her head.

Lucas held her to his chest with one splayed hand on her back. With the other, he tipped his still-open backpack toward her so that she could see the casino bag nestled inside. "I've got you covered. I picked this up for you."

She stiffened then threw her arms around him, hugging him tight. When she peeked up at him, her brilliant smile was a pretty decent reward. "You're amazing, you know that?"

"Not nearly as much as you." His head dropped, bringing his mouth dangerously close to hers.

Ellie's eyes fluttered closed and her lips parted.

Until he ruined the moment for them both with his thoughts. "When I saw what that bastard was about to do to you, I wished I hadn't stopped to snag the money, though."

"I'm glad you did. They don't deserve to prosper. At least what they did was for nothing." She blinked rapidly a few times. "I can't imagine even fifty grand is worth risking a life over. Never mind several."

Lucas cursed.

"What?" she looked up at him, half as confused as he felt.

Attraction, fear, danger and lust swirled around them in a deadly mix. A storm brewing.

"I think we should get going again if you're ready, E. Because I can tell you one thing..."

He swung to his feet and pulled her easily to hers, banking on his recently enhanced strength. At least all those gym hours counted for something. When they were upright, he snagged his jeans and drew them into place, securing them at his waist and shrugging into the backpack once more.

"These are bundles of hundreds in here."

"Yeah, I noticed. *Lots* of them."

"That's exactly my point. A standard bundle of hundreds is worth ten grand." He waited for that to sink in.

"That can't be right." She shook her head. "If it were, there would only be four and a partial. There are at least a dozen in there."

"Twenty," he confirmed. "I counted."

"What the—?"

"I'm pretty sure someone used you as a mule." Lucas frowned. "Maybe your win was real, maybe not, but the cashier definitely paid out far more than you were due."

"There's no way that's a simple mistake, right?" Ellie groaned.

"No," he confirmed.

"Fuck my life," she grumbled, then stuck out her hand.

Against his better judgment, he entwined their fingers.

Ellie surprised him when she yanked him toward her. Off-balance on his bad leg, he practically crashed into her soft breasts, flinging his arm around her to keep them both from smashing to the forest floor.

"Thank you for always being there when I need you." He saw her going to her tiptoes, read the intent in her eyes, and still he didn't take evasive maneuvers.

How could he, when he wanted to taste her so badly? Fuck, he craved her more than a pile of scallops on top of lobster ravioli—his favorite meal. And he could eat that every day for the rest of his life without ever getting tired of it.

The same might go for her.

Lucas groaned at the first sample of her lips. He savored her sweetness as if he were approving a fine wine from a sommelier at a five-star restaurant. It wasn't long before he was taking a nibble of her lower lip then fusing their mouths for a bigger portion of her.

It was better than he'd dreamed of, though he couldn't imagine how that was possible.

She arched into him, swiping her tongue across one corner of his lips then flicking it against his own. They thrust and parried as if they'd practiced this mock duel a million times before.

The rush of finally kissing her went straight to his head, and his groin. He wanted it to keep going forever because when he focused on bringing her pleasure, nothing else mattered. Not his leg, not her past, not the trouble they were smack in the middle of now.

Eventually, he had to breathe.

When they broke apart, both huffing like they'd run up the mountainside, all he could do was stare.

She was even more beautiful when she looked at him with unadulterated lust in her eyes.

"Take me home," she nearly begged.

He groaned, his cock twitching in his pants at the thought. Insane, he planned to do just that. Ellie Noble in his house! Hell, probably his bed, seeing as he only had one. How would he ever manage to keep his hands off her now that he knew how fucking great it felt to make out with her?

CHAPTER FIVE

Ellie had trudged for so long, concentrating only on putting one foot in front of the other, that when the trees began to thin, she hardly noticed. All she could think about was what it would take to bribe Lucas into rubbing her calves when they got to his house. Maybe if she offered the same in return he'd go for it. It'd be like sixty-nine for lame, bedraggled hikers.

His leg had to be killing him. He'd taken a few tumbles, ripping his jeans and skinning his knee along the way. Other than a vicious curse or two, he hadn't complained. So there was no way she was about to either.

Her dress had suffered too. The skirt had torn along the side seams, putting her thighs entirely on display, right up to her lacy red thong. Most of the beads had snapped off as branches ensnared the delicate strands. They'd also caned the upper swells of her bared breasts and caused welts along the exposed skin.

It was at times like these that she drew on the certainty that she was stronger than she'd ever imagined. This fleeting physical discomfort had nothing on her time held captive and how that had damaged her soul. If she could survive that, she could endure an uncomfortable walk through the woods with the one man—besides her brother, relatives didn't count—she'd most like to spend time with.

Especially if, as she imagined, Lucas was proving some things to himself about his capabilities tonight along the way.

"We did it, E. Holy shit." Lucas's voice penetrated her calcified brain. "My house is right over that hill."

As soon as he broke the good news, a rush of elation washed over her. She wanted to sprint, just to be there. Warm and safe, inside his home. Another part of her gave out, her limbs going noodly as they realized they'd done their job.

"Hang on, just a little bit farther." Lucas tightened his arm around her waist.

When had he slung it there? She didn't care that she'd missed it when he tugged her against his side.

Surprised, she realized she was holding him in the same way, both of them drawing strength and balance from the other. "How do we know for sure no one's waiting for us?"

Ellie didn't mean to second-guess him, but he'd told her to trust her instincts and right now she was worried they'd come all this way just to limp into a trap. Why else hadn't that guy chased them? Unless he'd been tearing her cute little house apart searching for the missing cash he'd been sent to pick up. When she thought about the dead men inside and the damage the lone remaining burglar had likely done, she wasn't sure she would ever feel comfortable there again.

"I've got ways to tell." Lucas winked at her. "I promise. You'll be safe here. Come on."

He steered her toward a small boathouse near a dock that jutted onto the lake. While she would love a tour at some other time, especially since he'd never so much as invited her over for one of the Men in Blue barbecues he'd occasionally held here, right now she only wanted to collapse somewhere soft and horizontal.

Giving him the benefit of the doubt, she ducked beneath his arm when he held the door open for her. The slightly musty shack held life vests, a changing room, spare oars and a mountain of fishing equipment that was a hell of a lot less organized than she would have imagined anything of his might be.

When he led her to a freestanding tackle box on one wall, she started thinking of polite ways to let him know she wasn't in the mood to see his antique-fly collection or catch their breakfast at the moment.

Lucas felt around its side, doing something she couldn't quite see.

And that was when a palm scanner popped out of the corner of the box.

"Wow." Sometimes it was hard to remember that this had been his life for so long. He seemed like a normal—mostly—guy. Not too different from the cops she hung around a lot these days. Ellie was starting to realize that he was a next-level crime fighter.

He smiled at her then said, "I may be retired, but I've still got a few tricks up my sleeves."

Once he'd verified about ten thousand different passcodes and who knew what else, the lid of the box opened. Enough computer equipment to make JRad come in his pants was stashed inside.

To her it might as well have been books written in Chinese.

The blinking lights, lines, graphs, maps and whatever else seemed to satisfy him, though.

"It's clean." He hummed his approval. "I'm going to disable the perimeter until we can get through."

That sounded like he had bombs planted around his property or something.

Maybe robofish in his pond.

Surreal.

The only other point of reference she had was her friend Shari and the things Jambrea had told her about the woman's resort, which could pretty much double as a fortress if needed. "Is it true that you used to work with Shari's brother?"

"Technically, I'm not supposed to confirm that." He left no doubt it was true.

"I don't even know what branch of the military you were in." She inspected him as if she'd missed one of his tattoos that would proudly proclaim him a member of some service.

"One that doesn't exist on paper." He cleared his throat. "I will say that John David had a reputation as the best person in our business. I still can't believe he's gone."

Lucas stayed quiet for a few moments, lost in thought, until he shook his head. "I guess none of us gets to stay in the game forever. He made it the longest of anyone I know. I didn't do too bad myself."

"Right now, I'm okay with settling for being alive. A comfortable place to pass out would be a bonus." She barely stifled a yawn now that she felt the tension of being on the run finally melting away from her.

"I'm totally in favor of that plan." He rubbed his stomach. "With the addition of some snacks."

Ellie couldn't agree more. "I hope you have ice cream."

"Do you like Rocky Road?" He grimaced. "Although I feel like that might be a little too close to home after the past few hours."

"I'm not particular." Ellie grinned.

"Let's get you inside then." He drew her to him and kissed her forehead lightly, inspiring an entirely different sort of bone-liquefying sensation to course through her. At least until he seemed to come to his senses and set her away from him once again.

"You too." She watched in awe as he repacked his monitoring station and hid the access panel then reached to the floor for a handful of dust to cast over the top.

"You go out first," he instructed. "I'm going to follow behind and step on top of your footprints so it will look like you were never here."

So many tiny details, and he knew how to manipulate them all.

If he kept up these friendly touches and cozy intimacies, how would she know if he meant them with newfound affection, as it seemed, or if he was simply trying to make her malleable?

Either way, it worked.

Outside again, she ambled by his side. Even after a couple of minutes resting, inertia made both of them stiff and awkward after losing their momentum. That warm bed and food was sounding better by the second.

Extra tongue-tangoing would round out her list of immediate needs, not that she dared tell Lucas that and risk spooking him. The idea that intimacy with her freaked him out after everything he'd seen and done in his life nearly had her giggling. Hysteria threatened. She tamped it down.

Lucas surprised the hell out of her when he led her up three or four steps, across the wraparound porch and through his *unlocked* front door. She stared at him with bug eyes.

"What?" He shrugged. "Anyone able to make it to the door won't be deterred by a simple lock."

"So how do you make sure you don't blow up the mailman or something?" she asked as she stepped inside his perfectly normal-looking house. Hardwood took center stage, with cobalt-blue accents that made for a rich and masculine space.

"There's a gate and lots of *No Trespassing* signs along the driveway." He shrugged. "Plus I haven't needed a lot of security lately."

"I'm sorry." It dawned on her that she was dragging him into her mess. Putting him at risk. "I should go. Can we contact the Men in Blue somehow? Maybe they have information about the robbers or someplace to move me. A safe house."

"You couldn't possibly be more protected than you are here." He put his hands on his hips.

"But *you* would be a hell of a lot better off with me far away." The will to argue was trumped by her need to collapse onto his sofa. But she didn't want to ruin the thing with her mud and blood and sweat.

"I don't know about that anymore, Ellie." He grew serious then. "We've tried the hands-off approach and I'm not sure it's working."

She flipped him the bird. "*You* tried that. I had no choice in the matter."

Instead of arguing, he grinned. "It turns me on when you fight back."

"I'm not usually a pushover, Lucas." She glared at him. "You saw me at my worst. Don't make judgments about me based on that or I guarantee you're going to be sorely disappointed."

He cleared his throat, acting the tiniest bit ashamed. It looked weird on him, considering how confident he typically was. Almost, though not quite, to the point of arrogance.

"To answer one of your earlier questions, yes. I have a secure line and I'm going to get in touch with the Men in Blue right now. We'll figure out the best course of action. Do you want to be in on the call?" he asked.

His offer was enough. "Nope. Whatever you guys decide, I'll do. You're the experts. What I want is to find your bathroom and take the longest, hottest shower in the history of the universe."

"I have a deep soaking tub with jets upstairs." He smiled. "Feel free to indulge."

Ellie practically whimpered at the thought alone.

Lucas hobbled into the kitchen and grabbed some fruit, a couple bottles of water and a block of cheese from his fridge. Then he gestured toward the stairs. "You first. I'm still unsteady going up these, especially right now."

"Can I help somehow?" She turned, about to offer her hand or something.

"I can do it on my own."

"Of course you *can.*"

He glanced away, then back, as if it pained him more to ask for assistance than it would falling on his ass with his hands full. "Would you maybe grab the food so I can use the railing?"

"Sure." Except he'd snagged more than she could hold in her much smaller hands.

Fuck it. Not like she had any modesty left at this point. She grabbed the hem of her dress and lifted the front flap of the shredded material, holding it out in front of her like a net.

Lucas deposited his scroungings, swallowing hard as he tried valiantly not to steal a glimpse at her exposed legs. Or her panties, which peeked out beneath the ruined dress. His gaze flickered toward her thighs a few times before he jerked his chin upward. "Go ahead."

Of course, that gave him a pretty up-close-and-personal view of her ass, which she didn't mind.

He stifled a groan.

When she spun around to make sure he was okay, she noticed his line of sight and beamed.

"God help me," he muttered.

Ellie waited until they were both at the top of the stairs before heading down the short hall to Lucas's bedroom. It was easy to pick out which one was his since it was the *only* bedroom. She figured his couch had looked plenty comfy. She'd get cleaned up then go crash.

"I hope you don't mind if I just say make yourself at home." He held his hand out toward the bathroom. "You can set yourself up in there a lot faster than if I try to do it for you."

"This is great—thank you." She smiled.

It would have been so natural to go onto her tiptoes and kiss him. Just a quick peck. But he turned toward a black box with a phone resting on top, right when she debated making her move. The chance vanished.

So Ellie limped into the bathroom, ripped her shoes from her feet and threw them directly into the trash. Her dress would follow shortly. She leaned over the massive tub to turn on the water. It would take a while to fill.

As she waited, she couldn't help but peek around. Not snooping, exactly. It just was such a rare opportunity to learn more about the man who'd kept her in the dark for months. No way would she dare to glance in the mirror. She could feel how ratty and full of leaves her hair was and her face couldn't be much better. So she distracted herself by cataloging Lucas's care products.

An assortment of items for amputees was lined up on the surround. Things she didn't really understand except to get an idea, by how many there were, of how much effort he was expending to adapt to his new life. She thought of the endless counseling visits, doctors' appointments, research on jobs and other therapy that had occupied her time lately. For Lucas, it must be way more daunting.

Every part of his personal space reflected some sort of change.

The bench in his shower, the slew of lotions and potions. Hell, even the pile of stump socks in his laundry basket. It was impossible to ignore here, where he spent so much of his time. Maybe he would let her turn his mind to more pleasurable things.

In the other room, she heard his efficient reporting to the Men in Blue. There, he was comfortable. Here, he still needed help adjusting. More determined than ever, she vowed to help him with that transition. If he'd let her.

"Mason, I think it's best if I keep her here." He spoke to one of Lacey's guys who had rank on the force. The other Men in Blue listened to him. If he agreed, she'd be staying. "People don't associate us. I wasn't on any of the documentation from Morselli's dungeon. We haven't been seen together for nearly a year."

Ouch. That part hurt.

It hadn't been for lack of her reaching out either.

Ellie leaned against the doorjamb, blinking back tears. Why had he cut her out of his life entirely?

With the evidence pointing to how radically his had changed all around her, it was clear that he resented her. Why wouldn't he?

Indirectly, she'd been responsible for this.

If she hadn't been in there that day...

If Ryan hadn't sent the Men in Blue and other task force members to search for her...

If Lucas hadn't been so damned brave...

He'd be whole, and she'd be gone. Instead of them both living half-alive.

Her heart sank as she realized the teasing they'd been doing in the woods was probably all they'd ever have. He'd been distracting her. Motivating her to keep going.

And it had worked.

Now it was time for her to return some of the generosity he'd shown her.

"There's two hundred grand in here..." Lucas dropped that bombshell on the rest of their city's finest. "Yeah, I counted it twice."

A short silence.

"Fuck. I think so too. They used her to smuggle it out." He growled. "But was it random chance? Or did they target her specifically. That's what we need to know."

Ellie poked her head out of the bathroom. "Lucas?"

If she didn't have some relief from the thick tension of the debriefing happening in the room next door, she was going to lose her mind. He might be used to operating in situations like this, but she certainly was not. Diversions would be welcome.

"Hang on a sec," he told the Men in Blue. "Yeah, E?"

"Sorry to interrupt. Mind if I use that tablet in the waterproof case by the tub?" She figured she could find a movie to watch or scan the Internet for information.

"Sure, go ahead. Just...don't log in to any of your accounts, okay?" He winced. "Sorry, but we don't want to give cybernerds, like JRad, who are playing for the other team a trail of breadcrumbs. Use my stuff. Everything you need should be on there already. The messenger app is open and I'm sure Lacey, Shari, Izzy, Jambrea and Lily are dying to talk to you. If you're up to it."

"Aren't they sleeping?" She glanced at the clock, surprised to find it was almost five in the morning. Lacey and Jambrea were nurses. They worked the night shift often to mesh their schedules to their guys'. Lily ran an exclusive BDSM club that had her on a similar cadence. And Shari was always up at the ass crack of dawn doing something on her land. "I guess not."

"They're worried about you." He smiled softly. "Us, really."

"I guess I should've known winning a jackpot like that isn't really the kind of luck I have." She dropped her forehead to the doorjamb.

"I didn't realize this was a pity party. Hang on. Let me pull up a chair so I can bitch about only having one leg without toppling over." He might have sounded harsh, but he grinned as he said it. Probably because he knew it was going to put her hackles up.

The man did seem to take perverse pleasure in her temper.

From across the room she could hear their mutual friends cracking up.

It felt good to burn instead of wilt beneath the gloom that had threatened her sometimes lately. No one could understand that better than Lucas. It made her happy to be treated like she wasn't fragile.

She figured it was best to get even. Except instead of firing off a double middle-finger salute, she flashed him a wicked grin.

"Uh-oh. No. She's not about to attack me. She's smiling. Now I'm scared." He rubbed his chest and damn if he didn't mirror her expression. At least with a hint of a tilt to his lips that only made him infinitely more attractive.

That was when she took her destroyed dress and began to walk it up her thighs, then her midriff, and finally over her head. She dropped it to the bathroom floor, leaving her in only her matching candy-apple red, strapless bra and lacy panties. It was freeing, to have the ability to tease a man while completely guaranteed that he would not hurt her.

"Son of a bitch!" he barked.

Still, he didn't look away.

"No. No, sorry. Everything's fine. Great. I mean, there's no need to rush over here or anything," Lucas rambled, something she'd never heard before or thought possible.

Could he actually be flustered? By her?

What would their friends find if they barged in soon?

Probably nothing.

The thought launched a zing of disappointment through her gut. So she spun, giving Lucas a perfect view of her backside. She reached behind herself, unclasping her bra and letting it join her ruined dress on the ground.

"E!" he hissed.

When she peeked over her shoulder, he had his hand smothering the mouthpiece.

So she decided to complete her revenge. If he could rile her, she could do the same to him. At least she hoped she could.

Ellie popped her thumbs through the skimpy waistband of her skimpier panties. She walked them down the curve of her hips then wiggled until she was able to step out of them.

"Holy shit," he groaned. This time when she glanced back at him, his hand was rearranging the growing bulge in his jeans. He could have looked away at any time—turned around or even simply closed his eyes.

But he didn't.

With a wink, she headed for his tub, out of his line of sight, ending her demonstration.

"Huh?" he said, obviously trying to catch up to the conversation he was having with the Men in Blue. "Sorry. I just...I got distracted for a minute. No, get your minds out of the gutter. She's not even in here. She went to take a bath. The hike tore her up some. Both of us."

And just like that, the results of her teasing evaporated.

He was all business again, reminded of how she'd been a victim.

Damn it.

On the side of the tub, a bottle caught her attention. It was one she knew well. Jambrea had given her the same thing for her birthday. It was a mix of lavender and other oils, designed for relaxation, mixed with a splash of bubble bath. Somehow, the thought of Lucas surrounded by suds had her chuckling.

She unscrewed the top and put a capful of the lovely mixture into the tub. Considering how monstrous the soaker was, compared to hers, she went ahead and added a second dollop.

Breathing deeply, she prepared herself then dipped a foot in. Lucas's patch job had worked wonders, but the sting in the areas he hadn't treated was enough to make her groan.

"You okay?" Lucas shouted from the other room. His conversation was nothing more than a comforting rumble when she was this close to the rush of water.

"Yeah," she lied. "Just felt good."

"Tell me if you need anything," he instructed.

Somehow she figured that didn't include a make-out session or an orgasm to help her relax before bed.

Easing herself into the water slowly, Ellie bit her lip to keep from hissing at each additional sting that resulted from submerging her dings beneath the waves. She didn't waste any time in pressing the button to activate the jets.

It took a while, but eventually she was up to her collarbones in blissfully steamy, pretty-smelling heat. It began to seep into her bones. For a while there, she thought she'd never be warm again.

Now that she was, she just lay there, boneless, as the rush of water massaged her all over.

And then the tablet near her head *bing*ed. After a minute it *bing*ed again. And again.

A smile curved her lips upward. She put her money on Izzy, the least patient of her friends. Not wanting to keep them in suspense—worried about her—any longer than necessary, Ellie grabbed the device and unlocked the screen.

Funny, Lucas had the same case she did.

Even the same color.

She'd picked it because it matched her eyes. Why had he? Was it his favorite color?

Or maybe it had been the only one left in the store when he needed one.

Ellie had spent lots of quality time in the tub, reading or surfing the net. It was one of the things that calmed her when she had a bad night. Could he have that in common with her too?

Sure enough, a little box with Izzy's name held a stream of messages.

Paging Ms. Ellie...

Yo, Ellie.

Answer me!

Are you okay?

Elllllliiiiiiiiiiiiiieeeeeeeeeeeee

Then the rest of her friends' names appeared in italics, with a note that they'd joined the conversation.

Lacey: Calm down, Iz. Maybe she went to bed instead.

Lily: Anyone want to take odds on where she'll be sleeping tonight?

Okay, that was enough of that. What if Lucas saw their messages?

Then again, so what if he did? Ellie had wondered the same thing, though she assumed they had different views on the best solution to that problem.

Lucas: Hey, ladies, I'm here. And fine. Mostly. My dress is toast, though.

Izzy: Unless Lucas has really taken up cross-dressing, which I might like to see, I'm going to assume this is you, Ellie?

Lucas: Ha-ha, yes. He told me not to sign in to my accounts.

Shari: NO! Not the dress! It was spectacular on you.

Lucas: Win some, lose some.

Jambrea: Is it true? There's extra money in the bag? Loads more? I can't believe it!

Lucas: I'm sure I don't get to keep it. You know, without people shooting at me and trying to abduct me and shit. Who knows if I even really won the $50K. I'm not holding my breath.

Izzy: Are you okay, Ellie? Really?

Lucas: Yeah. I will be. Kind of shaken up, but it hasn't really sunk in yet, you know? It still feels like a bad dream. If it weren't for Lucas... Mostly I just want to veg out, grab something to eat and then sleep for a year. My feet are killing me.

Lily: You definitely deserve a woman-of-the-year award for walking so damn far in those fuck-me heels.

Shari: Holy shit! Ellie, didn't you call your brother and let him know you're okay?

Lucas: No, Lucas is on the secure line with the guys. I have no way of contacting Ryan. Can you let him know, somehow that is cop-approved? If someone is looking for me, he could be in trouble too.

Why hadn't she thought of that before?

Shari: I don't think that's a problem. I'm kind of at his and Ben's place. We got the call and something seemed like it was up before I'd made it very far, so I turned around and came back. Thought he might be climbing the walls until he heard something. For the record, he was.

Lucas: Thank you for being there for him. I didn't mean to scare him.

Izzy: Not like you did this on purpose, babe! Ryan will chill out now that he knows you're safe.

Lily: And especially if he takes advantage of having both Ben and Shari at his disposal.

Shari: Hey now! He's right here. Watch your typing.

Lucas: Tell him I love him, and I'll call him as soon as I'm able, okay?

Shari: He says he loves you too. And that you should listen to Lucas and not give him a hard time.

Lacey: Oh, I think you should give him a hard time all right.

Lucas: Hey! My brother can see this. Gross.

Still, she laughed.

Jambrea: Ryan and Ben should give Shari a double-hard time! I highly recommend it.

Lacey: I second that. Mason and Tyler have made me a two-scoop girl for life.

Shari: OMG. Zip it.

Their antics did exactly as they intended—erased her worry. They'd gotten good at rescuing her from slumps or terror in the past year or so.

Lucas: I love you all and miss you already. Sorry I screwed up girls' night out.

Lily: I'll spank you next time I see you. Or, better yet, let Jeremy have a turn.

Ellie knew the notorious Domme was only teasing.

Lacey: We won't keep you. You need to chill out and rest. I'm so glad you're all right.

Lucas: Thanks. Hey, Jambi or Lacey...

Jambrea: Yes?

Lacey: What can I do?

Lucas: What are some resources for amputee education? Lucas had to stop and adjust his prosthesis a few times. I feel like I should know more. Where can I go to get up to speed?

Jambrea: AmputeeOT rocks.

Lacey: Damn, why do you type so much faster than me? I was going to say that!

Shari: Even on here you're ten times chattier than Jambi. *snort*

Lily: But still not nearly as much as my sister.

Izzy: Hey, I resemble that remark!

Jambrea: Just go to YouTube and do a search. I recommend AmputeeOT's videos to all of my patients.

Lucas: Okay, thank you! I wish I'd done my homework before.

Lily: It's not like Lucas was letting you be part of his world. If he were my guy, I'd have beat his ass by now.

Shari: Seriously, you've practically been a saint.

Izzy: Did something happen tonight? I'm getting a feeling...

Lucas: You and your feelings! No! Well, mostly not. Except for one little kiss. That's all.

It hadn't felt like such a small thing when she'd shared it with him.

Lacey: That's a huge step!

Jambrea: Was it good?

Lily: Of course it was. They're perfect for each other.

Lucas: It rocked. And now I think I should go. I want to watch some of these videos before the boys are done with their cop/spy talk.

Shari: Okay. We love you.

Izzy: STAY SAFE.

Lucas: Promise. I don't look for trouble. It finds me. ☺

They exchanged goodbyes, then she clicked off before they could start giving her advice for getting Lucas in the sack. She'd heard it before from them. Truth was, only one person was going to make a difference there. And it wasn't her who was putting the brakes on.

Too tired to think about that, she swapped apps, planning to scroll through the archives from the YouTuber her friends had suggested. Instead of a blank search page, the browser on Lucas's tablet had several tabs open already.

She went to click for a fresh one then realized she'd stumbled across some porn he'd recently been watching. Did he sit in the tub and masturbate while watching dirty movies?

Somehow the thought made her squirm beneath the pulsing stream of the jets.

Curious, she couldn't help but peek at what turned him on. Ellie poked the gray arrow in the middle of the video box.

And nearly dropped his tablet into the tub.

Not because the page featured the romantic category of the porn-clip consolidator. Or because it was too graphic. But because the woman on-screen looked remarkably like Ellie. People on the street had stopped her before, asking for autographs, thinking she was Taylor Swift, though she didn't think they looked *that* much alike. Maybe in the same way close family members of twins could tell each other apart and casual acquaintances couldn't, though.

Sure, there was some resemblance.

But this girl on the screen...she looked a *lot* like Ellie.

"Whoa." She barely resisted the urge to slide her hand between her legs and rub the ache developing in her clit. Especially when she watched a trim, sexy man go down on her look-alike. This she could get behind.

"Still doing all right?" Lucas called from the other room.

"Yep. Fine!" she squeaked.

Guiltily, Ellie clicked off of the video. He'd been nice enough to loan her his stuff; she shouldn't invade his privacy like that. Unless…

Could he want her as badly as she wanted him?

Maybe she should say "fuck it" and jump him. Living cautiously wasn't turning out how she'd hoped so why not be kind of reckless for once? She could be the aggressor. Lily did it all the time. Maybe Ellie could too.

To distract herself from thoughts that could ruin the tentative bridge she and Lucas had been building, she flipped again, this time to the correct tab and began to scan through the AmputeeOT archives.

Engrossed, and soaking up knowledge, she didn't realize how much time had passed before a knock came on the open door.

CHAPTER SIX

Lucas winced as he raised his fist to knock on the partially open bathroom door. He hated to bug Ellie, but their romp through the woods had roughed up his already sore leg. He had to at least wash out his liner and clean his stump again. An infection was a setback he couldn't afford. Soaking in the tub sometimes helped the soreness too.

Besides, he was afraid Ellie might doze off when exhaustion hit her full force. Relaxed, it'd be easy for her to close her eyes and slip beneath the water.

She'd been awfully quiet for a while now. He'd listened hard for the occasional splash she made when shifting positions as he developed a strategy for unraveling the motive behind her casino debacle with the Men in Blue. That had led to fantasies of what she must look like, naked and wet, a mere dozen feet or so away from where he stood.

Damn.

Nothing wrong with his third leg.

He could blame his reactions on the aftereffects of adrenaline, which probably did legitimately amplify his attraction. Still, he'd wanted Ellie since before he'd even met her face-to-face. The pictures he'd seen of her when they'd prepared to hunt her down in Morselli's dungeon had been enough to rouse his interest, and his cock.

Ever since, he'd been doomed.

Lucas cleared his throat. "Are you okay in there?"

"Mmm…" It sounded more like a purr than agreement. "This tub is huge. I feel like I'm at a spa."

He bet she could put the jets to good use and relax herself even more. Shaking his head to clear the thought, he barked more harshly than he'd intended, "I need to get in there soon. My leg is killing me. A bath is one of the only things that helps when it gets like this."

For a moment, silence.

When he realized how rude his tone sounded, considering he'd told her to get comfortable earlier, he added, "Sorry."

It wasn't her fault that he felt so on edge around her. She ended up on the receiving end of his short fuse too often. He had to get better at that. Reining in his emotions was difficult around her, tougher than it had been with anyone before. Everything she did inspired some kind of reaction in him. Most of them as explosive as the bombs he'd rigged from time to time. Epic.

"Screw you, jerk. I'm not giving this up anytime soon." Then, so quietly he almost didn't hear, she added, "Nothing's stopping you from joining me, though. There's plenty of room."

"I'll wait." He prepared to turn around and plop onto the bed until it was his turn. He winced as he considered how much he stank and how dirty he would get the sheets she'd probably be sleeping on soon.

"Don't be so fucking stubborn!" she shouted, surprising him.

Ellie rarely lost her cool. For that matter, the only times he'd seen her blow up had been at him. Like in the hospital right after his surgery. They'd collided when visiting Izzy and Razor's son—baby Ezra—in the maternity ward. He'd lost his shit when she showed up while he was there, and he'd tried to run. Okay, so it really had been more like rolling away from her, but he'd been humiliated when she saw him in the wheelchair.

Hell, he hadn't even had real pants on, just a sheet wrapped around his waist and the giant cast covering his stump.

Lucas hadn't been ready.

He might never be.

So when she had tried to stop him, to comfort him, he'd lashed out.

Her opinion was more important than anyone's. Even his friends'. Considering why that might be wasn't high on his list of fun things to do.

Fine. If she could act like it was no big deal to lounge around naked with him, then so could he.

He collected the rations they'd brought upstairs with them, then burst into the bathroom, his leg accidentally kicking the door from perpendicular to flat against the wall hard enough that it thumped into the towel rack behind it.

Way to make an entrance.

Ellie gasped then raised her hands to cover her breasts with fistfuls of suds.

"Were you bluffing?" he asked, his head tipped as he inspected every nuance of her reactions. Her hair was damp on the ends, where it dragged in the scented bath. A pretty flush spread over her skin. She blinked up at him, her mouth parted.

Sure, he'd startled her, but she wasn't scared of him. He'd seen fear in her eyes earlier and the look she flashed him now was pretty much the opposite.

87

"No," she whispered.

"This is a dangerous game, Ellie," he rasped.

"So?" She shrugged one bare shoulder, pink now that she'd absorbed plenty of heat from the water.

The air was heavy, either with steam that was making him sweat as if they shared a sauna, or with the unfulfilled desire that had been arcing between them like lightning.

He bet he knew which factor was most responsible.

When all he could do was stare at her and wonder if he was making the right choice, she grew bolder, something he found really did it for him. After months of thinking of her as wounded, she kept proving how much she'd recovered. He could learn a lot from her.

"You can stay on your side and I'll stay on mine." She waved her hands through the mountain of foam floating on the bathwater. "It's not like you can see anything. And, frankly, I wouldn't give a crap if you could. I've been on display in front of a roomful of men before. Guys who didn't look at me with even a modicum of respect. So I'm pretty sure I can handle being naked with you."

Lucas hung his head. It filled him with rage to know what she'd endured. But also with fear. Because he didn't know if he was as strong as her.

"What if I can't? Stand the thought of you looking at my leg, I mean?" He cleared his throat.

Her gaze snapped to his. "Are you serious?"

"Yeah." He'd never hesitated to shed his clothes before. He'd always been proud of his body. Sure that he attracted women. Hell, there were times in his younger days that he'd taken two or three at a time home with him, and had no problems satisfying them all.

Somehow, this was different. Higher stakes.

His scars were ugly. Something he'd taken for granted had changed forever. Irreversibly.

That was hard to swallow.

"Take your shirt off," Ellie demanded.

Well, that wasn't an issue.

He set the fruit, water and cheese on the surround. Then he grabbed the hem of his T-shirt. With one smooth motion, he stripped it over his head before wadding it up and tossing it into his hamper, hardly looking.

Naked didn't usually bother him. In fact, he liked to walk around nude, and even sunned himself on the boat on lazy summer afternoons, soaking up the sun's rays like a lizard on a rock in the desert. Plus, he was more cut than he'd ever been. Lean and defined. No matter how much he ate, it seemed he burned off the fuel during his therapy and workouts.

Not to mention the extra effort it took to do even simple things.

"You're the most gorgeous man I've ever seen," Ellie murmured as she studied his chest and the array of colorful tattoos decorating it.

"Uh, thanks, I guess." He laughed nervously.

"What?"

"I've had women call me sexy or handsome or a stud, never *gorgeous*." He shook his head. "I think that description suits you more than me."

"I noticed you seem to have a thing for tall, scrawny blondes with blue eyes and super-red lipstick. I'm not sure I own quite that shade, but I could bum some off Lily if that's your thing." She peeked innocently up at him from beneath her thick lashes.

It took him a second...

Then it hit him. "Holy fuck."

Lucas pinched the bridge of his nose between his thumb and index finger.

She'd just called him out for his porn selections. Why the hell hadn't he remembered what he'd used that damn tablet for last? He really must be slipping. Either that or, on some subconscious level, he'd wanted to show Ellie just how smoking he thought she was since she didn't seem to realize it herself.

"I could say it's not what it looks like." A coward, he wasn't. Usually. Especially not when she looked up at him like he was about to pop her favorite balloon or something. "But, yeah, I think you're hot and I've imagined what we would be like in bed together. A lot."

She beamed up at him, scooting closer so that she could fold her arms on top of the surround. Her chest pressed against the side of the tub, making the most of what she had, which was surprisingly curvy on her willowy frame. He tried not to get turned on, considering he planned to shuck his pants in the very near future.

"Want some help with those?" She reached toward the button on his jeans, like a snippet from his own personal dirty movie, if he could have made whatever he desired reality.

When he jerked back, he lost his balance, nearly busting his ass. Time slowed and he saw his life flash before his eyes. Wouldn't it suck to bash his head in and die without having enjoyed one last dip in a jetted tub with a gorgeous and willing woman?

What the hell was wrong with him?

Oh, right. There was still the matter of getting his pants and leg and everything beneath it off without completely creeping Ellie out.

Speaking of, she gasped then lunged forward, slopping bubbles and water onto the floor. Not that he minded. She grabbed his waistband and tugged, counterbalancing him enough for him to regain his equilibrium. "Lucas!"

"Shit. I'm fine." He brushed her fingers away from where her knuckles grazed the patch of skin below his belly button. Entirely too close to his cock for comfort.

Well, unless she planned to take things a lot farther than he did.

They both noticed, right about then, that she had emerged from the water. Her perky tits looked amazing decorated with suds and soaked from the bath. The urge to bury his face between the mounds, plump them with his hands and decorate them with love bites had him clenching his teeth to resist it.

"Jesus." Ellie relented, retreating to the opposite corner of the tub. She sank until her body was obscured from his gaze once more.

Half of him wanted to cry.

The other half cheered.

Besides, it gave Lucas an idea. Two could play that game.

"You sure you're not getting out?" He gave her a final opportunity to dodge the uncomfortable situation.

"Positive."

Stubborn woman. He kind of liked it.

"Fine. Then I'm coming in." He crossed his arms and widened his stance.

Still she didn't even flinch.

So Lucas sat on the edge of the tub and removed his shoes from both his meat foot and his prosthesis. Next he took the knife Ellie had returned to him after their hike and set it next to the food. His secure phone he left on a shelf above the tub, safely out of the splash zone.

Finally, he used his arms to anchor himself as he spun around and submerged his lower body.

It felt fucking weird to be getting wet with jeans on. Ellie's outraged shock was enough to push him over his aversion and inspire a chuckle. She sputtered in response.

Once he started, he couldn't hold back. He laughed loud enough that he startled himself with the impact of his joy reverberating off the tiled walls.

When was the last time he'd heard that sound? Maybe never.

"What the hell are you doing?" Ellie scooped up some water and launched it at him.

A rooster tail of droplets smacked him in the face. It only made Lucas clutch his stomach, which cramped from laughing so hard.

"Is it okay for your leg to be wet like that?"

"Yep. It's carbon fiber. Waterproof."

Now that her precious bubble shield blanketed him—preserving *his* modesty, as well as hers—he got to work on his jeans. Soggy, they were harder than usual to remove, though he managed.

Before long he'd worked the thick denim down his legs to his ankles.

Then Lucas disengaged the proximal lock on his prosthesis and slid it off. With that done, he tugged his jeans off the top of his prosthesis, below his stump, then kicked them from his uninjured foot. Everything was a pain in the ass these days.

"Fuck," he hissed.

"Are you stuck or something?" Ellie asked. "Serves you right for assuming I'd be critical of your body, dumbass. You'll be lucky if you don't slip and drown tangled up in your pants."

"Whatever. You'd save me long before that happened." It did weird things to his guts to know that was true too.

"Probably." She flashed a rueful smile. "So what's the cursing for then?"

"Damn, it just hurts. It's like taking your shoes off at the end of a *really* long day. Magnified a thousand times over," he admitted, wincing as he thought of her poor battered feet.

Slinging water everywhere, he put both his leg and his jeans on the floor next to the tub. With one final pass, he slipped his underwear off and added them to the pile. He'd have to be careful to step only on the mat until he could wipe the mess up.

Rubbing his knee through the socks and liner dampened the effectiveness of Lucas's hands, so he began to strip those off too. The stump socks he flung, adding them to the growing laundry pile. After rolling the liner down, he put the floppy gel sleeve on the tub surround so that he could clean it properly after they finished bathing.

Buck naked, yet hidden, he grinned. Settling in, he realized Ellie was staring at him with her brows drawn together, causing adorable wrinkles on her forehead.

"What?" he asked.

"I don't get you." She gestured toward him. "I've already seen you without your leg on. It's not a big deal."

"Oh sure, being an amputee is nothing." He frowned. "Trust me. From the number of people who stare at me when I go out, I know what a freak I've become."

"I can understand people being curious. You're different, sure. So am I, though my issues are invisible until I blank out in the middle of a grocery store aisle or something equally humiliating. That doesn't make you worse or anything." Ellie stared at him. "I realize I didn't know you before the accident. But, even after, when you were far more impaired than you are now—clinging to the hope you were going to go back to your old life on that mangled foot—you were never this insecure."

Lucas reached behind him and grabbed the knot at the back of his neck. He squeezed it as he considered how to explain. "I guess I've always been physically superior. I don't mean that in a douchey kind of way, but it's the truth. I didn't think much about running or any of the demanding things I had to do to excel in my training. Now, even the simplest things take a ridiculous amount of effort. Sometimes—despite having a great sense of balance, improving my core strength and practicing maneuvering with this damn thing on—I still fall on my fucking face."

"Everyone does. You get back up."

Ellie scooted closer to his right, so he edged to his left. If they kept this up, soon they'd cause a whirlpool in the tub from spinning around its perimeter in an eternal game of duck-duck-goose.

"Why do you keep pulling away?"

He knew she was referring to more than their current situation. "You deserve someone better. Someone who can lift you up, not drag you down."

Ellie closed her eyes for a moment. She drew a deep breath then stared directly at him.

"Are you sure it's not because you resent me? For my part in making you this way?" Her lower lip wobbled, and her voice had cracked as she asked.

Even in the days and weeks he'd visited her, taught her self-defense or hung out with her at their mutual friends' houses after she'd been caged, she'd never once cried in front of him. To know that he might cause her to do so now broke his heart. He'd hurt her when a lot of what he'd done in the past year had been to avoid exactly that.

"What?" His spine went ramrod straight. "Is that really what you think?"

"I don't blame you." She shrugged. "If it weren't for me..."

"Then we'd never have cracked the Sex Offender formula in time to create an antidote and stop its spread. We also wouldn't have had an ironclad case against Morselli without you." Lucas gaped at her, incredulous. "Don't you realize how many lives you—and the rest of the team—saved that day? The thought of you in that place...it tears me up. It does. But I've sacrificed a lot in my life for the sake of the greater good.

"The number of heroic men and women I've known who've given their lives to fight evil is more than I can count anymore. Even when normal civilians had no idea of the dangers they were in from unknown threats, they still gave everything they had. To keep it that way. Guys like John. Or my partner, Steve, who died on the floor of that dungeon."

He should probably shut up, since tears were spilling down her cheeks. But now that he was talking, he couldn't stop.

"So, no. I don't think what happened was your fault. Not in the least. And if I had to do it again, knowing everything I know now, I'd do it without a second thought. That stuff was pure evil. No one could understand that better than you. Millions of people would have been victims—either through addiction or by being abused by its users. This was a small price to pay in the grand scheme of things, even if it has a big impact on me personally. Never once have I blamed you for any of it."

"Then why—?" She couldn't get anything else out.

That was fine. He understood what she meant. She needed to know why he kept driving a wedge between them—to keep them both safe.

"Because I'm fucked up. And so are you. The potential for disaster is enormous. Would either of us survive the fallout of a bad breakup when we're both already jacked? Could we really make something work when we're each concentrating on ourselves so much? It's better to avoid making things more complicated between us.

"I know you can feel this crazy pull too. I don't know what to do with that. I never had the luxury of indulging in a real relationship before. I had a hell of a lot of affairs, sure. But never anything serious. It would have been too risky to have someone I cared for floating out there. A giant target. And learning how to do that, how to be a partner...I'm not sure I'm capable when I need to be selfish right now."

Ellie didn't utter a sound. When she only gawked at him, he mentally rewound what had spewed from his mouth unfiltered. "Shit. See, I'm sorry. I didn't mean to call you—"

"It's okay. You're right. I *am* fucked up. I jump at the slightest breeze when I'm walking outdoors. I have nightmares pretty much every time I fall asleep. It's absolutely *killing* me that your front door is unlocked right now, even though I know it's a silly thing that wouldn't keep anyone serious out."

The raw honesty pouring from her questioning stare had him rooted in place.

"So...what if I admit it makes me feel safer to be near you?"

How could he take that from her after everything she'd suffered through?

If he could make things better for her, shouldn't he?

Even if it made him less comfortable. Vulnerable.

Because too much more of this and he wouldn't be able to cast her aside again. Then they'd both be screwed, since everything he said still held true.

"Come here." He opened his arms to Ellie.

CHAPTER SEVEN

When Ellie neared to take him up on his offer, Lucas didn't hesitate to pull her in tight to his chest. The side of her face rested just below his collarbone. He didn't even shift when their thighs aligned.

It surprised him that Ellie didn't recoil when she couldn't deny his leg stopped short of hers. Knowing it and feeling it were different things. Every time he looked down was still a shock. He supposed he'd had thirty-five years to get used to his foot being there and less than one to rearrange his perception of his body. The difference between his mental picture of himself and reality caught him off guard sometimes.

Not E. She accepted him as he was.

For a while, they sat there, propped against the tub, letting the jets pummel their abused muscles, kneading them into relieved putty.

His fingers wandered through Ellie's soft curls, picking out leaves or twigs and unsnarling what he could of her platinum mane.

"Wash my hair?" she asked.

So he did. Slowly rubbing the shampoo into her scalp, taking pride in every bit more she relaxed against him. Content, he couldn't think of a single reason to move once he'd finished rinsing her off. So he didn't.

Lucas simply enjoyed her companionship.

Something he couldn't really say he'd ever sought from a woman before. That's what his brothers-in-arms had been for. Another enormous part of him he'd suddenly lost along with his foot.

"Lucas?" she asked eventually.

"Yeah."

"Pass me that apple and some water, will you?" She snuggled tighter to him when he shifted.

"I'll do better than that." He kissed the top of her head, maybe light enough that she wouldn't notice, then grabbed the water and handed it to her.

While she twisted the cap off, he took the apple and his knife in one hand. Unable to juggle them, yet unwilling to surrender his hold on her, he tossed the knife to his other hand and flipped it open.

The *schwip* of the blade extending rang in the bathroom.

Ellie's nails dug into his ribs. She turned her face into his pecs and slammed her eyes closed. Her lips moved as if she was repeating something to herself in a continual loop. Her breath came in fast, shallow bursts.

Lucas was afraid to move, even to conceal the knife. He didn't want to accidentally cut her with the extra-sharp blade if she lurched away. "You okay, E?"

"Uh-huh." She filled her lungs so deeply it had to be an intentional technique she used to calm herself. "The guard who was in my section most often used a switchblade at my throat to keep me from fighting when they forced me to swallow Sex Offender. I tried to resist. I hated how it made me feel. The things I did."

She shuddered hard enough to cause noticeable ripples in the roiling waters of the tub.

It hadn't taken five minutes before Lucas had failed her and brought some painful memory to the surface. "E, this is exactly what I'm talking about." His rage at her captors had leaked into his exclamation.

Ellie whimpered before glancing up at him.

"I don't want to scare you." His stare ping-ponged from her to the knife in his hand. He was afraid to budge.

"*You* do not frighten me." She turned and faced the knife. "My memories do. They're phantoms I can't fight."

Ellie extended her hand and wrapped it around his. She tugged until he followed, slowly. Little by little, she brought the razor-edged blade closer to her. When it got within a few inches of her face, he prevented her from moving it farther.

"Put it against my neck," she whispered.

"Hell *fucking* no!"

"Do it." She pulled again and still he resisted.

"E—"

"Do what I say for once!" she snarled at him. "Give me control. Please. Let me have it back."

Lucas must have gone temporarily insane. Carefully, monitoring her every twitch, he did as she asked. The bright steel touched her, making her eyes close and her breathing hitch.

When she ensnared his wrist, he nearly cracked and yanked back. But instead of cutting herself, she shouted "No!" and shoved the knife away.

Instantly, he transferred it to his other hand, as far from her as he could get it. And though she tracked his movements, she didn't seem as terrified.

Ellie looked up at him, smiled wanly, then kissed his cheek. "You have no idea how good it feels to rewrite history like that. I obsessed about it.

Daydreamed about how I'd overpower him the next time he threatened to slice my head clean off. I would have used that fucking knife to slice his dick off. Of course, I never was able."

Could Lucas fully comprehend her logic? No. But he witnessed the transformation coming over her and figured it wasn't his place to judge. Whatever remedy it took to facilitate her healing, he was willing to administer it.

Shifting, he brought his hands together, his arm still looped around her, pretty much squishing her to him. With a few quick strokes, he sliced the apple into reasonable wedges then washed the blade off with a single splash before tucking it away again.

Relief had Ellie melting into his chest.

Without speaking, Lucas fed her some of the apple, barely resisting the urge to lick her lips when a trickle of juice escaped a particularly crisp bite. She ate from his hand with complete trust and absolute faith that he wouldn't harm her. It was a beautiful gift.

He took his share before collecting the block of cheese. This time, when he revealed the blade, more subtly this time, she averted her stare for a moment—like someone choosing not to watch the needle go into their skin when having blood drawn—but didn't lose her mind. Again, he divvied up the food, taking perverse pleasure in the way her lips curled around his fingers as he nourished her.

Lucas realized it was probably sick that caring for her made him feel more like his old self than he had since his accident. Somehow, though, granting her strength increased his own like an echo that kept bouncing between them, benefitting them both.

The more comfortable she became, the more her hands roamed.

From his ribs and chest and abdomen, she moved lower.

Not in an overtly provocative way. More like *she* was intending to soothe *him*.

Could she tell how conflicted he was? Simultaneously, he wanted to shove her away and tug her closer. Selfless versus selfish. How fucked up was that?

Particularly when selfish won out.

Lucas allowed her to explore. Her fingers trailed over his thigh then lower, reading the topography of his scars like twisted Braille. The entire time, they stared into each other's eyes as if to see who would cry uncle first in this game of emotional chicken.

It was likely to be him.

Certainly, it made him defenseless when she touched his stump. No one but doctors had done that. However, her gentle massage felt so motherfucking good that he couldn't budge or order her to stop.

"E," he moaned, his eyes closing while his head tipped back to rest against the edge of the tub.

"Too hard?" she asked in a low hum that had him in danger of taking things way too far.

As if they hadn't ventured there already.

"No. Keep going." He tried to think of anything except how right it felt to have her with him. Touching him and not screaming in horror. Overwhelming bliss left no room for doubts or worry about the future. All he could do was sit back and enjoy.

When her fingers paused in their swirls, he moaned. Though the sound morphed into something like a growl when he realized why she'd slowed. She had risen to her knees, carefully straddling his thigh so that she could reach his mouth with hers.

Ellie plastered their damp torsos together and kissed him.

For a moment, nothing else in the world mattered except their full-on, skin-to-skin contact.

He opened his mouth, allowing her free rein over his body since she'd already taken something inside him hostage permanently. If she noticed his hard cock occasionally tapping her thigh as it bobbed in the roiling water, she didn't seem afraid and certainly didn't retreat.

Some of his fears eased, though they didn't vanish entirely. If a knife made her flash back to her time spent imprisoned and brutalized, what would having sex do to her?

He wasn't an expert, but he figured they shouldn't rush into anything.

If she'd been anyone else, he'd have lifted her into his lap and filled her from below. Imagining the tight clasp of her silky pussy as he plunged deep inside her made him groan between her parted lips, which he now plundered, unable to hold himself back.

Then again, if she'd been any other woman, he never would have let her get so close.

When she finished gliding her mouth over his, she rubbed their noses together and patted his shoulders. He stole a few more pecks before she withdrew.

His eyes opened then, allowing him to peer directly into the bright pools of her eyes. Rich and still, they said so much, allowed him to believe in her as much as she'd trusted him with the knife. Surely, she could cut him as deeply. But she didn't.

Ellie put only enough space between them as was necessary to return to doing a fantastic job of rubbing his stump. The ache in his knee eased, releasing some of the tension in his remaining calf muscle. When she slid lower, he swallowed hard, waiting for the moment her touch glided over his truncated flesh.

It was weird. When her fingers wandered over the bottom of his stump, which used to be the back of his leg, everything got kind of topsy-turvy. It didn't matter, though, when she made him feel pleasure from every direction.

Lucas stretched his arms out along the top of the tub, to either side of him, his fingers clamping on the edge. It was the only way he could stay still.

"Am I hurting you?" she asked.

"God, no," he practically panted.

Gentle caresses from her fingers made him wonder at the way she seemed to worship his body. How could she keep from being repulsed by what he was now?

"What are you…some kind of devotee or something?" He apparently was a little *too* relaxed if his rogue thought winged from his mouth so freely.

Ellie paused. "What does that mean?"

"Never mind." He figured the chances she'd let it drop were a hell of a lot lower than the odds she'd beat on the slot machines the night before.

"Tell me."

Fuck.

"There are people out there with all kinds of kinks," he started.

"No kidding." She wrinkled her nose. "I had to hear more than I wanted about my brother's—and the things he and Lily and Ben did together while they were working to take down the Sex Offender ring from the inside—during the statements we gave to the police. I was too scared to be alone, so he stayed with me and we did ours together. Awkward. If I could do it again, I'd have kicked him out so he didn't have to know every detail of what they did to me. At least the stuff I could remember."

How could Lucas have forgotten that? Ryan had gotten sucked into the same sex ring as his sister. Kind of on purpose. To try and get her out. Lucas would bet unwarranted guilt over his own injury hadn't been the only kind eating Ellie up inside.

"Besides, Lily tells me plenty about her Domme sessions when it doesn't breach confidentiality." Ellie shrugged. "I think it's cool that she provides a safe place for her clients to find what they're looking for."

"Well, there are some women...and men...out there who are exclusively attracted to people with disabilities." He lifted one shoulder. "To each their own. Let's just say that I'm glad you didn't flip to the page of my browser that has messages from strangers who cross the line after viewing articles about me online."

"I watched some videos Jambi and Lacey recommended earlier." She bit her lower lip. "It did seem like there were a lot of comments that ignored the content and went straight to some perverted stuff that seemed like unwanted advances."

"If I had a dollar for every time someone asked if they could lick my stump..." He sighed, laughing a little.

"Look, I don't have anything against mutual fetishes." She put her fingers on his cheeks, making sure he couldn't avoid the truth in her eyes. "But that's *definitely* not what this is. I care for you. Not because of your leg, or in spite of it. It's actually one of the least important factors in how I feel about you. So get that crap out of your head. I don't think you were really serious, but I don't want you to be so damn shocked that I'm not grossed out or that I don't pity you either. Do you think so little of me?"

"I think more of you by the second." He took her hand and slid it to his mouth so he could press a soft kiss on her palm. "And I started with an extremely high opinion."

"Thank you," she murmured. Then as if they both needed a break from the seriousness, she smiled.

The full impact of her happiness stunned him, so he didn't react fast enough when she said, "And I can't wait to see how this improves your estimation."

She moved fast, considering her hands had plunged back under the water.

Abandoning her massage of his leg, she moved a couple of inches to her right. Her fingers encircled his cock instead. The top of his head nearly blew off as she spiked his blood pressure with a single light caress.

"E?" The question was strangled.

"Shh." She silenced him with another chaste kiss at odds with her skilled grip. Her hand fisted him and began an entirely different sort of rubdown.

Lucas should have stopped her.

His voice refused to cooperate with his brain's instruction to tell her not to stroke him so fucking well. By the time she'd reached lower with her other hand to cup his balls, he had forgotten entirely about doing the right thing.

Instead, all he cared about was releasing the flood of lust she'd inspired in him for the better part of a year. Simply by being.

Every story his friends had told him of what she was up to had increased his longing to blockbuster proportions, as he was sure they'd intended.

"You know, Lucas, there *is* something of yours I want to lick." She turned coy, showing him an entirely new side of her. One that he couldn't resist. "Sometime when it wouldn't mean drowning in the process."

"How can you, after what those assholes did to you tonight? And before?" He winced. "I never want to make you uncomfortable or scared. We don't have to do that."

"It's not the same thing at all. Do you really think it is?" She paused and looked away. "Unless it bothers *you*. The things I've had to do..."

It would be easy to prove to her that he loved every second of what she was doing. As soon as he was sure he wouldn't cause her any additional harm. "E, no. That's not it."

"If I scratched off every act I've been forced to perform from my list of things I enjoy, there'd be nothing left. It's like the difference between running from my house tonight and going for a jog on a pleasant spring day."

"Well, shit." If she put it that way...

"Can we not talk about this right now, Lucas?" She redoubled her attention in a very successful attempt at distracting him. "I'm doing exactly what I want to be doing right now. Is it what you want too?"

He couldn't keep up with what she was saying. All he needed was more of her rhythmic pumping. So he lifted his hips, fucking into her hold.

"You like that?" She knew damn well he did, but her satisfied smirk made him enjoy her ministrations even more.

"Hell yeah." His jutting cock had to be proof enough. The intuitive accuracy of her handling, doing exactly what felt best, kept diverting blood flow, making him feel huge and heavy, compared to her delicate grip.

With other partners, he could have lasted like this forever.

Something about Ellie's intimate contact had him riled in an instant. She didn't boost his stamina when she leaned in and tasted his neck with a combination of licks, sucks and glancing rakes of her teeth. Direct hits on one of his most sensitive areas, as if she had a user manual for his body.

Lucas kept his hands where they were, practically drilling holes in the tub. Afraid to bury his fingers in her hair or trap her to him in any way, he allowed her to play with him however she liked. When he bent his knees and put his sole on the tub floor for better footing, he tipped slightly to one side.

It caught him at the oddest moments, probably because he had his brain completely switched off as instincts took over. Refusing to let his momentary lapse steal his enjoyment, he concentrated on Ellie and the bliss her touch brought him.

Except that had him rushing toward orgasm entirely too fast.

Her fingers bumped the ridge made by his engorged head while the water swirled over his sensitive tip and his balls, which drew closer to his core with every pass of her hand over his straining shaft.

When she added a flick of her thumb to the underside of his cock at the apex of each stroke, he knew it wasn't going to be long before she made him come. Hard.

"E," he warned.

Instead of slowing or drawing away, she began to pump him in earnest, making it clear what she desired from him. And he was perfectly happy to oblige.

Lucas opened his eyes and stared at her, watching her breasts bounce as she worked him beneath the surface of the bathwater. Ellie bit her lip as if she focused on making her strokes as smooth and languid as possible while increasing the pace of her jacking.

When she approached again, this time to take one of his nipples gently between her teeth, he couldn't resist another second. He growled her name then quit resisting the rapture she brought him. He surrendered to the inevitable tingle building at the base of his shaft.

In a rush, his orgasm crashed over him. His cock jerked in Ellie's hold as streams of come launched from his body. Though he couldn't see them, he knew she'd milked him dry because he could feel the pleasure zinging through every molecule of his body, lighting a fire for her that wouldn't easily be snuffed.

When he sagged, completely relaxed, she gave him one final tug.

"Next time I want to see you shoot. With an orgasm that powerful, it probably was an impressive display," she purred. It shouldn't have shocked him that she was so organic and open in how she dealt with pleasure, yet it did. He'd always thought of her as innocent despite the unwilling experience he knew she had.

Her frank admission had his cock twitching already.

Ellie started to stand, a proud grin gracing her adorable face.

Oh no. He wasn't about to be the only one utterly wrecked.

"Where do you think you're going?" He put his hands on her waist and lifted, shoving her against the wall. All that weightlifting was finally paying off. Not that her slender body was a burden, but his enhanced strength helped him keep his balance as he situated her.

To her credit, she didn't freeze. Instead, she perched on the edge of the tub, with her shoulders resting on the tile, and spread her legs, welcoming him between them.

Lucas could smell her arousal—sweet and somewhat sharp. Just like her.

He longed to bury his face in her folds and devour her. But he didn't. For now, this first time he touched her, maybe the only time, he had to see her face. Make sure she wasn't getting lost in the shadows of her memories while he—hopefully—delivered pleasure instead of terror.

It was critical that he got this right.

So he held her waist in one hand as he eased his other between her thighs. With his good foot planted on the bottom of the tub and his knee steadying him from behind, he wobbled a little. But their connection kept him upright.

At the first glance of his fingertip against her labia, she shivered. Not in fear, either, if her encouraging moan was any indication. "I didn't tease you, Lucas. Don't make me wait. It's been long enough."

He stared at her in awe. How could she be so resilient, so willing to have faith in his abilities and his ultimate goodness? The latter of which he figured she'd highly overestimated.

It was only because he cared so much for her and her long-term well-being that he abstained from taking her right then and there. Lucas settled for slipping his fingers through the slickness of her arousal before nudging against her tight opening.

When her body yielded to him, little by little, his fingers sank into her hungry pussy.

She clamped around him, already drawing on his digits with rhythmic pulls that made him feel better about coming so quickly in her grasp earlier.

Ellie moaned. She opened her eyes, stared straight at him and commanded, "Rub my clit, Lucas. Don't fool around. Make me come. Please. Touching you, watching you, turns me on so much."

"Shit yes," he growled as everything unnecessary melted away.

For a brief moment, they were just a guy and a super-sexy girl getting it on, like he'd done so many times before. Looking for quick, hard relief. Except this time was like fucking in the middle of a lightning storm, even though all he had inside her was a couple of lousy fingers.

Their energy neutralized his worry, doubt and...anger.

Temporarily, he felt free of every burden.

It was as if he could run unfettered again.

Or at least it seemed that way.

Lucas aimed his elation at Ellie. He tried to refund to her even a portion of the ecstasy she'd granted him. Not only when she'd jerked him off, but also when she'd acted as an antidote for his lingering depression, granting him a much-needed respite.

She was the best medicine he could have hoped for.

So he complied with her wishes, even though he would have liked to drag out their exchange indefinitely.

He tested several different motions until he found one that drove her wild. When he flicked his thumb over her clit while drilling his fingers into her, her thighs began to tremble around him. With one hand, she reached up and cupped her own breast, surprising him with the amount of force she used to stimulate the berry-colored nipple.

He'd have to remember that for later. If there was ever another time he allowed himself to live this dangerously—and risk them both crashing and burning when things didn't go as planned.

Damn, she practically squeezed his fingers from her undulating sheath when she clenched on him that time. It would feel amazing if she did that to his dick.

Willing himself not to get fully hard again, he dedicated himself to bringing her to climax.

It didn't take long.

Ellie screamed, her eyes flying open and her fingers tangling in his hair. Then she shattered.

Her arousal drenched his hand, making him glide easier in between the clamping of her muscles, which nearly froze him solid within her.

An unnatural, feverish glaze came over Ellie's eyes. She became animalistic, roaring her completion in a way that would have been unbelievably hot if it had been a product of regular arousal. Though it was the first time he was seeing the reaction firsthand, he'd seen plenty of similar responses on the tapes they'd lifted from Morselli's dungeon.

His heart stopped in his chest. Would she be okay? Was this *her* new normal?

It should have occurred to him sooner. The discussions he'd had with JRad about how, even now, Lily sometimes had reactions during sex that were influenced by the one time she'd taken Sex Offender. It changed something permanently within the people who'd been cast under its spell.

If it did that to Lily after a single dose, what would it do to Ellie, who'd taken more than just about any other still-living person on the planet?

Unsure of how to react, Lucas retreated. He kept her from falling, but stopped touching her otherwise, making her descent from her orgasm sharp and unsupported.

"Lucas?" She called for him, confused.

"I've got you," he promised.

He simply didn't know what to do with her.

What was the right thing?

It might be too late for him to do that. He should have talked to her about this first. Maybe to Jambrea or Lacey, to find out what the medical repercussions might be. Shit, he'd gotten carried away and done exactly what he shouldn't.

Lucas pushed himself up onto the opposite end of the tub, sitting on the side near the bath mat, leaving Ellie to recover once she could sit up on her own.

The bathwater had grown chilly. It was time to face reality and the consequences of what they'd done.

Ellie mimicked him, heading for the exit. He steadied her until she climbed out of the tub on her own. But when she realized he didn't plan to follow right behind like a dog in heat, her face fell.

"Wow. I think I missed something. What just happened?"

"We got each other off." He played dumb.

"I thought that was the opening act, not the whole show." She snagged a fresh towel off his rack and wrapped it around her, hiding her spectacular body from his view. "Why are you stopping? You can't possibly have had enough, after how long we waited for that. Did you?"

"It's probably best if we get some sleep, don't you think?" Lucas exaggerated his yawn.

Couldn't she feel the effect the drug still had on her? Was it wrong of him to touch her now? He would never take advantage of what those monsters had done to her. The only way he could avoid it was to let her go until he could be sure she was thinking rationally.

"I don't know when the Men in Blue will call back with info, but when they do, we may not have a lot of time before we need to act on it."

She put her hands on her hips. "Don't act like this is a necessary sacrifice. Or for my own good. I know what's best for me. It involves you and me and doing more of what we just tried."

"Things have been insane today...er...yesterday, E." He knew it was a lame excuse, but he wanted to give them time to adjust. And her the chance to come to her senses if she wanted to, or needed to. "I don't think we should rush anything."

"If we went any slower, we'd be going backwards."

She stared at him until he angled his torso away from her and drew clean water to douse his liner. He slathered it in Hibiclens to inhibit bacteria growth then took extra time rinsing it.

She seemed to get the point.

He'd tapped out for now.

"Have it your way, then." A huff came before she pivoted to exit the bathroom. "But I'm taking your bed. Have fun on the couch."

Ellie grumbled beneath her breath about stubborn bastards, making him grin as he finished his routine. She stomped down the stairs, though he wasn't worried she was going very far nude. The lock flipped on his front door before she returned. The sound of a pillow being fluffed reached his straining ears.

"Sweet dreams," he whispered too softly for her to hear.

Then he took forever tidying the bathroom before settling in for a long, freezing shower.

CHAPTER EIGHT

*E*llie thrashed on the cement floor of her cell
without a thought about the bruises she'd leave
behind on her elbows or her legs or even down
her spine, since she'd gotten downright bony lately.
They didn't feed her much here, despite how ravenous
she always was. A side effect of Sex Offender, she
thought, though her logic was still fuzzy from the last
dose they'd given her.

The men who paid Morselli to rent her drug-crazed
body wouldn't appreciate the marks on her ivory skin.
At least not ones they hadn't put there themselves. Or
ones she gave herself when fucking them like a
madwoman. She wondered how much more of this her
body could withstand before her heart detonated in her
chest.

"Don't be a pain in my ass," the guard grumbled as
he tried to quash her flailing so he could administer
another dose.

"Take that shit yourself and you'll bend over and
ask for it. Even from a guy with an elephant dick.
Especially from someone like that, though you won't
find many around here." She spit at him. "You'll
welcome anything that gives you a moment of relief,
including getting fucked up that flabby, glow-in-the-
dark butt of yours, long after you've started to bleed.

Doesn't that sound like fun? No? Then quit forcing me to do it, you disgusting excuse for a human being."

Okay, so antagonizing the guy probably wasn't wise. But she couldn't stand to be quiet anymore. Playing meek hadn't gotten her out of this hell. No good-behavior early release either. They could take her freedom, but they couldn't make her like it, or even pretend to. Not until they jammed that shit down her throat again.

They'd raped and beat her so often that even the thought of punishment no longer frightened her. Sometimes she hoped they'd go too far and kill her. At least then she'd be liberated.

"You know the other bitches around here beg for more of this shit. Too many started killing their cellmates, hoping they'd get both cuts, so we had to isolate everyone. Not only the guys either. Women too." The dungeon warden examined her for a second. "Why don't you crave it like that? You're the only one left from the batch of originals, you know that?"

She hadn't. Was she bordering on extinction?

That stupid devil-man had managed to injure her when she thought she was numb to the damage he could inflict. Was her turn coming? Would this be over soon?

Or was she destined to eternal torture for some unknown reason?

Somehow, she seemed to have enough natural immunity to resist addiction to Sex Offender, maybe even to dampen some of its effects. Now that was a terrifying thought. Could it affect others even more than her? If so, she didn't see how they didn't rip themselves to pieces searching for relief.

Hell, maybe some of them had.

She'd been trying her best to convince this guard to try it, just once, for a while now. If he did, as weak-willed as he was, he'd be destroyed. Like she probably already was. Even if she managed to escape, she'd never be normal again.

It was the only wish she had, though, so she clung to it.

"Do us both a favor and take it on your own today," he snarled at her as if they were buddies instead of mortal enemies.

"It'd be faster if you took a taste." She tried to focus on what she was doing instead of the fire in her skin, an aftereffect from yesterday's high. If she closed her eyes she could imagine herself getting stung by a swarm of bees, all over her body, or maybe running through a field of poisonous nettles.

It was tempting to seek relief in another hit, but that would only bring more pain tomorrow.

No thanks.

Except she didn't have a choice.

"Fine. We'll do it the hard way." He was fast. Or maybe her reflexes were dulled by continual drugging.

Before she could dodge, he'd fisted his hand in her hair and yanked her head down, smacking it on the floor as he straddled her. Pinned to the floor, she bucked, trying to dislodge him with the superstrength that was one of the few benefits of Sex Offender.

It didn't matter, though, when he pulled a giant knife from his belt.

"I don't give a shit if you're one of the Scientist's pets." The blackness in his eyes made her believe every threatening word he told her. "There are hundreds of others nearly as good as you around here. If I slip and cut your fucking head clean off, no one will care."

119

Ryan will. *She thought of her brother. Only that could make her quit endangering herself. For him, she would try to live another day.*

When their parents died, she was the thing that had kept him going. Without her, what would happen to him?

She didn't want that responsibility on her soul.

Ellie stilled as the freezing steel dug into her neck, scratching her. A warm trickle ran along her skin, making her squeeze her eyes closed.

"That's better." *The guard throttled her neck with his other hand, cutting off her air until she struggled, before letting up on her windpipe.* "Why defy me when you know I'm going to win? I do every day, don't I?"

Because it was the only way she had to keep her spirit nourished.

Hope that she would someday get free still blossomed deep inside her, in a place she kept so secret they couldn't find it and crush the dying embers of her belief.

Tired of their game, he reached in his pocket for the tiny vial that held the precious drug. After popping it open, he tipped it against her lips. She kept her mouth closed long enough that he jabbed her throat a little more. Then he mashed on her face hard enough that she feared he might break her front teeth if she didn't open. The thought horrified her.

So she relented.

Chemicals mixed with her saliva, allowing the drug to be absorbed almost instantly into her system. If it hadn't muddied her brain, she would have known the types of reactions occurring since she'd studied so long and hard for her job as a lab tech for pharmaceutical firms.

Now it was for nothing.

She could never go back to that career, knowing what it could be used for. How it had ruined her life. What a stupid mistake—going to work for the Scientist—though she hadn't realized what her enigmatic company was beneath the cloaks they'd used to obscure their true purpose. When their salaries were nearly double the national average for employees without experience, it should have been a clue something wasn't legit.

Ellie paid for that dumb mistake every single day. Every minute.

A surge of power went through her, enabling her to flip her guard onto his back.

She would have grabbed his knife, but he'd caught on to her tricks long ago and thrown the damn thing through the bars to one of the other minions outside her cell. Fuck!

"You know it's not the weapon you wanted anyway, Pretty."

She hated when he called her that.

But, damn him, he was right.

The ache started inside her. First as a white-hot pinprick, then growing until it was a supernova of lust in her core. Compelling her to fuck. Screaming at her to find relief for the discomfort in her pelvis and breasts. Desire taken beyond pleasure to pain. If she didn't appease it, it would drive her mad.

Insane men and women had fled past her cell before being put down like rabid dogs by the guards many times during her stay. That wasn't how she wanted to go out.

Ellie nearly ripped the guard's pants in her desperation.

She didn't remember taking his puny cock out or hovering over it, jamming it inside her. But by his grunts, she knew she had.

Before this place had become her existence, she had only ever gone to bed with a few men. And she'd never fucked like this. Foolish and naïve, she'd never really comprehended the meaning of that word. This *was* fucking.

All she cared about was calming the cyclone whipping her into a frenzy. The person she used to satisfy herself meant nothing. It disgusted her to treat another human being that way, even if they had forced her into it. The repulsive cycle of abuse was something she tried to untangle, but she rarely was clearheaded enough to make sense of it.

Right now, she didn't give a shit.

Ellie flung her head back and whipped her hair from side to side as arousal coalesced into an impending orgasm. Finally, relief. At least for a moment. Coming would only sate her for a few instants at first. It would be half the night before her body settled enough to abstain even for an hour without it being pure torture.

Hate made her motions exponentially more harsh.

The guard didn't seem to mind.

In fact, as she gave in to a great racking orgasm, it seemed like he did too.

His face scrunched, turning an unhealthy shade of purple before he cursed then twitched beneath her, as if she'd jolted him with a live wire instead of crushed his cock with her artificially enhanced arousal.

Simultaneously she felt relief and sickness.

Would she ever be able to experience one without the other?

First she had to escape.

Which didn't seem likely, thanks to the evil bastard beneath her and the other mercenaries like him, who had taken things too far to turn back now in their scheme to create a new superdrug. When he withdrew, he grunted then watched his come spill from her body.

A glimmer of his humanity made an appearance. "It'd be better if you went the way of the others. Are you sure you don't want me to give you more?"

Was that some sick attempt at a mercy killing? They'd already increased her dosage to try to hook her. Another portion so soon would be the end of her for sure.

"Fuck you."

"Have it your way. See you tomorrow, Pretty."

The guard reached the door to her cell but didn't close it entirely. Instead, he shouted down the hall, "Send in the first client. Keep 'em lined up. Especially the sadists. Make sure she's worth all the trouble she gives me."

Ellie would have sobbed if she could have stopped rubbing herself long enough to think about how miserable she had become. Her night hadn't even begun. It would be hours and hours more of this before she was left alone again—starving and freezing.

In the twenty seconds or so since she'd had that loser's cock in her to the time her newest assailant entered and dragged her to the filthy mattress in the corner, she nearly went insane with yearning. If the guy she pounded hadn't paid a premium to be there, she would have considered how she used him so violently a brutal rape.

What kind of sick fuck would enjoy that?

And why couldn't she stop wanting more?

***

123

"Ahhhhhhhhhh!" Raw terror and outrage escaped Ellie's throat in the form of a bloodcurdling scream mixed with a battle cry that burned every bit of her esophagus.

She flailed—kicking, punching and clawing at air in every direction.

If Lucas had been asleep, she probably would have scared him to death.

Hell, even from the boathouse, he couldn't have helped but hear that screech.

Unfortunately for them both, he was sitting right beside her, despite her earlier decree. She wasn't surprised to find him there. He was nearly as obstinate as she was. Frankly, she appreciated having him close, though she probably wouldn't tell him that.

It looked—from his faintly glowing e-reader, the crumpled sheets drawn to his waist, his tablet in a docking station, which flashed a similar info display as the thing in the tackle box earlier, and the squashed pillows behind his lower back—like he'd been camped out for a while, resting against the headboard. Protecting her as she slept.

Too bad he couldn't slay nightmares.

"Oh Jesus. E!" He angled toward her and reached out, stopping with his hands hovering a few inches away from her shaking shoulders, as if afraid of touching her. Using what she thought of as his calm-and-collected voice, he soothed her. Had he perfected this tone while talking down a hijacker sometime in his spook career?

Right now, she didn't give a shit.

She simply appreciated his talent, zeroing in on the reassurance he rained on her, instead of the fragments of vivid recall that threatened to drag her under the blackness.

"You're here, with me. No one's going to hurt you. At least not in that way." His stressed displeasure was enough to seep through the shell-shocked buzz rattling her brain every time she woke from one of those dreams.

It shouldn't have been funny that she was still frazzled over one threat when they faced an entirely new one that she hadn't even come to grips with yet.

A mildly hysterical giggle escaped her when he shook his head. "I'm going to do my best for you, E. I just don't know what you need. Can you tell me? How can I help? Please let me make it better. That was horrible. I couldn't wake you. Is it always so bad?"

She blinked up at him then shifted, grasping his still-outstretched hands when words escaped her. Too many questions, not enough hugging. Besides, she didn't want to make him think she was any more fragile than he already did.

With a yank, she toppled him onto the bed beside her. In fact, he kind of squished her.

Fresh visions of being pinned beneath men who'd opted to take Sex Offender before attacking her rioted through her mind. But only for an instant.

This was Lucas.

He would never hurt her. Shield her, yes. Harm her, no.

Relaxing, she lifted her arms to hold him tight to her when he would have retreated.

"Sorry, E. Sorry. I didn't mean to trap you." He rolled to his back, though her grip ensured that he didn't separate them.

"Don't go," she croaked, only now realizing how much her terror had dried out her throat.

There was so much more she wanted to say. Forcing out sound seemed impossible at the moment. Unless it was another howl, which tried to escape. She swallowed then kept it bottled inside.

"Are you sure?" Tentatively, he laid his hands on her back and began to rub in gentle circles that did more to erase her panic than months of therapy had.

"Yeah." She cuddled into him, burrowing her face into his chest, listening to the reassuring steady beat of his heart. "Hold me?"

Lucas didn't respond verbally. His arms came around her, slowly and gently. It would have been impossible to mistake his tender cradling for the rough restraint of her captors.

Ellie's teeth clicked together as they began to chatter. Goose bumps rose on her arms. It was like this always. A giant crash followed her night terrors. It sucked the life out of her sometimes. Having Lucas there to rock her and whisper how brave he thought she was, how precious, lifted the weight of the world off her shoulders, if only for a few minutes.

She wished she could do the same for him.

Why hadn't he been sleeping?

It took quite a while longer before her limbs defrosted enough to curl around him more naturally in return. Her hand splayed on his rock-hard abs over the arched *Don't Laugh* tattoo she planned to ask him about some other time.

After holding him in her hands earlier, she knew for certain it wasn't a commentary on his size.

Even her feet nudged closer to him, facilitating the tangling of their limbs as well as she could. Maybe if he never let her go, she wouldn't have her nightmares again. A girl could dream. Well, the good kind anyway.

A deep sigh raised then lowered her entire torso. She went floppy in his hold, draped over him, completely worn out by the gamut of her emotions. If only she could be sure she wouldn't relapse into her same nocturnal horror, she could easily float away into sleep again.

"Better?" he asked, his question strained.

"Much. Thank you," she rasped, which probably didn't do a lot to reassure him. Would this only make him see her as more damaged? Probably. Shit.

When he rocked slightly away from her, she whimpered and clutched him with an instinctive grab that had him promising, "I'm not going far. Just getting you some more water. Okay?"

Peeking over at the nightstand, she saw the half-empty bottle there and nodded. Any farther than that and she would rather be parched than give him up. As he leaned and reached, their chests separated and the air being circulated by the gently rotating ceiling fan above them pebbled her nipples.

Holy shit. She was naked.

And he might be too.

At the very least, he hadn't bothered to put a shirt on after he finished cleaning up.

Considering her clothes were ruined, she'd planned to bum a T-shirt off him. Except she'd fallen asleep by the time he finished what had to have been the longest shower in the history of the world. A chilly one too. The decided lack of steam had given him away.

Maybe there was hope yet.

She never stopped believing in the power of that virtue when she'd been locked up without a reason to think she was any more likely to escape than to meet the Easter Bunny down there. A relationship with Lucas didn't seem too improbable after that.

Gladly, she accepted the bottle from him and levered herself onto one elbow before chugging the entire thing in a few unladylike gulps. Stray droplets she licked from her lips when she'd finished.

His stare never wavered from her mouth.

"What time is it?" It seemed like she'd been asleep for only a few minutes.

Sunlight streamed through the sliver of his windows left exposed on the edges of his blinds.

Disoriented, she searched for a clock.

"It's about two thirty in the afternoon," he confirmed. "You really zonked out."

"But you didn't?" She wondered, "Do you think people are going to find me here? Should we be taking turns on guard or something?"

"You watch too much TV." He cracked a smile for the first time since she'd rocketed from her dream into reality. "Everything's okay for now. We're lying low, not drawing attention. The Men in Blue are on it, tracking some stuff and doing their homework. Don't worry about that."

"Okay." She nodded, sitting up while pinning the sheet to her chest. "So why weren't you sleeping with me? I mean, next to me. Or on the couch like I told you to."

"You didn't mean that. Did you?"

"No."

Blushing at something that silly after what she'd done and had done to her seemed ridiculous. She did it anyway.

Lucas smiled softly as he cupped her cheek in his palm then swiped his thumb over one last, lingering drop of water she'd missed on her lower lip. "Maybe

I'd rather spend my time looking at you. You're so pretty."

"Don't call me that, please." She shuddered. "It was the name the guard used for me."

"Shit, I'm sorry." He reached for her hand. "How about beautiful? Gorgeous? Stunning? Mesmerizing? Sometimes I can't look away from you."

"Sure didn't seem that way earlier." Her annoyance was returning now that she could shove her dream into the basement of her mind and recall how irritated she'd been before she passed out. "Try again, Lucas. Don't bullshit me either."

He glanced away and then back, the flirting he'd been doing erased. She almost regretted that.

Until he came clean.

"I've been struggling with phantom pain in my foot. You know, the one that's not there? It hurts like a son of a bitch. Feels like it's all pins and needles or like I need to stretch it, or like it's a winter day and I've forgotten to put a sock on. Sometimes, like right now, I'd swear it's on fire. Depends on the day. Well, night, actually. I think I messed with my body's internal clock. 'Cause it's going nuts right now although it usually only happens when I'm trying to sleep." He frowned.

"And there's nothing you can do to stop it?" She hated hearing he was suffering.

"Not unless you can figure out some way to make my severed nerves settle down and get with the one-footed program." He shrugged. "I've got some pills to manage it with, but they make me fuzzy-headed. I hate them."

"More than you hate hurting?" She put her hand over his and squeezed. After spending months under the influence of a powerful drug, she could understand.

"Yes. Especially when we should be alert."

"You just said..."

"I know. But I'm not taking any chances with your safety." He let her gaze into his warm chocolate eyes.

"Thank you." Nothing could mean more to her, or show her how much he cared, if it wasn't that. So surely he'd appreciate that she felt the same way about him. "You have to rest, Lucas. Believe me, I know what lack of sleep will do to you. Especially when you're running a deficit over a long period of time. You're pushing yourself so hard to get better. Quickly."

"I'm okay."

"I don't think you are." Scooting her hand, she put it on the top of his thigh, watching as he squirmed slightly.

"It's getting better." He cleared his throat. "I tried some things, like mirror therapy. You trick yourself into thinking the limb is still there. It's supposed to reset the map of your body in your brain or something like that. That sounded kind of like quackery to me, but seems to be helping. Just, for some reason, it's not cooperating right now."

"What else helps?" she asked. "Anything?"

His answer came too quickly to be genuine. "Nah."

Ellie smacked his belly. It might as well have been a drumhead, given the resulting *thwack*.

"Hey." He held his hands up, palms out. "Okay, fine. Massage helps too. Like the one you gave me before. I'm supposed to do that to myself three to five times a day."

"Yeah, I bet. Coming usually helps me settle down too." She beamed, intentionally misunderstanding.

"Not *that* kind." His tone said exasperation, but his smile and twinkling eyes proclaimed his appreciation for their exchange. "It's also helping me build tolerance to touch on the sensitive areas of my stump."

"Why don't you call it a residual limb?" she wondered.

"I guess that sounds too tidy to me." Lucas shifted, rubbing his thigh through the sheet as if talking about his leg made him more aware of it. "My scar is kind of nasty. Because of the way the bone was crushed and how they tried to save as much as possible, despite the necrosis that developed while I was—"

"Being stubborn." She bit her lip. "I know. Jambi told me about what she saw that day in the hotel bathroom. You're lucky the infection didn't kill you, you know."

"So I've been told. Repeatedly."

"But now you're older and wiser, right?" She nudged him toward her goal.

"What are you getting at?"

"You know something that helps, so let me do it for you."

Ellie didn't dare whip the sheet off of him, though she could have. She'd had her choices stolen enough to know that forcing someone wasn't the way to make them comfortable.

"I just told you it's...ugly."

"And I already told *you* that I don't give a shit." She glared at him. "Why don't you believe me? Have I ever lied to you? I've been nothing but honest, even when it was humiliating. Shove me away again if you have to. I'll just keep coming back. I'm a glutton for punishment like that, I guess."

"Fuck." Lucas scrubbed his hands over his face then through his hair, putting his colorfully tattooed sleeves on display. "It's not you, E."

"I'm starting to believe that's true." The thought didn't make her any happier. She hated that he was in pain and had licked his wounds solo for so long.

"If you don't want to anymore, after you see it, that's fine." He cringed.

"Show me."

Slowly, he drew away the thin material keeping him from sight. The fact that his cock and balls were equally on display didn't seem to bother him in the least. Distracted, she forgot to look at his leg for a minute.

Lucas caught her spying on his junk and laughed. "I guess you're right. I didn't have to worry. You're never going to see it anyway."

"Sorry." She slapped her palm over her eyes to block the temptation. Then peeled it away, her gaze aimed lower.

"Oh, Lucas." She didn't hesitate, reaching out to trace the long gash that went kind of crookedly across the front of his limb, unlike the clean incision she'd seen on AmputeeOT's videos earlier. No wonder this hurt. "Do they say this will fade with time? The pain, not the scars."

"It should, but we're at the stage now where it's been long enough, that if I don't see improvement soon, it could be a lifelong problem." Tension strung his shoulders tightly together. The idea upset him. As it should.

"We're a terrible pair, aren't we?" She sat cross-legged, putting his thigh in her sheet-draped lap as she began to run her fingers over him, helping him adjust to the presence of her touch. As he relaxed more and more, she deepened the caresses, massaging the muscles there.

The fact that her breasts were on display, an easy thing for him to focus on, didn't bother her in the least. She had nothing to hide from him anymore.

Lucas groaned then nodded. "We are. Both of us crippled in one way or another."

"I'm not sure I appreciate that label, but...okay, yeah." She peeked down at her handiwork. It *was* a bit of a shock every time she saw his reconfigured body. But only because he'd kept himself concealed from her for so long.

"I own my issues. I told you I'm fucked up." He added softly, "I just don't like other people to know about it if I can help it."

"Is that why you've gotten so many tattoos lately? Are you trying to compensate for the parts of your body you're unhappy with? Is it like, wallpapering over your scars?" she asked, though not with derision. More like fascination. Her fingertip stretched out, tracing some of the swirls around his elbows before returning to her work on his leg.

"I guess. I always liked ink on other people. In my line of work, it was strictly forbidden. Too identifiable. But, now, that's not my life anymore. I can do some stuff I couldn't before."

"Well, I like them. They're hot." She bit her lip, embarrassed she'd admitted out loud what her dilating pupils had already probably communicated to him. "I have one too. Want to see?"

"I should say no. You don't need to be any sexier to me." He reached out, trailing his knuckles over the upper swell of her breast. "Besides, I kind of saw it earlier. Not clearly. I admit I was focused on other parts of you when you tortured me with your little striptease. Which I will get back at you for sometime, by the way. But it seemed pretty sweet."

"Looking forward to that." She smiled as she gave his leg a few lingering rubs before twisting at the waist to grant him a clear view.

On her shoulder there was a Victorian-style birdcage with broken black feathers lying on the bottom. The door was open and a bird rocketed from inside, wings spread, rising above it. The beak and plumage of the bird were vividly colored where it had been reborn postcaptivity. Its tail feathers, which hadn't yet cleared the open door, were the shade of midnight.

"It's beautiful." He wrapped his arm around her waist and drew her into his lap so he had an up-close view. "And sad. Determined and hopeful. It's you."

Lucas kissed the design softly, bringing tears to her eyes.

She nodded. Of course he would get it.

Angling herself so that she faced him, she looped her arms around his waist and hugged him. "When you got me out of there, I felt like a snake shedding its skin or a bird molting, sloughing off the person I'd become to survive. That's not who I want to be. I want to make the most of life, now that I know how fragile it really is. For me, that means finding someone to spend my time with, enjoying every moment and, as much as possible, refusing to dwell on the past."

Ellie peeked up at him from beneath lowered lashes.

Did he know what she was saying?

"You think you're ready for a relationship?" He swallowed hard, making her fingers itch to stroke his stubbly jaw.

"Yes. With the right person." This time she refused to glance away.

Lucas sighed. That couldn't be a good sign.

"What?" She tipped her head as she studied him.

"I don't know how to ask this really." He rested his forehead on hers.

"Just say, 'Hey Ellie, want to be my girlfriend?'" She teased him, hoping to make him squirm a little. "I'll say yes and then we can celebrate with a round of spring-bending sex. How about it?"

This time he laughed. She loved the sound of it, rich and honest. It didn't last very long, though.

His brows furrowed and his eyes grew serious. "Despite the fact that I'm a decade older than you, and how our lives are completely out of whack right now, I would love that, but..."

"No buts." She put her fingers over his mouth. Until she realized he was serious. Something was bugging him. "You're not kidding... Crap, sorry. What's bothering you?"

"Before, when I got you off—"

"Mmm," she hummed and rocked closer to him, just remembering how skilled he had been at manipulating her in all the best ways.

Lucas took her hand in one of his and entwined their fingers. He paused then said in a rush, "Could you feel the effects of Sex Offender on you still?"

The temptation to deny it was strong. Founding a relationship—if that was what they were doing—on anything but sincerity, frankness and candor wasn't part of her blueprint, though. "Yes. The doctors believe it's a permanent mutation. Because I took the drug so many times. They're not sure, though, since my case is one of the first. I'm pretty much the only person to have survived after that kind of massive, repetitive usage. Most people OD'd before they got to where I was. Does that bother you? Is *that* why you stopped—?"

Suddenly she felt entirely too close to him. How could she not have realized how much she'd disgusted him? That he'd rejected her without her even realizing it.

Ellie scrambled backward until she nearly fell off the edge of the bed.

"Hey, come on." He reached for her, but she shied away.

"I accept you as you are, and you pull that bullshit with me, because *I'm* different? I can't control it or undo what they did to me, any more than you can regenerate your stupid leg. How the hell is that fair?" His rebuff stung. She wasn't sure if she wanted to cry or punch him in the nuts, but she was leaning toward violence when he held his hands up in surrender.

"Give me some credit here." Lucas inched closer. "It's not that I'm repulsed or something."

"Sure?" Bitterness seeped from her now that he'd lanced the wound. "Because I've probably fucked half of the men in a three-state radius. How I didn't end up pregnant or infected with any incurable diseases *is* kind of a miracle. There's no part of me that hasn't been violated repeatedly. Nothing about me would be yours alone. And as if that weren't bad enough, I'm some kind of sex junkie now. Every time you turn me on, you'll be reminded of those facts. I guess that's not really what a man wants for his significant other, is it?"

"E, stop."

Ellie continued rambling, spewing an assortment of hateful things she'd thought plenty of times about herself, although it twisted her up to imagine Lucas aiming that kind of malice at her.

"E!"

He shocked her with his speed and his strength. Lucas grabbed her shoulders and hauled her close then tumbled them to the mattress. He held himself above her on straight-locked arms that allowed him to stare directly into her eyes without pinning her to the mattress.

Before she could continue her demeaning rant, he sank lower and fused his mouth with hers.

The sweep of his lips transformed her ire into something warmer and welcome. He slanted his mouth over hers and tickled the seam of her lips with his tongue until he cajoled his way past her prickly defenses. Maybe she had overreacted. He had trod directly on her insecurities, mashing all her hot buttons at once.

This was a much preferable way to burn. Ellie arched against him, inviting him to steal much more than first base.

A gentleman at heart, he didn't. Once he'd shut her up, he rolled off, flopping onto his back.

With nowhere to hide, his cock proclaimed that Lucas wasn't as unaffected as he might like to appear.

Thank God.

Ellie sucked in a lungful of air to replace the oxygen they'd depleted during their marathon make-out. She turned just her head to peek at him from where they now lay side by side.

"I was sort of hoping you might like the idea of having a superfreak in bed. Or that my newfound sexual appetite might be the silver lining, not another black mark."

Discreetly, she sniffled, trying her damnedest not to cry in front of him.

"When you put it that way, it doesn't sound like such a terrible thing." Lucas wiggled his brows, making her laugh despite her misery. "But, Ellie, even down a foot, I'm man enough to give you as much pleasure as you can stand. I don't fucking need to cheat by banking on the aftereffects of Sex Offender."

Wait. Was this his ego talking? Had it been bruised by her condition?

"I...I didn't think of it like that." She frowned. "Is that what you thought? That I wasn't enjoying what we did because of you? Only because of the drugs?"

"I didn't know what to think. I'd be lying if I didn't say it surprised me. You looked so... *Damn.* Like Nymphomaniac Barbie or something."

That certainly seemed like a compliment when he said it so reverently.

He took some time to choose his next words carefully. "So, what exactly does it do to you? What does it feel like? Are you in control? I'm terrified that if I'm in to what we're doing to each other, I'll think you are too when really it's just a chemical reaction, not your true desire causing you to respond to me."

"Oh." When she thought about it from his perspective, she could see exactly why he'd balked. His noble nature wouldn't allow him to take advantage of someone's condition like that.

"Hmm." She tapped her fingers on her belly, where she'd stacked her hands. "When I'm turned on it's like...going to the grocery store when you haven't eaten yet. Lots of stuff starts to look good to me. But I have enough control over those urges to only buy the things I would normally, even if it's uncomfortable to suppress a craving."

He cursed under his breath.

"But before...with you...it was *amazing*." Part of her figured that would have been true even if she'd fooled around with him prior to her run-in with Sex Offender. "It was more like when you eat a small lunch, knowing you're going out to a fancy restaurant later. It was a good kind of deprivation, with a payoff almost as fantastic as something chocolatey for dessert."

"Hey." He reached over and tweaked her nipple, making them both crack up. Then, he double-checked, "So you really liked it? *You.* Not you under the influence of that shit."

Ellie didn't respond reflexively, she really took time to analyze in hindsight. The way she'd acted with him might have been amplified, but the desires were hers. Truly.

"Yep." She stared up at his handsome face as she confessed, "I've wanted to do that for a while now."

"Me too." Lucas dropped a kiss on her shoulder. "Maybe sometime—now that we know each other's deepest, darkest secrets—we could try it again. And if you're ever...needy...I want you to tell me so I can take care of you."

"Like ring a bell every time I need you to toss me a bang?" If she didn't laugh, she'd cry.

Fortunately, it turned out that Mr. Serious Pants actually had a sense of humor buried under his perfectly pressed clothes. Or maybe his injury was teaching him to lighten up. Either way, she liked the new Lucas.

"So, can I ask one more thing, or are you tired of my questions?" He wasn't being flippant. Over the past seven months he'd faced endless interrogations and concern from everyone around him. He knew how exhausting it could be to mull over your worst problems constantly.

"Go for it." She smiled.

"Do you think this is how you'll always be?" He rubbed his thigh. "Has it faded since you got out? Or will it weaken over time, like I hope my phantom pains will?"

"Nah, I think I'm pretty much destined to be a sex fiend for life. My doctors say I'm always going to have an abnormally high sex drive." Ellie choked down her embarrassment and told him everything. If he was going to be the one for her, he had to go into this knowingly. "I get horny *a lot*. And if I don't do something about it, it can hurt. Bad."

"Ah shit." He rolled onto his side, propping his head on his palm and slinging the other arm across her middle. "Did I leave you in a rough place this morning? You should have told me."

"It's not your fault." She laughed, though it was strained. "And don't feel bad either. I took care of myself a few times while you were in the shower."

He groaned. "I would have loved to watch you play with that sweet pussy. In my bed. Son of a bitch."

The thickening shaft of his cock nudged her hip, giving her all sorts of ideas. But she had to finish this discussion now or she'd never find the nerve again. "I'm kind of an expert-level masturbator at this point. I can't tell you how many vibrators I've worn out since you hauled me from Morselli's dungeon."

"They don't make shit like they used to. Cheap junk." He grinned down at her, making her hungry for another taste of his smile. "Good news. I don't break so easily. Hell, I'm practically a cyborg. I can take you."

"So, all this talk..." She rubbed against the full length of him, trying to ease some of the heat spreading through her. Unfortunately that only made it worse.

"Yeah?" His eyes grew slumberous, as if he imagined the possibilities like she did.

"It's turning me on."

"Me too. What do you think we should do about that, E?"

"How about a medicinal fuck?"

CHAPTER NINE

"Like actual sex?" Lucas grimaced.

Not a good sign, Ellie figured, considering she'd just suggested they get down and dirty.

"E, I know you're going to be pissed, but I'm asking anyway. Are you sure you're ready for that? You know, like penetration. My cock, your pussy..."

He made the universal sign for sex with his index finger poking through the ring of his thumb and forefinger on the opposite hand a few times.

A laugh blasted from her tight chest. Because he made discussing difficult topics easier. And because he was right. She *was* scared in tandem with being horny. When it came down to it, she hadn't mentally prepared herself for getting it on with him today. Hell, she hadn't even known she was going to see him again.

Though obviously she wished it hadn't been because he was hauling her ass from another fire, she couldn't be sad about spending this time with Lucas. So she didn't want to do anything that would screw up the memories they were making, in case that's all she had later.

"As much as I hate to say this...no, I'm not positive." She sighed, deflating. "I haven't...*you know*, with anyone since I got out."

"Except your stable of dildos."

"Well, yeah." She smacked his abs. "I have some pretty cool ones—colorful glass ones, high-tech ones, waterproof ones, big ones. Lily bought me a really fancy one from Europe for my birthday. Jealous?"

"Hell yes." His eyes darkened as if the thought of her bringing herself pleasure really did it for him.

"Too bad I don't have any of my stuff with me. The one from Lily and JRad has a remote control feature that could be fun. Or I could put on a show for you." The idea burst from her lips before she could put the kibosh on it. Prior to Sex Offender, she never would have been so bold. Now she kind of liked that she could be. With Lucas, anyway.

After spending so long thinking of her ordeal as ruining her, she clung to any silver lining she could draw from the experience.

"I had something else in mind." He leaned down and kissed her. Long and languorously. "But I will *gladly* take a rain check on that, E."

He certainly had more experience than she did. Or had.

At least now she knew what possibilities there were. And she couldn't wait to experience them with someone attentive and skilled. Someone who would focus only on bringing her satisfaction, not pain. Unless it was the fun kind.

Lucas was so considerate and respectful of what was best for others that she knew he'd be an excellent lover. One she couldn't wait to experience and treat to some well-deserved ecstasy of his own.

When they were ready.

Jumping in too soon could spoil everything. So she let him guide them to the destination he'd selected. He didn't seem in any hurry to get there, though, as he continued to kiss her senseless.

Ellie lost track of time as they made out. A simple pleasure that she could indulge in for hours.

The only thing she'd found to quiet her buzzing mind most days was sketching in the pad she picked up seemingly randomly a few months back. It had called to her with an urgency that surprised her. Maybe the drugs unlocked some hidden well of creativity she hadn't known she possessed.

If the relief she derived from her art was like wearing earmuffs on a noisy street, kissing Lucas injected Zen directly into her soul. When he aroused her like this, it was like he gave that continuous underlying buzzing of her body's sexual system something to focus its extra energy on. Effective, his calming influence made her crave more of it.

With newfound purpose, she reached over to him, tangled her fingers in his hair, which—though still short—had grown some from his military cut. He groaned when she leaned into his embrace, taking as much as she was giving.

Ellie sucked on his tongue, thrilled that she could delight him even as she sated herself. And when she tried it in reverse, he let her raid his mouth, tasting him and claiming him all at once. He was delicious. By far the sexiest man she'd ever dared to kiss, never mind fuck.

It awed her that Lucas seemed to enjoy their interaction as fiercely as she did. Maybe not all of the intensity of their connection could be blamed on her chemical makeup.

His hands began to travel from her shoulders down her arms, caressing to her very fingertips before reversing their trail up to her collarbones. She shivered when he allowed his hand to dip, teasing the upper swells of her breasts with a barely there sweep.

The reverence he infused in each tender stroke was offset by a possessiveness and boldness that made her feel simultaneously cherished and desired. Not lusted after in a seedy way, like the men who'd relished her helplessness under the spell of Sex Offender, but as an equal who was wanted for who she was as much as—or more than—what she was willing to do with him.

Lucas growled into her mouth. He never once looked away from her gaze, letting his admiration shine through in his stare. He nibbled on her lower lip then paused, as if checking for her reaction.

She would have smiled, but he made it difficult with his teeth holding her mouth hostage. It felt amazing to be claimed by him.

When she didn't flee, instead kissing him deeper and more urgently, Lucas advanced their boundaries once more. His hand hovered over her breast, so close that she could feel the heat radiating from his broad palm.

Ellie followed her instincts. She arched her spine, lifting her chest so that she fit herself to his hand. The resulting pleasure was so sharp and deep that she gasped.

He withdrew instantly, eliciting a whimper from her. "No."

She dug her nails into his shoulders somewhat deeper than she'd meant to. Already her altered body was magnifying the effects of her natural arousal. For once, it didn't frighten her. She embraced it. And Lucas. "Please don't stop. I need more."

It wasn't an exaggeration, either.

Ellie legitimately *needed* additional contact. Once triggered, the Sex Offender mutation drove her to orgasm for relief. Otherwise, her entire body would begin to ache until pain seemed to radiate from her very bones. They'd gone far enough now to kick off the sequence. If she didn't finish it, she would pay.

Sometimes it happened at inconvenient times, like when she was out shopping. It was one reason she'd holed herself up in her house far more often than not the past year. After having to dart to the restroom to relieve herself more than once, she'd suffered. Embarrassed and ashamed, she'd eventually caved to the urgings of Lacey and Jambrea and gone to her doctor. That was when they'd discovered the permanent impacts of her time in captivity.

With Lucas, it didn't seem like such an imposition.

No, he made it feel like she'd hit a bigger jackpot than the one at the casino the day before.

Because he knew exactly how to handle her to spin the extra arousal into something she could enjoy.

"Tell me if it's too much," he whispered before cupping her breasts in his hands. "You're so responsive. It makes me feel superhuman to be able to turn you on like this."

Ellie's heels drummed on the bed when he began to knead her flesh. Sparks of electricity ran throughout her entire body. She felt alive. Her senses enhanced. Everything about her seemed to finally fall into place, like she'd been operating in the wrong gear and suddenly got it right, rocketing her forward, right off the starting line.

"More!" She couldn't even draw enough breath to add "please" to her demand.

The devilish grin Lucas tossed her had her squirming beneath him. He told her over and over

147

how beautiful she was. How brave. He eased himself above her, still keeping a gap between their torsos, probably so as not to alarm her.

Ellie admired his strength and stamina. The man certainly had put his time in at the gym. Even balancing on his knees and elbows while his fingers began to toy with her nipples, he didn't waver once.

The intensity of their kisses increased when their mouths collided once more. She ate at him, trying to communicate just how madly she wanted him.

If they hadn't discussed it previously, she would have been groping between their bodies for his cock, to shove it inside her. Then who knew what she might have thought later, when she'd recovered enough to be logical again.

Fortunately, he didn't allow her to overstep their agreement.

Lucas abandoned her mouth despite her moan at the loss of the intimate connection with him. He made it up to her by proceeding to lick along her jaw then down onto her neck.

The instant his open mouth glided along the column toward her shoulder, pausing here and there to nuzzle, kiss and nip her, her pussy clenched. God, that felt amazing. Her eyes rolled back as he proceeded to home in on the places that made her quake the most.

Meanwhile, his hands never stopped toying with her breasts.

The thick length of his hard cock rested on her mound, making her sure she'd been a fool to answer him honestly earlier.

She could have Lucas inside her with a shift of their hips.

When she tried to make it happen, he stopped toying with her to *tsk*.

"Don't distract me, E." He bit her a little harder, which only made her cry out his name and hug him closer to her.

"Hurry," she begged. Already the pressure was growing inside her, demanding relief. "Need to come."

"I'll bet." Lucas murmured naughty things directly into her ear, "I can smell your arousal...so sweet. Hell, I can feel your heat on my cock. Just wait until I fuck you. It's going to be so damn good, for us both. We'll probably kill each other with how hot it will be."

She didn't doubt him.

"Do you think I can make you come just by sucking on your perfect tits?" he asked.

Ellie was more than willing to let him try, though she didn't think even she was that desperate. She'd always been a clitoral-stimulation kind of girl. Unable to form a coherent response, she shoved on his shoulders instead.

His rough chuckle made her press her thighs together. A trickle of arousal squeezed from her core. Soon she'd be soaked for him. She hoped he had another set of sheets.

Or at least the thought flashed through her mind an instant before he blanked out everything but the feel of his mouth toying with her collarbone and finally angling toward her right breast.

He removed his hand, swapping it for his lips.

When he lapped across her rock-hard nipple with the flat of his tongue, she moaned.

The deep, sensual sound spurred him on. Lucas latched on to the tip of her breast. He closed his lips around it and tugged, varying the suction so that her nipple pulsed in his mouth.

"Oh shit!"

His answering laugh rumbled across her ruched skin, only enhancing the sensations he imparted. Unwilling to leave her unbalanced, he switched his attention to the other side of her chest. His fingers toyed with the slick skin he'd left behind, which was so sensitive to his touch that she nearly wept with the bliss he left in his wake.

The haze of rapture fogging her mind made the world beyond him and her unfocused. She didn't realize at first that he was shifting his position until she felt his thigh settle into the space between her legs. When he leaned forward, he pressed against her pussy, nearly making her come on the spot.

"Lucas!" she shouted.

He hummed his approval against her breast, redoubling his efforts as if he knew he was within reach of his goal to make her shatter from his careful tending of her chest alone.

As Ellie rose on waves of pleasure that lifted her higher with each swell, she tensed. A tendril of fear snaked into her gut. It was too powerful. Would it dash her to pieces like a shipwreck against rocks in a storm?

What choice did she have now but to ride the tide?

She stiffened, feeling herself climb inexorably toward orgasm.

Her breath got stuck in her lungs and her hands fisted in Lucas's sheets.

Of course he noticed the glimmer of panic detracting from the beautiful sensations he granted her.

"It's okay, E." He lifted his mouth from her body long enough to reassure her. "Let go. I'll take care of you. I promise."

She trusted his word.

So she forced her fingers to unfurl one at a time until all she could concentrate on was the intoxicating pull of his lips on her breasts and the way he rocked, pressing his thigh into her clit and saturated pussy.

Resisting would have been impossible.

Ellie shuddered. She looked straight into Lucas's eyes and begged, "Help me."

He growled then mashed his leg against her, while at the same time plumping her breasts with his hands. His teeth raked against her nipple before he suckled her harder than he had before.

That was all it took to push her over the edge. Her climax erupted from her core, frightening her with its intensity even as it threatened to burn her alive. The room seemed bright, even with the curtains drawn, as if her pupils had dilated to the max.

From Lucas's hiss, as he watched her explode, she assumed the change was visible. Every part of her yearned for more pleasure. Her orgasm had only kindled the conflagration of lust now raging inside her. She wanted him.

When she reached for Lucas's cock, he shifted out of her grasp.

"Next time, E." He kissed her then, feeding her as much of his ardor as she could stand. When they were both breathless, he said, "I'm not going to let you make decisions when you're like this. Next time. When you're sober, we'll talk about what you really want."

"It hurts." She attempted to curl into a ball to stop the cramping in her abdomen, but he was in the way.

"Okay. I've got it, E. Hang on. Just a second." He didn't waste any more time explaining. Instead, he slithered down her torso until he was sprawled between her legs.

Of course he'd never leave her to suffer.

He pressed her thighs far apart to make room for his powerful shoulders and grant him the best possible access.

"I'd love to spend hours teasing you," he moaned.

"Don't!"

"Maybe after I've made you come a few more times." He blew across her oversensitive pussy as if trying to ease into contact.

The air flowing over her only acted like fuel on the fire of her arousal. It flared, and she responded without thought.

Ellie reached down and wrapped her hand around the back of Lucas's neck. She pulled him to her, though they both knew he was strong enough to resist if he chose.

He didn't.

Instead, he dove into the slick folds of her pussy, licking and nuzzling her between animalistic sounds that made her believe he enjoyed his feeding frenzy nearly as much as she did. It didn't take more than thirty seconds before he'd set off another orgasm, making her spill additional release for him to drink as if he were dying of thirst.

"Shit, yes."

He groaned against her when the vibration of his praise caused another shock wave to run through her. Their cycle of ecstasy and relief blended. She couldn't tell anymore when she was coming and when she wasn't.

Maybe because he kept extending her pleasure with his perfectly placed laps against her clit. When she hooked her knees over his shoulders and crossed her ankles behind his back, he chuckled.

"Better?"

It was, in a way, but still... "Mmm. More."

Greedy, maybe. But she wanted to revel in the fact that someone wanted to bring her pleasure, finally, instead of taking it at her expense or forcing her to service them.

"Yes, ma'am."

He got back to work. More gently at first, until she could tolerate the direct pressure of his mouth and the hand he slipped between her legs. The tip of his finger nudged her flexing opening, reminding her of how good it had felt earlier that morning when he'd used his thick digit to pump into her. "This okay?"

"Yes!" she shrieked.

So he advanced, pressing against the rings of muscles clamped so tightly at her opening that he had to work her open, cursing in between gentle kisses and sucks on her pussy.

The combination of his caring, the pressure of his hand and the attention he paid to her clit finally resulted in the capitulation of her body to his demands. He sank inside her bit by bit, his finger spiraling inward to facilitate embedding in her spasming channel.

Of course, when he inspired another orgasm, he only increased the difficulty of his own job. Her sheath gripped him, keeping him from making more progress until it had subsided again.

And still she was hungry for him.

"Again, E," he groaned against her soaked pussy. "I could watch you come all day. You're so fucking hot."

She no longer cared that she was beginning to perspire, her entire body covered with a light sheen of sweat. Or that her wanton display might frighten him off, since he made it so clear that he enjoyed every minute of satisfying her.

But now that he'd knocked the edge off her frenzy, she wanted something else.

He deserved some pleasure of his own.

Ellie slid her legs from his back and nudged his shoulder until he leaned to his left and looked up at her.

"Have enough?" His voice was strained and his respiration elevated. His eyes didn't look nearly as crazy as hers did when she saw them in the mirror after getting turned on—and she suspected that being with him took the lingering effects to a new high—but they glittered with his appetite, determined to feast. On her.

The sight had her going all shivery again.

"Not yet, but I want to be on top for a while." She brushed her thumb against the shimmer left behind by her arousal on his cheek. "Can I?"

"Hell yeah." He put his arms around her hips and rolled, dragging her over him.

If she hadn't situated herself on her knees, hovering above him, fast enough, she could have smothered him. He didn't look like he would care.

"Ride my face, E." He groaned, extending his tongue and letting her do the work, grinding over him in a sinful figure eight that had her forgetting momentarily about her devious plan.

His hands cupped her hips, helping her to glide across his mouth. His nose and chin bumped over her when she grew wilder in the arcs she made with her pelvis. Just a little more and then she would see to him, she promised herself.

It was tough, though, when he distracted her. He was a face-fucking connoisseur.

Ellie leaned back, planting her palms on his chest, curling her fingers some to feel the muscles there. The angle doomed her.

As soon as her release washed over her, she started to spin around, changing the direction from which she straddled him. She'd gotten about halfway when he realized her intent.

"No, E. You don't have to do that." He gripped her tight, keeping her from the thick, pulsing erection she spied lying heavily on his abdomen.

"Want to." She brushed his hands away, or attempted to. His steely grip prevented her from claiming her prize.

"If you do that, you'll be right by my leg. That's not what you want when you're turned on, is it? I don't want to gross—"

"Lucas. Shut up." She reached to the side and poked him in the belly, not that she even made a dent. "There's only one of your appendages I'm concerned with at the moment, and it sure as hell isn't your leg. Stop arguing. Let me suck your cock, and I'll be happy to have you get back to finishing what you were doing."

Already she ached for his fingers inside her again.

Or something bigger.

Why had she shut them down earlier? How could she be afraid of sex with Lucas?

It wasn't like what they were doing wasn't intimate as fuck already.

She knew he wouldn't negotiate with her now, not when she was out of her mind with rapture. As soon as she was clearheaded, she planned to make sure he knew that the next time they hooked up it'd be in every way.

For now, she'd settle for giving him the best BJ of his life...she hoped.

This time, when she moved, he let her finish situating herself over him, facing his feet.

Ellie walked her fingers down his ripped abs before lightly stroking him. She loved the way he twitched beneath her hand.

He groaned then went back to work, keeping the pain at bay by replacing it with white-hot arousal.

Sex had never felt this good. Even since she'd been altered by Sex Offender, she'd never had such a gratifying experience. Fucking Lucas had her entire dildo collection beat hands—or was that cocks?—down.

She leaned forward, resting on top of him as if he were the most comfortable couch in the world. In truth, he kind of was. His muscles were covered by soft, warm skin that lulled her with the pure enjoyableness of contact with it.

Lying on top of him, she studied his hard-on close up. It was every bit as large as it had seemed when she'd cupped him in her hands in the bath earlier. Maybe even more than she'd expected.

Dark with his arousal, it was also decorated with heavy veins that would feel amazing rubbing inside her.

But it wasn't until she opened her mouth and drew him in, savoring the unique flavor of him, that she felt something inside her shift. The insatiable horniness that had rampaged inside her dulled some as she sipped precome from the slit in the tip of his cock.

Lucas roared beneath her, redoubling his efforts. He impaled her with several of his fingers as his tongue danced across her clit. There'd be time to go slowly later, but she could feel them reaching the apex of her arousal and wanted him to join her in one final epic orgasm.

He must have realized she was hovering on the precipice of something major too.

"Hang on." He nudged her hip just as she opened her mouth to swallow him to the root.

"Don't wanna." It was hard to talk around a mouthful of him so she shook her head, making him curse and flex his hips upward.

"Just a couple seconds. Are you okay?" he asked her. "Can you get something for me?"

She knew it stung his pride to have to ask, so she didn't give him any more shit than necessary. "Of course. What?"

"Go grab my electric toothbrush from the medicine cabinet."

When she looked at him over her shoulder like he might be the crazy one in their couple, he smacked her ass.

"Hurry back."

She liked the resulting sting more than she probably should have. And if she hoped for any chance of him doing it again, she figured she should do what he wanted.

On the way, she didn't mind sassing him, though. Didn't he know he'd just cockblocked himself? "I

157

figured you could wait until you were finished eating me out to brush your teeth."

When she opened the mirrored door and saw the shape of the appliance's handle, she figured she knew what he had planned and immediately upgraded his sex-god rating from amazing to superstar.

"Why would I want to have the taste of you out of my mouth?" He shook his head at her. "Get over here, E."

He sat on the edge of the bed, a condom in his hand.

"Are you sure you wouldn't rather use that on your dick and do this the old-fashioned way?" Couldn't blame a girl for trying, right?

"Saying no right now is the hardest thing I've ever done. I hope you appreciate it later, though." He reached out and drew her into his open arms.

"I will." She kissed his forehead, then his nose and finally his mouth.

Sometime, while they made out, he snatched the toothbrush and rolled the condom down its handle. Armed with a makeshift vibrator, he tossed her to the mattress.

She squeaked, surprised. Not a hint of fear went through her when he approached, though. Her smile must have conveyed that to him.

"Thank you for trusting me," he murmured as he flopped to his back and drew her over himself once more like a blanket.

"Thank you for being trustworthy." This time she didn't hesitate. She took him inside her mouth and slid her lips in a tight ring to the base of his shaft in a single swoop.

"Fuck!" he shouted, then followed suit, wasting no time in lining up his impromptu toy with her opening.

When he inserted it into her, giving her something to hug inside her, she went wild, sucking on his shaft as if it was her favorite thing to do in the world. With the exception of having his erection buried in her pussy, she figured it might be. Well, maybe tied for kissing him. He *was* an *excellent* kisser.

Distracted by her thoughts of the plethora of ways to enjoy Lucas, she didn't prepare herself for the vibrations that pulsed through her when he turned the device on.

Thankfully, she managed not to bite his dick off when she yelped then jumped in his hold.

Ellie reached lower and cupped Lucas's balls in her palm. She rolled them the way that made him groan loudest as she slid her mouth up and down his shaft with rapid, staccato pulses.

When he began to fuck up between her lips, she figured he was close.

The whir of his toothbrush inside her, coupled with his tongue tapping her clit, ensured she was about to explode again. This time ecstasy built within her into something terrifyingly intense.

She allowed herself to relax, knowing Lucas would protect her and catch her if she fell too hard.

Instinctively, her body rocked, forcing herself onto his toy when she went one way and sucking him deeper on the return stroke. The tip of his cock poked the back of her throat and she allowed him to pass. Swallowing around him, she found his limit then smashed through it.

"E!" was all he could manage before his erection began to pulse. His balls drew tight to his body and launched his release down her throat. She didn't waste a single drop, draining him completely, even as she joined him.

Shuddering so hard she thought she might crush his toothbrush, or maybe fly off him with the heights he raised her to, she came so hard that she felt the Sex Offender reaction receding.

Together, they had conquered it.

Ellie collapsed on top of Lucas, knowing he was plenty strong enough to take her weight and then some. Her hands rubbed him everywhere she could reach, his thighs and knees mostly, not shying away from his residual limb. She drifted, completely blissed out, until she felt him withdrawing the toothbrush and squirming from beneath her.

He twisted around so they were eye to eye.

"Hey," he said.

"Hey, yourself." She smiled lazily.

"Doing okay?" He ran his fingertip down the bridge of her nose then over her brows.

She closed her eyes, snuggling deeper into his bed. "Never better."

Surprised, she realized it was true. Being with Lucas made her problems fade away. He was the antidote for all of the shit in her life. And she never wanted to give him up.

His proud smile even pleased her. There was no way he could deny how amazing he was for her. To her. How useful and needed. If she could give him that, it couldn't be wrong, could it?

Lucas fit himself to her, wrapping his arm around her back and snugging her tight to his chest. "What do you say we try to bank some hours of rest to make up for the ones we've lost lately?"

Spending the next fifteen hours or so cuddled together in his bed sounded like a decadence she was willing to indulge in. Especially if he woke her the same way he'd put her to sleep.

"Sounds great." She leaned in and kissed him, savoring the mingled flavors of her arousal and his spicy taste. "Just don't let go, okay?"

"I swear, E. You couldn't pry me off with a crowbar." He ran his hand through her hair, petting her until she grew drowsy and dropped into the easiest sleep she'd had since she escaped.

CHAPTER TEN

An insistent beeping woke Lucas from a dead sleep. He sat bolt upright, reached instinctively to his nightstand and snagged the secure phone from its charger. Disoriented, he couldn't immediately tell what time it was. He hadn't slept that hard in...well, ever.

Though it had been nearly a year since the Batphone—as he liked to think of it—had been active, his body responded on autopilot, as it had hundreds of times during his career.

The cell buzzed agitatedly in his fist. Still, he didn't connect the call immediately. He allowed himself a millisecond to appreciate the fine woman splayed next to him, completely nude, in his bed. She was more beautiful than any of the artwork he'd seen in the great museums around the world, which he'd made a point of visiting when his assignments permitted. Something about paintings drew him. He had no artistic talent himself, but he appreciated the hell out of others'.

Ellie's blonde hair curled softly around her shoulders as she burrowed into his pillows on her stomach, giving him a fabulous view of her high, tight ass. The only thing better would be if she were awake so that he could stare into the endless blue of her eyes, which reminded him of the Caribbean Sea on a hot summer day.

Lost in his mushy thoughts of her, he jolted when the phone rattled his hand again.

He answered before it woke Ellie, who needed her rest. She'd looked so strung out, even before their impossible hike. There was no way she'd been sleeping lately. He could relate.

"Good morning, sunshine." Tyler Lambert's sarcasm greeted him. He was Mason's partner on the force and in their personal life where they shared a lucky woman—Lacey.

"It was until you interrupted my beauty rest," Lucas grumbled.

"Hang on, you were actually still sleeping?"

Ty knew how much trouble Lucas had been having lately in that department. Some nights he'd even volunteered to look after Razor and Izzy's newborn, Ezra. The little guy was getting so big now—heading for a year old—but when he'd been in his up-all-night phase, they'd hung out some. His parents had been grateful for the break. Of course, they'd probably thought Lucas was going home and crashing after they relieved him at the end of his shift, since he had nowhere in particular to be these days.

"It's after eight. I figured you'd have been up half the night already. When you didn't answer our texts, we got nervous."

"Sorry." He couldn't believe he hadn't heard the notifications come through.

"Especially Ryan." Ty lowered his voice. "Is Ellie in bed with you? Can you put her on for a second? Ryan needs to hear her voice. He's going kind of nuts since we won't let him visit in case they're watching him."

"Uh..." Would E want her brother to know they were sleeping together?

Damn, it wasn't like there were many secrets between the close-knit group of friends.

Still, he'd rather it be her choice.

Lucas looked over his shoulder to find her stretching languorously before blinking up at him. When she saw him watching her, she smiled. He covered the mouthpiece of the phone then asked, "You want to talk to Ryan quick?"

"Can I?" She sat up pretty fast, not seeming to mind her breasts being on display for him, despite his seeming inability to look away from the perfect spheres and the faint marks he'd left on her porcelain skin with his scruff the night before.

He'd have to be more careful with her from now on. Or not, since the sight of his possession did some crazy things to his insides. Good things.

Lucas lifted the phone back to his ear. "Put him on, Ty. She's here."

"Way to go, buddy," Tyler cheered.

"Er, thanks."

"What's that all about?" Ryan asked in the background.

Deciding it was time for him to get out of the mix, Lucas tossed the phone to Ellie, who snapped it up then scooted closer to him. She rested her cheek on his shoulder and released a contented sigh when he began to draw idle patterns on her back.

He couldn't get enough of touching her.

Tasting her.

Soon enough, fucking her.

Ellie angled the phone away from her mouth to steal a quick kiss. He couldn't help but deepen it, wishing he had been able to rouse her in an entirely

165

different way. They might have gotten a little carried away.

Next thing Lucas knew, Ryan's voice was shouting through the speaker, "Ellie? Ellie, are you there? Are you okay? Sis!"

Snapping back to what she'd been doing, she grinned then turned her attention to her brother, damn the man. "Hey, Ry. I'm here. Just half-awake." As if on cue, she yawned.

Her brother's response was muted this time.

"Yeah, I slept through the whole night. Well, actually part of yesterday too." She sounded proud of herself.

Lucas allowed himself to share in that. He knew he'd pleased her beyond her wildest dreams. Her surprise when he'd finally sated her had bruised his heart.

All this time, he could have been granting her relief. If he hadn't been so scared of rejection or caught up in his own image issues, they'd have been a couple a long time ago. What a waste.

He didn't plan to make that mistake again.

If she was willing, he was going to have her. As much of her as she could give.

The siblings chatted for a while, mostly Ellie reassuring her brother that she was okay and that Lucas was taking good care of her.

"I love you too, Ryan. You want to talk to him?" she asked.

Lucas waved his hands in front of his chest. A lecture from her brother wasn't really in his lineup for the day. Shit, she was extending the phone to him anyway.

"Hey, Ryan." He was a grown man. A soldier. He could deal with a single cross-examination from his girlfriend's brother. If that's even what Ellie was. Probably—he should check that out with her. Though he hoped it was true, from the way she was staring at him with a soft, silly smile curving her naturally rouged lips.

"Lucas." The other guy didn't sound quite as jovial as usual, or as...meek. "Watch out for her, will you?"

"Of course." That was easy enough.

"And don't mess around with her feelings. Those bastards fucked with her body. They took everything she had in that respect, but if you break her heart—secret agent or not—I will figure out how to hurt you."

Had to respect a man who looked out for his family. Lucas wouldn't have done any less.

"Understood."

He tried to give Ellie as little as possible to go on from his side of the conversation, but her narrowed eyes said she knew the score. Not only that, she seemed pissed that her brother would interfere. Probably because she felt she could take care of herself.

Lucas knew she could.

But it never hurt to have allies. Hopefully, her brother would be one of his.

"Okay, good." Ryan seemed surprised that he'd gotten Lucas's agreement. Naturally submissive, Ryan didn't often take such a direct stance. "Well, then...you want to talk to some of the guys? They've got some stuff to run by you. I'm heading into the other room with the rest of the bystanders to let them do their official police stuff or my head will explode."

"Yeah, sure. Put them on." Lucas smiled at Ellie and she returned his grin with enough wattage to make the sun envious.

167

"Can you do speakerphone with that thing?" she wondered. "I'd like to hear what's going on too. Save you from repeating it later."

He nodded then hit the button, laying the phone on the rumpled covers in front of them.

Maybe when they'd finished this briefing, because that's certainly what it was, they could renegotiate the boundaries of their sexual arrangement. After yesterday, he thought she might have changed her mind about what she wanted to experience.

God knew he would bury himself inside her immediately if she was ready.

"Huh?" He started when Ellie nudged his knee with hers.

Her hands wandered to his leg and started the massaging she was so damn good at. He never should have told her that he was supposed to do it periodically throughout the day. Though it seemed less weird every time she did it.

Which was probably her intent. Damn her for being so smart. So perfect for him.

"Sorry, I'm here."

Lucas scrubbed his hand over his face. He had to get in the game. Where Ellie's safety was concerned, he couldn't fuck around. As tempting as it was to think of the past two days as a vacation from reality, the truth was that she was on the run.

He'd better get his shit together fast. Because if something happened to her on his watch, he'd never be able to forgive himself.

"Okay, so. Here's what we were able to dig up." Mason kicked off the meeting, putting his side on speaker too. "JRad found some online chatter that makes it sound like there could be a heist going down. But the scale seemed off."

"You mean because I won fifty thousand but they gave me two hundred, right?" she clarified.

"Oh, hey, Ellie," Mason said. "No, the other way around."

"Fuck," Lucas groaned.

Ellie bit her lip and glanced up at him. Though she didn't ask for details, he explained anyway, "E, he means that the job is a lot bigger than what you scored."

"Yep," Razor chimed in from the Men in Blue's side of things. They were probably gathered at one of the guys' houses. Their ladies too. "The cash you smuggled out for them—"

"Don't say it like I did it on purpose." She frowned. "I would never do something like that. Just because you're a cop doesn't mean you can talk to me like that."

"Ow!" Razor must have gotten slapped upside the head by one of the older guys. A common occurrence for the recent rookie. "Sorry, Ellie. I was just joking."

"Not funny," Lucas growled. Mason backed him up from the other end of the line.

"Anyway." Matt—one of Jambrea's men—got them refocused. "The cash you have seems like it was a test. For a bigger operation. Kind of like they were trying to show that whoever is looking to join in with the head honchos running the heist has the skills to get the job done."

"This is bad." Lucas pinched the bridge of his nose.

"Why?" Ellie tipped her head.

"Because they're not going to let it go," Mason answered. "They can't afford to. It's not only about the cash. It's their reputation, which surprisingly means a lot to a criminal."

169

"Are you fucking kidding me?" Ellie threw up her hands.

Lucas thought she looked adorable, and it kind of turned him on when she cursed. The combination of her classy looks and trashy mouth did it for him. Besides, the motion did awesome things to her boobs.

But he was more concerned than ever now. "Do you know who they were targeting with their show?"

There were only a few organizations in this region that could pull off something like that. Unfortunately, they were also the best at evading the cops. They had plenty of experience. It was possible Lucas could use some of his government resources for additional support if it was someone who operated across state lines.

"Not exactly." Clint—Jambrea's other guy—spoke slowly enough to make Lucas wary.

"What's that mean?"

"We don't know who it is," JRad admitted. "We believe the local goons who tried to step up had instructions for a drop. If they made it there, they would have been considered for the real job."

Lucas felt something icy and sick go through his guts. "No. *Fuck* no!"

"It might be the only way to shut it down," Tyler said.

"You're talking in code again." Ellie chewed on one of her nails, which didn't have much to lose before she'd start bleeding.

"I'm pretty sure these assholes were going to be crazy enough to suggest that you and I take this pile of money to some badass motherfuckers and do some snooping around for them." Lucas clung to Ellie as if he could protect her from the entire world with his arms alone.

"It's one plan," Razor confirmed.

"A shitty one." Lucas wouldn't do it. No way would he put Ellie in danger. "Think of something else."

"Wait," Ellie interjected.

"E, no." Lucas tried to shush her with his fingers over her plump lips, but she nipped his hand. "Ow!"

Someone on the other end of the line chuckled.

"What good would it do for Lucas and me to hand over this money?" she asked.

Lucas closed his eyes, already knowing where they were headed.

"If we can set them up and bust the main heist, we could take down a lot of high-level guys operating in this part of the country," JRad explained. "It would be a huge win."

"How can we *not* do it if we have the opportunity to make a difference in the world?" Ellie spoke exclusively to Lucas. She stared into his eyes. "You built your whole career doing exactly this. Why would you ask me to be any less honorable than you have been?"

"It was my job. You didn't sign on for this." He took her hand in his and squeezed gently. "You're also not trained. Shit happens."

He lifted his leg as if it weren't obvious, laying directly between them. "Even for trained professionals, stuff can go bad quick. I'd never let you do this."

And that was the worst possible thing he could have said. Even Razor made an audible grunt from the other side of the line before mumbling something that sounded like "you blew it, dude".

"What *I* do with *my* life is not your decision to make, Lucas." Ellie dared him to tell her otherwise.

Even he wasn't that stupid. He could try it, and they'd be over before they'd really even got started.

"Look, I spent too long at the hands of evil people to turn a blind eye when I could do something to stop these guys. This isn't the only horrible thing they're going to do in their lives. I could be keeping someone else down the road from going through something like I did."

He wished she were wrong, but she wasn't.

"If I can help, I want to do it," she told him, and the Men in Blue heard.

"Thank you, Ellie," Mason said.

"So where's the handoff?" Lucas asked. If he was prepared enough, he could skew the odds far in their favor. He had equipment. He had friends. He had knowledge and experience. He hated that there was any risk at all, but he could minimize it.

"Well, that's the part we need some help with." JRad picked up the thread of conversation.

It reminded Lucas of his old team, the way they thought so much the same, like they were using a single hive mind. He figured most guys who spent so much time together, a lot of it with their lives entrusted to their partners, ended up the same way.

It made him miss his team. He'd distanced himself from them when he couldn't bear to see the pity and anguish in their stares anymore. But maybe it was time he started reconnecting, showing them that there was more to life than their war games.

Attuned to him already, Ellie noticed the change in his bearing and snuggled closer.

He hugged her tight. Maybe she could be his new partner in life.

"It seems like there's someone working this from inside the casino," Tyler said. "It's the only thing that makes sense. No one miscounts that kind of dough. So we think it was a test. They were only going to get the coordinates if they were able to snag the money."

"It's in the bag." Lucas groaned, then stared across the room to where it lay on top of his dresser.

If Ellie weren't next to him, he'd hustle over there to snag it in some combination of his hop-crawl-scramble method of getting around. He wasn't quite ready to put on that show for her, though, and his leg would take a minute to don.

"Dig around, we'll wait," Mason instructed.

Without him asking, Ellie crawled off the bed—flashing her perfect ass at him in the process—then retrieved the sack.

"It's not obvious, whatever it is." He talked mostly to himself. "I sorted through here twice. There were no neon signs or a note that said 'meet us here at high noon', or even a business card or anything like that."

Ellie reached into the bag then paused. "Can I touch it?"

"Go ahead." He nodded but didn't add what he was thinking. *They already know who you are, E.* Because that thought alone was enough to send shivers down his spine.

Lucas had the skills to take her and run. They could live a comfortable life somewhere overseas and never be found. A tiny, remote island all to themselves sounded ideal. But he knew without asking that she would never leave Ryan or the support network of friends that had become her second family.

Shit.

While he was daydreaming about running away for the first time in his life, Ellie was flipping through the cash. She picked it up, shook it, smelled it. Stared at it in awe. It was a life-changing amount of money

173

for someone with no job and a lot of medical bills piling up.

Lucas made a mental note to see about getting her a reward for helping the authorities.

She deserved it.

Hell, she deserved everything good in life.

"Is it normal for some of these to be highlighted?" she asked after a while.

"No," every one of the Men in Blue plus Lucas said in unison.

"Wow, did you guys practice that?" She smiled, completely at odds with how Lucas felt. He'd hoped maybe they wouldn't make the connection and she'd be out of the mess by default.

"Tell me what you see," JRad ordered, his Dom side peeking out.

Ellie shivered then responded quickly, making Lucas's eyes narrow. Was she in to that? Or was it a learned response from Morselli's dungeon?

Efficiently, Ellie reported back, "It's in the serial numbers. Different characters all over. Numbers too."

Lucas sat by, letting her take charge as she read them off to JRad, who plugged them into one of his crazy software programs.

Within minutes, he had a short list of possible addresses.

While Ellie and Lucas listened, the Men in Blue eliminated them one by one from the records.

Until they hit on a name that had the hairs on Lucas's arm standing up.

"Lucky's Bar at 777 Clover Boulevard." Razor snorted. "It's *got* to be that one. There's a special event listed on their website at seven o'clock tonight, with no information other than the time."

"I wouldn't say this was very fortunate for us at all." Lucas shook his head. "Does Ryan know you're sending her in there?"

"*Hell* fucking no," Razor nearly shouted, as if Lucas were crazy.

"Don't tell him, either," Ellie insisted. "He'll only worry and there's nothing he can do. I'm going."

Lucas crumpled the sack in his hand, staring at her and measuring her resolve.

"Don't look at me like that either." She shoved him hard, but he didn't budge from her side. "I'm not going to change my mind."

"She'll be okay with you to protect her. These guys are crooks, not murderers, mostly. They'll need her for the job, Lucas. Getting rid of her doesn't make any sense." Mason's logic might have been soothing if they were dealing with something slightly less important to him than his woman's safety.

Wow.

Where had *that* thought come from?

He wasn't sure, but he didn't deny to himself that it felt right.

Whether she knew it or not, she was destined to be his. And he was hers.

"I don't know."

Lucas doubted himself. It was a foreign experience. One he hated. But the stakes had never been so high before. His own life meant nothing compared to hers. If something happened to her, he was as good as dead himself because he'd never recover from the guilt.

"Maybe one of you should cover her. I'm still getting used to things. What if she needs me and I trip or something? I'm not sure—"

"We can't risk them recognizing us," JRad said gently. He knew the toll it could take when your partner was at risk. Lily had been in Morselli's dungeon too. She'd nearly lost her life there. "If I had to pick any man not on the force to watch over Lily, it would be you. And I have to say that first part because they have guns, and they're right here."

Matt, Clint, Razor, Mason and Tyler laughed.

"Not you of a year ago either," JRad kept going. "You right now. You're ready for this. You've been working hard, getting yourself back up to speed. Hell, you hiked almost four miles through rough terrain wearing completely the wrong prosthetic foot for the job and managed to tough it out. You're the best man for this job."

"You're the *only* man I'd trust." Ellie leaned up to kiss him on the cheek.

It might have been a maneuver intended to soften him to her. If so, it only worked on certain parts of him, like his heart. Below the belt, not so much.

"You kept me safe the other day. We make a good team," she continued when he didn't immediately agree. "Otherwise, it'll be me alone. And that's way worse."

It was. And he knew she'd do it too.

"Fine. Fuck," he snarled. "We'll be there. Tonight. At seven. We'll tell them we're on to their game and that we want in. Ellie's proven she can be the mule. I'll tell them we want a cut for not turning them in."

"Act less threatening than you really are." Razor tried to be helpful. "You're kind of scary when you're in agent mode."

"The kid's right." Mason backed Razor up. "Grab equipment from your stash. Maybe set something up with JRad later so we can listen in or watch. That would be even better. We'll be ready with backup in case something happens. But when you're on-site, face-to-face, make sure you tone it down. Remember to act casual. These losers aren't in the same league as the baddies you're used to. You're just a street-smart, greedy punk. Not a hero."

Lucas figured there was a specific reason Mason had chosen that word. It implied sacrifice. They didn't want him doing anything stupid.

Well, too fucking bad. This whole plan was the dumbest thing he'd done in his life.

And if went sour, everyone would pay.

Missing a leg or not, he would hunt down every last person who dared to harm a hair on Ellie's head if she wasn't at home, waiting for him, to stop him from going vigilante.

"Got it," he told the Men in Blue.

"Good. So maybe you want to get back to resting up for tonight, then? We won't keep you." Mason's smarmy tone made it clear he knew what they'd been up to in order to induce such fantastic sleep. He must have been moving as he talked since his speech was uneven. "Say hello to Lucas and Ellie, everyone!"

Just before the connection was severed, a chorus of "hello", "miss you", "stay safe" and "love you" poured through the speaker.

When it was just the two of them again, Lucas realized there was a sheen of tears in Ellie's eyes.

"Are you scared? We can call them back. Tell them we're out."

"No. I'm grateful and so lucky to have people like them in my life." She crawled into his lap and wrapped her arms and legs around him. "People like you. I would never disappoint them by doing less than the right thing."

How could he not find that type of spirit attractive?

Hint: He couldn't.

Lucas buried his fingers in Ellie's hair and drew her to him for a kiss that wiped his mind of everything but her and how incredible she made him feel, simply by being near her.

If doubt still niggled the back of his brain, somewhere deep in the instinctual zone he'd perfected during his career, he silenced it. There would be plenty of time for running the odds later.

Please let them come through this unscathed.

CHAPTER ELEVEN

It gave Lucas hives when things went too easy. This was definitely one of those times.

Even after making a stop at the mall so Ellie could pick up some appropriate clothes to replace the too-baggy T-shirt and shorts he'd loaned her, he hadn't been able to delay them significantly.

At precisely seven o'clock that evening, he strolled through the front door of Lucky's Bar with Ellie on his arm. She hadn't taken any of the opportunities he'd given her to turn around. In fact, she'd implied that if he didn't stop asking her, she'd torture him by playing with herself and not allowing him to touch her when they got home.

He didn't intend to piss her off that much since he had big plans for tonight.

That was, if they didn't get wiped out by the fuckwads they were meeting.

Before Lucas had even made it all the way into the dimly lit, smoky interior of Lucky's, he knew who they were aiming for. The thugs were too inconspicuous to be natural. It was like a debadged tan sedan with mud slung just over the license plates. Trying too hard to blend.

Lucas steered Ellie by her elbow toward the pair of men. The taller of the two wore a too-new baseball cap and the other had on a pair of ridiculously dark sunglasses.

Lucas did his absolute best to mask his limp. Fuck, they were sitting on either side of the booth, so he and E would have to split up to join them.

He hated this more and more by the second.

"Last chance," he murmured to her.

"Keep going," she responded with a low rumble completely incongruent with the lovely smile on her face.

"Gentlemen," he said as he approached the table. The two guys who'd noticed them the instant they entered acted pleasantly surprised, as if they had run into old friends out for drinks.

"Have a seat, please." The Yankees fan motioned. Lucas gave Ellie's hand one final squeeze then ushered her into the seat with the obvious second-in-command.

"I think we have something of yours," Lucas said as if he were talking about a Tupperware container the guy had left at his house during their last potluck, or something as trivial as that. He plopped the sack on the table. Of course, the real bills had been replaced by high-quality counterfeits he'd cooked up while stashing the originals in the boathouse. He'd included a tracker for fun too.

The fake bills and transponder were all top-of-the-line, international-quality spy shit. Nothing these guys would be able to detect either. JRad had nearly come in his pants when he'd seen the gizmo up close. This way, they'd have an idea of where these losers were hanging out, so the Men in Blue could bring down the entire network of conmen and robbers.

"I'm surprised to see you found it." Sunglasses shook his head. "I would have thought it would be with someone else. Those three guys we know."

Lucas thought about the two corpses the Men in Blue had cleaned out of Ellie's house. He bet the third sucker wasn't doing much better right about now.

"Funny thing about that." Ellie dazzled them with her smile. She stuck to the script they'd rehearsed as best as possible, given that they hadn't known exactly what to expect. "Sometimes you discover what you're looking for in unusual places. Or maybe you figure out that what you were hunting for isn't what you need at all."

The taller guy nodded at her. "I do think that's true."

He steepled his fingers as he took a long, hard look at Ellie, then Lucas.

Neither one of them flinched. They must have passed his unspoken test.

"Would you like to go to the casino with us this weekend?" Yankees fan asked Ellie. "I've heard you're quite the lucky charm."

She laughed. Lucas hoped he was the only person who could sense the slight tinge of bitterness to the peal. She'd been dealt some rotten hands by fate lately. But he hoped to turn that around for them.

If she'd let him.

Lucas jumped into the conversation to seal the deal. The sooner they finished with these goons and got the hell away from here, the better he'd feel. "It's true. She won a jackpot last weekend. If we go with you, though, I'm sure they're going to pay lots of attention to her. High roller and all, you know. The house will want to win back their money. I'm sure that would be no fun for you. It'd almost be like you were invisible, you know?"

The man nodded solemnly. It was a solid plan. They'd be perfect for the job. Unsuspecting, the casino would be blind to the real drama happening in the cashier's cage. If Lucas were planning this heist for real, he would use a decoy exactly like Ellie.

She would steal everyone's attention.

Be the diversion they needed.

"Let's make a night of it," Sunglasses said. "We'll be in contact soon to arrange the details. Sound good?"

"Sure," Lucas answered for them both. "But if her good luck rubs off on you, I expect you to split the winnings with us fifty-fifty. It's only fair, after all."

Yankees nodded, though the glint in his eye told Lucas the man never intended to pay what he owed. He'd kill them before they could collect. Or he *would* if the Men in Blue weren't on to them, waiting to spring their trap. As soon as they had evidence in hand.

"That's a deal." The man grinned as their food was brought to the table.

"Well, we won't keep you from your dinners." Lucas stood then extended his hand to Ellie. She took it, her fingers like ice in his grip. "See you this weekend."

"It will be our pleasure." Sunglasses guy leered at Ellie when he said that, making Lucas long to rebreak his crooked nose with a punch or two to his smarmy face. Maybe once they had the cuffs on the douche bag, he could sneak in a jab or two.

Lucas let his hand trail behind him. Ellie's body blocked part of his, giving the thieves something to concentrate on beside his slightly uneven gait. He hated using her fine ass like that, but it had to be done.

Once they were outside, she started shivering despite the balmy air of late spring. He wished he had a jacket to drape around her. For warmth and just to keep whatever filthy eyes were on them from seeing too much of her.

When they got to his car, he checked around discreetly for any signs of tampering. When he found the strand of hair he'd placed over the passenger door broken, he stopped Ellie from getting in. Peeking in the window, he noticed a manila envelope on the seat.

That could not be good.

Lucas took a piece of gum from his pocket, unwrapped it and handed her the paper covering. "Would you mind throwing this in the trash can over there?"

He pointed to a receptacle in the park, nearly half a block away.

If his car blew when he opened the door, he wanted her out of the blast zone. He didn't think that was the intent of this package, but he didn't want to take any risks with her. She was too precious. To him, and to the world.

This hadn't been in their plan, so she hesitated.

"Go, E."

She bit her lip then nodded, spinning on her sexy, low heels and hustling to the spot he'd indicated.

When she was safe, he opened the door. Nothing.

Then he retrieved the envelope and withdrew the thick paper from within.

Photographs.

He recognized the very, *very* dead man in them as the one who'd been left behind at Ellie's house, searching for the money. Their message couldn't have been clearer. Fuck this up, and they'd end up with fresh holes in their heads too.

Unfortunately, Lucas figured that was the plan, no matter what. The Men in Blue better know what they were doing. He held the car door open for Ellie, signaling her to return.

Neither one of them spoke the entire way home, just like they'd practiced.

***

When they got to his house, he pulled his car into a shed that encompassed a secure zone, scrambling any transmissions. He checked it for bugs then scoured every nook and cranny for something out of place.

Only when he was sure that it was clean did he give Ellie the all clear. "We're good now. You did amazing, E."

"Oh, thank God that's over." She sagged against him as they crossed the driveway toward his house.

Lucas didn't remind her that their involvement was only beginning. Instead, he picked her up, causing her blue-and-violet watercolor-silk sundress to flutter around her ankles.

She giggled then smiled up at him as he carried her toward his house. The feel of her slight form, deceptively strong, in his arms thrilled him so much that he refused to put her down, even if he took his time as he went cautiously up each riser.

Lucas lifted his meat foot first, then the prosthetic one, putting both feet on each tread instead of walking left over right as he would have before his amputation. Extra insurance against tripping, and dropping Ellie. That probably wouldn't put her in the right mood for what he had planned.

Sure, this had been an easy assignment, one that would have been beneath him not long ago. After being sidelined for almost a year, though, he couldn't believe they'd done it. He hadn't lost his touch, and now he was going to celebrate the victory, even if it was only a temporary win.

Worrying about the next stage of the sting could wait until later.

Much later.

Successful missions always made him horny. Today's was no exception. His cock was rock-hard in his pants.

Lucas kicked open his front door then swung Ellie inside as if they were two normal young lovers who'd spent the day outside, enjoying the beautiful weather and each other. When he carried her inside, he paused only to steal a kiss that turned into a series of them instead of one isolated taste of Ellie's lips.

He'd never have enough of her.

Their postadventure adrenaline must have been coursing through her as well. She moaned into his mouth at the slightest contact with his lips. Her fingers clenched on his neck and shoulders, silently asking for him to deepen the exchange.

Before they went too far and he tripped her Sex Offender reaction, he confessed, "E, I want to have sex with you."

"Like…" She mimicked his seventh-grader sign language for fucking from the day before.

He couldn't help but laugh. She made him happier than he could remember, just by being. It was easy to hang around her and, he had to admit, they did make a good team.

"Yeah"—he kissed her again, hungrily—"like that."

185

"What're you waiting for, then?" She grinned up at him when he broke away to draw in a shaky breath. How could she do this to him so quickly, so powerfully?

He had no idea, but he liked it.

"You're sure?" He'd swallowed hard when he asked, though he would wait forever if that was what she needed. It wasn't like he hadn't enjoyed their carnal explorations so far. Just being next to her, skin on skin, did something to him that he knew he'd never be able to undo.

Didn't want to either.

Lucas carried her only as far as the living room. He wasn't going to make it upstairs before he had to have her. She seemed completely in favor. The wide, black-leather couch was plenty comfortable and roomy enough for what he intended.

When he sank on top of Ellie, careful not to crowd her, she put her thumb over the camera hiding in the button of his shirt. "You might want to shut that off before we go any further."

He chuckled at the show they'd been putting on for the Men in Blue. How could he have forgotten? Because she made him lose his mind every time.

Somehow he knew, no matter how often they were together like this, that would hold true.

Lucas plucked the camera off his shirt, turned it around so that his face was captured in the live-streaming footage then said, "Goodbye, JRad. We'll call you in a while. Do me a favor and erase that last bit so Ryan doesn't see it."

"Okay, spy time is done. Gotta go." Ellie nudged him with her knee so he took his cue and shut the gadget off, tossing it onto the coffee table.

"Now, where were we?" He grinned down at her.

"I was about to tell you that I get hormone treatments to keep the SO mutation in check. As long as I'm on them, I can't get pregnant." She smiled sadly up at him. "I'm not sure how I feel about that most days, but right now it's seeming like a benefit. Unless, you know, you'd rather use condoms with me because of how many guys—"

"Fuck that," he snarled. "Don't act like what *they* did makes *you* dirty."

"I've been tested. I got lucky. I didn't catch anything they weren't able to treat." She looked away then.

Lucas's heart hurt for her. He leaned forward and kissed her softly. "I'm going to fuck you. Bare. I don't want anything between us ever again. Okay?"

Moisture gathered at the corners of her eyes and she nodded, though still without meeting his stare.

So he kissed her tears away.

"You have no idea how humbled I am to have you. That you let me be with you like this. I'll cherish you, Ellie. Never doubt that. And"—he hesitated, wondering if he should bring it up; his gut told him to share with her parts of himself that he hadn't told anyone about in nearly twenty years—"if you ever want to be a mom, there are lots of kids out there who need loving parents, waiting to be adopted."

"Why does it sound like you know that from experience?" She perked up.

Figured she would get what he was saying without really being told. "Because I was a ward of the state. An orphan. Grew up in the system. Never staying any one place very long."

She reached up and laid her hands on either side of his face, but didn't bother telling him she was sorry.

Both of them knew words like that didn't help the bone-deep kind of sorrow.

"It's one of the reasons why I was chosen for my agency," he told her. "They don't accept guys with family, girlfriends or wives, kids. Nothing that can be used against them, you know? I had nothing, so it was easy for them to mold me into whatever they needed."

"Well, now you've got me." She leaned up until she could seal their mouths together, kissing him with every ounce of tenderness she could muster. And that was a lot.

"Do I?" he asked, afraid to hope. What would happen after this weekend when their lives went back to whatever passed as normal these days.

"Uh, yeah. We *are* about to..." She busted out the fucking sign language again.

It was the perfect thing at the perfect time.

Lucas's laughter chased their troubles away. If she could be strong enough to move forward, so could he. After just one more confession. "So, um, for the record. I haven't"—he flashed their running joke at her—"since before I met you."

"You mean since your injury." Her eyes grew wide as she considered that.

"Obviously, yeah, part of the reason for my dry streak was my leg. But...I had some offers, you know, from the fetishists and regular women too," he admitted. "I just didn't feel like taking anyone up on it. I didn't think it would be fair when every time I got turned on, all I could think of was you."

"Aw, that's the sweetest thing anyone's ever said to me." Ellie beamed.

They laughed more together.

Then chuckles turned into kissing. A ton more kissing. So much more that he sort of lost track of time and where they were. When he realized he was pinning her to the couch, he lifted up.

Ellie groaned and yanked him back on top of her with her hands on his back. "I'm fine, Lucas. Don't assume I'm weak just because of what happened to me. I don't operate that way around you."

"There's a difference between thinking less of you and making accommodations," he tried to explain between another round of furious making out. It seemed like, if his mouth were apart from hers for more than the time it took for him to suck in a breath, he might die.

"Well, I don't want you to treat me differently than you would any other woman." She surprised him by reaching around and slapping his ass. Hard.

The sting spurred him on, as she'd probably intended. "That's too damn bad, E. Because you're not like any other woman to me. No one has ever made me want them as badly as you do. And I don't only mean in bed."

There, he'd said it.

She blinked up at him a few times.

Then a wide, sly smile lit up her face. "Keep talking like that and I might even let you"—more signing—"in the back door."

Lucas laughed so hard he thought he might cry. He had no idea how she could do that to him. Yet he was not only amused, but also so horny he thought he might come in his pants if he didn't get down to business soon.

"E, when I get around to fucking you in the ass, you're going to be the one begging for it." He nipped her lower lip. "Right now, I'm craving your pussy. I can't wait to be buried inside you. Fully connected."

"Oh. Yeah. Do that." She took on that dreamy, dazed look that made him sure she'd passed the point of no return. He had to take care of her now or she'd suffer from his teasing.

And that was definitely not in his plans.

He considered simply shoving her dress up, unsnapping his jeans and digging in. But he wanted it to be something better than that for her. Something she would remember.

Lucas wanted to make a good first impression since he hoped she'd want to do it again. Hopefully often. He didn't hesitate to admit in his own mind that he also wanted their encounter to be different in every way possible from how crudely she'd been treated by men in the past.

So he took more time than he would have liked in sliding her dress from beneath her ass then helping her sit forward so that he could draw it over her head. It fluttered to the floor, landing in a pool of silk.

When he took in the sapphire-blue, matching panty-and-bra set, he suddenly wished they'd had more time for her to roam the lingerie stores at the mall. "Fucking sexy."

She smiled crookedly up at him. "You like?"

"Definitely." He admired the way the color enhanced her eyes. "But I'll like it even more when you're naked."

Lucas wished he'd taken time to light candles and pick some wild flowers from the field out back. *Next time,* he silently promised her.

He carefully unclasped her bra then peeled it from her like fancy wrapping paper on a precious present. The same for her panties when he eased them down her legs. She bent her knees up so he could tug the underwear from her dainty ankles and over her feet.

When he saw how torn up her soles still were from their hike, he winced. She hadn't complained once while they were out.

"Don't worry about that now. Only pleasure, Lucas. That's all I care about." She reached up and began unbuttoning his shirt while he took care of his jeans.

Except he couldn't pry them off his prosthesis. *Shit.*

"Just take your leg off—it's fine," Ellie reassured him.

Except it wasn't.

It might have been stupid, but it made him feel more complete. And, especially his first time with her, he wanted to be everything he was capable of. "Hang on."

He left her side for a minute to doff his leg and slip his pants over the top of the prosthesis, but then, as soon as they were off, he put his leg back in the socket and ratcheted the proximal lock tight once more.

Ellie lost a little of the glow she'd had a moment before, but she didn't argue with him about it.

Instead, she opened her arms, welcoming him— no matter how many feet he had.

He went to her, loving the shock of feeling her breasts and belly pressed to his torso again. It would never get old—the moment they connected flush each time they shared themselves like this.

Lucas stared into her gorgeous blue eyes and took in the rouge of her cheeks and red lips. Even without makeup, and dotted with bruises and cuts on her chest from their romp in the woods, she was easily the most beautiful woman he'd ever seen.

And she was looking at him like she was going to either tear into him or beg him to fuck her in the next few moments. She was his dream woman, for sure. Passionate and tough. Fierce yet vulnerable. She did things to his heart that felt especially dangerous for a man used to being a loner.

"You need this, don't you?" he growled against her neck as he bit her gently.

"Yes." She moaned and flexed so that she fused their bodies tighter together.

"But you *want* it too, right? Me?"

"Stop talking so much and put your mouth to better use." Ellie drew him down with a steady pressure on the back of his head. But when he neared, she didn't kiss him or force him toward her breasts, as he expected. Instead, she whispered in his ear, "I've been dreaming about this moment for close to a year. Don't make me wait any more, Lucas. Please."

Nothing could have made his dick harder than that sweet admission.

Lucas smiled down at her then brushed his mouth over hers as his hand snuck between them. He'd planned to see how wet she was and prepare her for penetration.

When he touched her pussy, she gasped and moaned. She was soaked. Completely ready for him all on her own.

Her follow-up groan held a hint of pain, the last thing he wanted for her while they were making love. "Please hurry. I don't need anything else but you buried inside me."

There would be plenty of time later to prove that he was capable of finesse.

So he did as she asked and took his cock in hand. Aiming the blunt head toward her opening, he settled into the space Ellie enlarged when she hooked one leg over the back of his couch and spread her thighs, putting the other foot directly on the floor.

Her flexibility impressed him.

Ellie shrugged one shoulder at his raised brow. "I've been doing yoga a lot to relax. I guess I've become more flexible than I realized."

"Another point in your favor." He grinned then stared directly into her eyes as he fit the tip of his erection to her slippery pussy. The opening to her body kissed his head, as her channel already clenched restlessly.

Even the barest of contact like that bowled him over. If it weren't for her steadying hands at his shoulders, he might have gotten disoriented. She tilted his whole world on its axis. And he hadn't even joined them yet.

Any movement on either one of their parts would fit them together. Lucas took Ellie's hands and interlocked their fingers, bringing their entwined hands to rest on either side of her head. "If it's too much..."

"Lucas," she growled.

"Okay, okay." He pressed forward, praying for her body to yield easily to his. He didn't want to hurt her or have to use any appreciable amount of force. But, damn, she was tight. And so hot. She was practically scalding his erection with the heat they generated together.

"Relax, E." He dropped lower, watching her carefully for any signs of panic.

There were none.

"Trying." She cried out when he clenched his ass and pressed harder against the muscles prohibiting him from bonding with her. "Need you so much."

Her desperation finally got through to him.

Taking it slow was only torturing her. Well, both of them, but her especially.

So he distracted her with a kiss that he hoped conveyed his caring while he lunged, driving himself a couple of inches within her grasp. They both shouted as their bodies adjusted to each other, stretching and swelling as necessary to ensure a perfect fit.

He swore his dick had never been this hard in his entire life.

Even barely within her, he had to clench his jaw to keep from getting carried away. If he wasn't careful, he could easily find his pleasure within her body in seconds. She suited him that well.

Ellie whimpered then writhed beneath him, encouraging him to move.

So he gave her what she was asking for by withdrawing a tiny bit before drilling deeper, inserting another inch or two into her hungry pussy. He kept on this way until he'd introduced his entire shaft to her body.

When the pad of muscle above his cock tapped her clit, she shuddered.

The resulting shock wave ran through them both, making them groan in unison.

Ellie opened her eyes, which had been scrunched closed. The pure adoration in her gaze was enough to puff out his chest.

He began to move within her. Slowly, lazily, making sure they both could enjoy every instant of this ride.

The rings of muscle inside her undulated around him, threatening to milk the come from his balls before he was even remotely ready. He had never felt a woman who gloved him this well. The ridge of his cockhead locked against the muscles at her entrance every time he pulled out, thrilling them both.

And when he plunged to the hilt within her, he felt like he was bottoming out, counting on her elasticity a bit to make room for his full length and girth.

Ellie seemed as blown away as he was. She stopped speaking coherently, surrendering instead to a form of communication that was more about instinct—the rhythm they moved to and the intensity of their gazes—than verbal exchanges.

Everything they did was slow and thorough. From their continual kissing to his grinding inside her, to the full-body caresses that resulted from the intimate positioning of their bodies.

Though it might satisfy his animal urges to piston wildly within her, he wanted to show her that they didn't need that kind of aggression to make each other feel good. Beyond *good*. Spectacular.

Best sex of his life.

The only thing they needed was to nurture this connection they shared and the rest would follow behind. Though more than that might be fun some other time, tonight all he wanted was the purity of their basic bond to shine through, expressed by the natural interactions of their bodies.

He couldn't say how long they stayed like that, the press and release of their muscles causing his cock to shuttle back and forth within her sheath. But there came a point when her breathing became ragged, and her eyes grew ferocious. It tweaked every instinct in him to see her claiming him every bit as much as he was taking possession of her.

In fact, it tipped him too close to the edge of orgasm. He wasn't going to be able to recover.

Ellie didn't seem to mind.

She tightened around him, as if reflecting his own passion back at him. They fed off each other's energy, each ramping up in sync with the other. Lucas was about to warn her that he couldn't hold back when she froze, then went wild beneath him.

Her pussy clamped on him so tight he wondered if she would leave a permanent dent.

It would be worth it.

Then she screamed his name, staring directly into his eyes, and let her climax pull him under with her. He shoved his cock through her tight channel and locked them as tightly together as possible before he allowed himself to join her in release.

The rippling of her pussy milked him, drawing semen from his balls in pulse after pulse that felt more satisfying than anything he'd ever felt before. Their releases seemed as complementary as everything else they shared, hers amplifying his and his seeming to prolong hers until he swore he had poured half of himself into her.

When he glanced down at where they were joined, he saw some of his come leaking from her body, which was filled to capacity.

Lucas noticed that as soon as he had flooded her pussy, she began to quiet. Her eyes regained their summer-sky-blue shading and her entire body seemed to relax beneath him. If he thought he'd counteracted her arousal reaction the day before, it had been more like exhaustion compared to this...true relief.

"You okay, E?" he checked in, the change in her drastic enough to concern him some.

"Mmm" was her only answer.

"Was that enough? I can do other things..."

"No, it was perfect. *Is* perfect." She rubbed his back, helping to bring him down gradually from the epic high that they had shared. "All I want is to lie here next to you and float after that."

"Me too."

He kissed her nose then arranged them in a more comfortable position. Neither of them moved to dislodge him from her body, so he stayed embedded in her pussy as they drifted off, completely satisfied.

Together, safe and happy, he couldn't have asked for more.

It seemed a single perfect orgasm could be enough to sate her after all. Who would have guessed?

Even more curiously, he could say the same. With other women, an entire night of rowdy sex had never made him feel as content as holding Ellie now did. Only when her body relinquished its grasp on his softening flesh and he slipped free of her did he reach down and disengage his proximal lock, sliding off his leg, socks and liner, before using his other foot to shove them to the end of the couch.

Relieved and exhausted, he sighed.

"Goodnight, E," he murmured.

The only response he got was a soft, adorable snore.

197

CHAPTER TWELVE

Ellie felt like she was suffocating. The man on top of her in the pile of bodies wouldn't budge. She was going to die here. Smothered by lust monsters hardly better than those cooked up by Dr. Frankenstein or zombies who wanted pussy instead of brains.

She fought as hard as she could, but it was no use.

Breaking free was impossible.

"E!" someone shouted. It should have been Lily, who'd ducked under the closing gate a brave soldier—Lucas—had used his own body to stop so she could crawl beneath it to search for Ellie.

Instead...

"Lucas?" she asked in a hoarse voice as confusion reigned around her.

She stopped pounding on the person above her when she realized how badly she could be harming him. He wasn't the enemy. He was the man who'd saved her.

In so many ways.

The fight went out of her. She tried to sit up but was trapped by Lucas's strong, lean body, which had been trying to protect her by keeping her from injuring herself as she dreamt of the evil she'd lived through. When he realized she'd come back to the present, he sat up quickly, giving her space to breathe.

She would have much rather had him close.

The pitch-blackness was only interrupted by the green and red lights on his TV and entertainment consoles. A faint glow that could be a night-light illuminated the doorway into the kitchen.

Ellie tried to swallow and found her mouth and throat so dry she couldn't even speak without croaking.

"Need a drink?" he asked.

She nodded, her fingers worrying the edge of a cushion she clung to as she tried to shake off her terror and remember she was somewhere safe. With someone who had affection for her, at least.

In her semiconscious mind, Ellie dared to think the L-word, but quickly scrubbed it away. It was too soon for that, wasn't it?

No, she was certain she knew what kind of man Lucas was and it was definitely the kind she could love. Whether he would say the same of her, she had no idea.

Lucas went to stand then lurched to one side, crashing into the coffee table hard enough that it surrendered a giant crack. Who knew what it had done to his hip?

"Son of a bitch!"

She reached for him. It was too late; he'd withdrawn, recovered and popped to his feet—well, foot. Leaning slightly to one side, he found his balance.

"I still forget sometimes." He ran his hand through his hair. "Hang on."

Ellie blinked up at him, lost in her own thoughts too much to question what he was up to. As she watched, he hopped to the kitchen using the sofa and the dining room chairs as handholds along the way. His agility was impressive.

Her eyes narrowed as she heard him grab a glass from the cabinet, then run the water for a moment. When he tried to come back, she heard sloshing then splatters as her drink overflowed and lost a significant part of the contents in the first couple of bounces.

If he kept up that way, there'd be nothing in the glass by the time he made it to her side.

He paused then looked at her with a horrible twist to his sinful mouth.

Ellie rose, intending to take the cup and help him back to the couch.

But when she did, he snarled, "Sit your ass down. I can do this."

Whoa. Still raw from her nightmare, she couldn't take his bitterness on top of everything else.

"I'll do whatever I like." She crossed her arms, hoping to hide her nude breasts from his view, suddenly feeling entirely too exposed. Her voice was an ugly rasp when she said, "You might as well leave that glass on the dinner table there because I won't be drinking from it if you talk to me like that."

"Whatever," Lucas grumbled then dropped to his hands and knees.

She watched as he crawled back to her without spilling another drop. Considering how effective that was, she wasn't sure why he hadn't done it that way to start. Could it be another ego thing with her watching?

Ellie hoped not because she thought it was pretty awesome to see how he'd adapted. To eliminate some of his tools simply because he was afraid of how it would look to her...well, that would be ignorant and she wasn't in the mood to deal with stupidity at the moment.

"Here," he said when he reached the sofa and lifted the drink to her.

She didn't want to be a bitch, but neither did she think it was okay for him to snap at her simply because he was having some image crisis. His nasty attitude wasn't increasing her opinion.

"I told you I'm not taking that. I'll go get my own." She stood and stepped over him. Or would have if he hadn't snagged her ankle.

The aggressive clutch tripped something in her. Reflexively she kicked to break his grip. Her breath came in huge pants and the room spun around her. Her foot connected with his cheek, which only horrified her more when her flash reaction faded and she realized whom she was with.

End result, they both ended up crashing to the floor.

"E, are you all right?" Lucas scrambled to her side, his eyes wide and his hands hovering over her as if afraid to touch her.

"I'm fine." Now they were both mortified.

"I'm sorry," he said at the same time she did. Then he added, "I'm going to go..."

Where? They were sharing his modest house. One she loved—with all the hardwood and cobalt and emerald homey fabric accents—but there wasn't a ton of space.

"Lucas—"

"I need some time to myself. You can take my bed," he offered.

She shook her head. No way would she sleep there, surrounded by his smell and his soft sheets. All the reminders with none of the benefits of his company. "I'm fine on the couch."

He winced as she scurried from him and practically dove beneath the quilt he must have pulled over them while they slept. She realized why he'd

202

rather have her spot when he didn't stop to find his supplies and his prosthesis, instead rising to hop to the stairs then climb them using some oddly graceful combination of his knee on his residual limb and his foot on his other leg.

Unable to look away, she watched in awe as he navigated the stairs his way. Quick and efficient. Demonstrating his strength. But when he got to the top and saw her staring, he shut down completely, as if she would judge him for acclimatizing to his surroundings and his new body.

"Dumbass," she muttered beneath her breath, but it didn't matter—he'd already vanished down the hallway like a wounded animal slinking into the night.

Ellie got up, locked the door then returned to the couch, taking a deep breath to inhale his dissipating scent before it vanished like he had.

***

Ellie didn't sleep at all without Lucas by her side. Neither did he, if the periodic tossing and turning or sighs she heard from overhead were any indication. By the time golden morning light poured through the window, she had given up. Shrugging into her dress from the night before, since the rest of her new wardrobe was still in the trunk of the car, she shuffled into the kitchen and started a pot of coffee.

She was nursing her second cup, doodling on a napkin at the table, when Lucas appeared.

"Morning," he said, not bothering to put a *good* in there.

Awk-ward. With a capital *A*.

On one hand, she wanted to race to him and smother him in kisses. Both because he'd given her the best sex of her life and because her heart hurt for him. They'd both shown their wounded sides in the middle of the night. There weren't going to be any instafixes for either of them. Plus, he was sporting a faint shiner, courtesy of her foot. Shit.

But...if they couldn't work through their issues together, then falling any harder for him would only be begging for heartache. Because she could admit she was already pretty much in love with the man and that gave him unimaginable power over her. Something she was wary of.

"I know I fucked up last night," he said. "But the silent treatment? Ugh."

Ellie couldn't help but laugh at his exaggerated *yuck* face.

"I'm thinking about what I want to say." She toyed with the handle of her mug as she considered her options. "I guess I just want you to know that no matter what happens between us on the sexual side of things, I'll always consider you a friend and I don't want to chance screwing that up. I missed you these past six months."

"I think I liked the silent treatment better." He stomped into the kitchen to get his own coffee and a bowl of cereal before plopping down across from her.

After he'd shoveled a few spoonfuls into his mouth, and chewed them somewhat more vigorously than required, he said, "Don't act like the link between us isn't there. It's electric and way more potent than that *friend* bullshit."

"I know," she admitted. "But if we can't make that work, at least we could have something."

"I don't think so." He shook his head. "Every time I'm near you, it's a stronger pull."

"Okay, fine." She tapped the end of her pen against the tabletop in a rapid tattoo. "Then why are you still hiding from me? I've shown you all the ugly parts of myself and you're going to go and act like I'm gonna be some judgmental bitch about your disabilities? That's totally unfair."

"Damn, E." He dropped his spoon into the bowl with a clatter. "You are *so* stubborn! It's not about you. I trust you. Hell, I even told you about how I grew up. It's just that...sometimes...I'm still not ready to deal with this, okay? I'm not nearly as strong as you are. Don't hold that against me."

"Let me know when you're ready to be a little more honest with us both." She flipped her pen around then started drawing again, more viciously this time.

They might have argued about it more if his phone hadn't buzzed just then.

"Shit." He banged his fist on the table, making her jump.

So she collected her mug and her drawing and took them out into his sunroom, where she could try to regain her calm while he talked to the Men in Blue.

The guys on the phone must have sensed something off because they insisted on coming over for a debriefing and check-in. Ellie didn't see how that was wise, considering the place would be teeming with cops and they were trying to scam some scammers, but she figured they knew best.

***

A few hours later, it shocked the hell out of her when people started showing up.

Not through the front gate or up the driveway, but on golf carts from the other side of the lake.

"I own a cabin about a mile that way." Lucas pointed. "It has more surveillance equipment and a secondary exit—or entrance, in this case—to the property through a tunnel in the wine cellar. I have a motorcycle and some other supplies stashed there in case I ever have to make a run for it for some reason."

He shrugged as if that were a normal thing.

Was she fucking a superhero or something? Too bad he couldn't fly—then they wouldn't have gotten in a fight the night before and things wouldn't be threatening to unravel before her eyes.

When it seemed like he was about to say something, maybe to bridge this horrible gap between them, the back door opened and Ryan rushed inside. He scooped her into his arms and squeezed her tight enough to make her squeak.

Over her brother's shoulder, Lucas was watching them with a sad smile. Was it because he was wishing he had a sibling of his own? Or because he was happy she had someone to fall back on if things between them got blown to smithereens?

Either way, Ellie knew she couldn't let him walk away from what they'd been building because it was too good to throw away over something as superficial as his image issues.

Later, after everyone left, she would try to convince him of the same thing.

When Ryan finally put her down, Ellie was immediately hugged again by Shari and Ben and Ben's niece, whom he had sole custody of since his sister had not survived Morselli's dungeon. Ellie embraced her brother's roommate a little tighter when it was his turn. She knew what he still struggled with, and it could just as easily have been her brother grieving instead.

Shari eventually cut in, handing her an enormous paper bag. "I thought you might want some art supplies to help you cope with the stress while you're here."

Though her friend might have meant the heist, it was clear she didn't when she glanced between Ellie and Lucas, who hadn't taken his gaze from her for a single moment.

"Thank you." The woman was a lifesaver. This would allow her to stay calm, especially if things between her and Lucas deteriorated.

Shari leaned in closer and said, "I put some of your collection in the bottom of the bag, in case you need some way to release the tension without relying on your host."

Ellie's face flamed. She would have told Shari she had a much better substitute, but Lucas's smirk was enough indication that he had a pretty good idea of what had caused her flush. Screw him. If he was still acting like an idiot later, maybe she'd put on that show she'd teased him about.

Then she'd see what he had to say.

When the hell had she become so bold? Probably about the time he'd made it clear that the two of them together were clear frontrunners in the world's best-sex-in-the-history-of-mankind contest.

"Uncle Lucas?" Julie went up to him and took his hand between both of hers. It looked so strong and enormous, compared to the innocent girl's.

"Yeah, sweetie?" He crouched down to her level.

"I saw a rope swing in the backyard. Uncle Ben and Uncle Ryan said I had to ask if I could play on it. Can I? Please?"

"Sure." He beamed at her. His adeptness with children was just another endearing factor about the man. Damn him. "Want me to push you really high?"

"Yes!" she screeched, making the adults grin. It'd taken the child a while to return to her playful self. All of them had been wrecked in some way or another by Morselli and the Scientist. At least Julie seemed the most resilient. "I want to touch the clouds."

"Well, maybe not *that* high." Lucas laughed as he let her drag him out into the sunshine. Ben and Ryan followed along.

From the sunroom, Ellie and Shari watched the other Men in Blue join their guys out back, suspiciously not far from the grill, while Lacey, Jambrea and Lily headed in toward them.

Matt and Clint—Jambrea's men—unpacked rations for an impromptu barbeque while the ladies joined Ellie indoors under the guise of whipping up some side dishes.

After a round of hugs from everyone and some baby talk from Ezra, who rode Izzy's hip, they all stared expectantly at her. Lily went ahead and said it for them all, "So...are you two doing it yet or what?"

"Um, yes. Kind of." She couldn't help but smile at that revelation.

Her friends cheered louder than they had when she'd hit that cursed jackpot last weekend.

They were so noisy the guys must have heard them from outside and turned their way for a moment before resuming their chatter.

"Shh...shhh." Ellie held her hands with her palms down and lowered them toward the floor. "It's not all sunshine and roses. I mean, it was, until last night."

By the time she'd finished explaining, the group of women was giving her plenty of suggestions for how to overcome Lucas's hang-ups. Not a single one of them doubted that working through things was the way to go.

"Honey, I can see him looking over his shoulder at us every ten seconds. He can't stop staring at you. He just needs some time to adjust." Shari smiled at Ellie.

"Speaking of"—Jambrea winced as if she hated to bring it up—"how are you doing? With the physical aspects of the relationship, given your condition?"

Spoken like a true nurse.

"Honestly, he's better than any of the hormone therapy I've been getting. It's amazing. He makes me feel so good. Almost normal, except way sexier than I used to be." She giggled as she shrugged nervously. "But...I was wondering..."

"We've heard it all, Ellie." Lacey slung an arm around her shoulders. "Do you know how many people we see in the ER each week who get stuff stuck up their butts? What could be more embarrassing than that?"

Lily looked between them before offering, "I can leave if you want to talk to them in private. I know what it's like to respect someone's confidentiality, though, and I'd never break yours. I hope you know that."

"It's not that I'm worried about anyone knowing, I'm just sort of thinking I might be nuts." She shrugged. "Stay, stay. I trust you all. Is it possible that when he comes in me, either in my mouth or my pussy, the Sex Offender effects are diminished?"

Shari couldn't help herself. "He's got magic jizz?"

"Oh. My. God." Ellie put her face in her palms. "I knew that was crazy, right?"

"Actually, no. It's not." Jambrea tugged on Shari's hair. "Quiet, ho."

209

When they broke into a mock fight, Ellie turned to Lacey instead. "It's not?"

"Jambrea and I have interviewed all of the recovering Sex Offender addicts at the hospital. Even Lily." Ellie held out her hand to her friend. Only people who'd experienced the ravaging effects of the drug could truly understand. "There aren't that many of you because, you know, it was so addictive. Most people who used it OD'd. But I can think of four who have told us the same thing you just did."

Lacey and Jambrea exchanged a look over Shari's head.

"What? What was that?" Ellie asked.

"It could be coincidence. We have a correlation going, not a causation-type situation. There's no proof for sure..." Jambrea hedged.

Lily squeezed Ellie's hand as she prepared herself to hear what they said next. "Tell me."

"The women who've reported this phenomenon are all in love with their partners," Lacey said. "You know a lot of the addicts were, and still are, prostitutes. None of them have described the effect when they're with clients they have no affection for. And even some of the women who are married haven't. But the ones who have rated themselves a ten out of ten on our survey when we asked about being in love."

"That's ridiculous. That's not how chemicals work." Ellie had been a lab tech before all this. She knew about reactions. They were standard equations. No deviations for something as intangible as emotions.

"You know," Jambrea added, "the more I think about things, the more I think I know a doctor you should talk to. I met him one time when he took Matt, Clint and me out to a fancy restaurant as a thank-you

210

present. Remember when they saved that college girl who got kidnapped? The photographer?"

"Oh yeah." Ellie shivered as she realized she had a lot more in common with the woman now. "Wasn't her name Elsa? It was similar to mine, I think."

"Yes," Jambrea confirmed. "Well, anyway, her brother-in-law is Dr. Kurt Foster of Elembreth University. He invented this thing called the Dream Machine that's tearing up the field right now with its effectiveness in treating people who suffer from repressed memory, and especially sexual therapy through dream analysis. Anyway, he didn't used to believe in love at all because he only looked at base-chemical reactions. Long story short, he's convinced now—thanks partially to his wife, Becca—though he still thinks there are reaction types we simply don't understand yet that drive some of these unbreakable connections between people. It's fascinating stuff."

Ellie could see how it would be. "Could I get his card? Or his number or something?"

"Sure." Jambrea smiled. "How about I send an email when I get home, introducing the two of you? I think it could be really beneficial for you both."

"Thanks." She gave Jambi a quick hug.

"So until you and Dr. Hot Stuff crack the scientific reasoning behind it, I'd just recommend you keep draining Lucas." Lily shrugged. "If it ain't broke…"

"Damn it. It sort of is, though." Ellie frowned.

"Not for long." Shari smiled at her. "Trust us. You'll get through this. It'll be a fun trivia question at your bridal shower someday: What was your first fight?"

"*What?*" Ellie snorted as she shook her head. These ladies were too much.

"Yo, woman!" Razor shouted to Izzy from across the lawn. "The burgers are ready. Where's my potato salad? Don't forget the brownies either!"

They all cracked up at that, knowing poor Razor was about to get his balls handed to him yet again.

***

Sharing the fresh grilled food, they laughed and talked. A brilliant relief. Ellie sat quietly next to Lucas, wishing the heat of his thigh pressed to hers weren't their only contact. They spoke to their neighbors instead of each other, making her wonder if her friends had everything wrong after all.

Across the table from her, she watched Ben and Ryan offer Shari tastes of their food until she was too stuffed to finish what was on her own plate. From beside them, she could see Mason and Tyler rolling their eyes. More than once she heard them rag on themselves for being too stupid to make a move on Lacey earlier than they had and how they wished they hadn't wasted years of their lives before acting on what was between them. Matt and Clint seconded their opinions. Loudly.

Hopefully the third trio in their group would get the point soon.

Ellie could see how well they meshed. Why couldn't they?

She didn't want to make the same mistake. Just when she was about to whisper her revelation to Lucas, he got up from the table, clearing her garbage without being asked, before he joined the rest of the Men in Blue, who were tossing a football around near the lake.

When the ball popped off Clint's hands and went into the water, things turned into a cross between catch and a wet T-shirt contest featuring a host of sexy, ripped law enforcers. She, Izzy, Lily, Shari, Lacey and Jambrea swooned appropriately from the shore.

Ellie couldn't tell for sure, but at one point she thought she saw Razor reenacting their fucking faux sign language at Lucas. Oh God, had that been caught on camera? If it meant that the guys were treating Lucas as one of their own, not holding back or acting like he was too fragile for their jabs, she would gladly suffer a little embarrassment.

***

After a while, the guys headed in. Most of them had stripped off their shirts and were sunning themselves as they lounged near their women. The first really hot day of the year made them eager to soak up the sun's rays.

Laughing and dripping lake water, Lucas climbed up the bank then headed toward the pile of towels on the picnic table beside Ellie. She handed him one, admiring the way happiness transformed his sometimes too-serious features. He really did have a killer smile, dimples and all.

In silence, he began drying off his leg, pressing and holding where he'd gotten his liner and socks wet. His smile faded as he worked. Because of her?

"If you want me out of your hair, I'll go with JRad or one of the other cops until it's time for the sting," Ellie murmured so that their friends couldn't hear.

"Like hell." Lucas spun to face her so fast he had to take a moment to catch his balance, which only

213

seemed to piss him off more. "You're staying with me. It's safer and...because...this is where you belong."

Ellie tried not to grin.

"Shit, E," he groaned, "I'm an idiot. I freaked out last night and I'm sorry it came between us. I can't promise that I won't get frustrated sometimes, but I'll try not to shut you out. Forgive me?"

When he came closer and put his fist beneath her chin, tipping her face up, she couldn't deny the sincerity in his searching gaze.

"Yeah. But if you go into dumbass mode again, I reserve the right to kick your ass with your own foot until you snap out of your funk. Deal?"

"Deal." He grinned.

She nodded then went onto her tiptoes.

He met her halfway, kissing her full-on despite their friends and family not more than a hundred feet away. She'd missed the support of his arms around her and the heat of his lips sweeping across hers. Too much more of that and she'd be running inside for that vibrator Shari packed.

Lucas noticed her hesitance and separated them, but didn't let go of her. The public display of affection was as good as a promise ring in the eyes of their friends.

Unsurprisingly, a chorus of catcalls, whistles and hollers echoed from the gathering, in appreciation of their little show.

"I think that's our cue to pack up." Mason clapped his husband, Tyler, on the shoulder even as he hugged their wife, Lacey, to his chest.

But it wasn't until Julie began to sing "Uncle Lucas and Aunt Ellie, sitting in a tree..." that the two of them finally broke apart, grinning like fools.

CHAPTER THIRTEEN

Ryan, Shari, Ben and Julie had been the first to arrive and they were the last to leave. Ellie's brother took a long time saying goodbye to his beloved sister. No one could doubt his devotion to Ellie. He'd raised her, risked his life for her and been forever changed by the experience himself.

Ben hovered nearby with a sleeping Julie resting against his massive shoulder. The clutch Ryan had on Shari's hand as he said farewell to Ellie made it clear how tough it was for him. After nearly losing her once, this had to be killing him. Hopefully Ben and Shari would help him through it.

It was the only time Lucas saw Ellie waver in her resolve to aid in the takedown of the robbers.

When the four of them, who would make a pretty awesome family in Lucas's opinion, piled into the golf cart that would take them back to the secret entrance to his property, Ellie called to her brother one last time, "I love you. It'll be okay."

"Better be." Ryan glared at Lucas.

Spending time around their friends had made Lucas realize he had essentially no tie to Ellie, or her to him. Even their lip-lock would be easy to blow off if things went south after this. It bothered him. By the time they were alone again, the need to claim her coursed through his blood.

He'd never felt that way before about a woman, though it didn't surprise him that she would be the first. The only. Their bond had seared away everything but her while they fucked. It also made her opinion count when he'd never given a shit about what people thought of him in the past.

And that was why he'd fucked up so royally the night before.

Lucas took Ellie's hand and tugged gently, leading her to a soft blanket he'd laid out under the most enormous oak tree back there. It was close enough to the lake's edge to have a great view and even be in range of hearing the soft laps the gentle waves made as they kissed the shore.

When he sat beside Ellie, he scratched around the top of his liner, which had gotten soaked while he was horsing around with the guys earlier.

"Why don't you take that stuff off if it's bothering you?" Ellie asked with feigned nonchalance. Here they went again. "It's still warm and bright enough out here that it'll dry in no time."

He hated when she made sense, especially when he had other priorities at the moment.

"Maybe I'd rather remove some other things, like your clothes," he growled as he leaned in and captured her mouth in a kiss rougher than he usually gave her unless they were in the middle of sex. For the first time, he didn't doubt her ability to handle him.

She'd faced the full brunt of his temper, even when it had been unfairly aimed at her. Could she withstand the heat of his unshielded attraction?

They were about to find out.

Lucas buried his fingers in her hair and she tipped her head back, parting her lips so that he could sip from her as he liked. But when he toyed with the buttons on her dress, she slapped his hands away.

"Nope." Ellie shook her head.

"What kind of game is this?" He could see her eyes changing from cerulean to the deep, stormy blue that accompanied her body's transition to her ultra-aroused state. She wanted this. *Him.*

So why was she stopping them?

"I'm not stripping until you do. You're going to end up with a rash or sores if you leave that thing on wet." She knocked her heel into his prosthesis. "Be a good boy and I'll make sure you get a treat. Otherwise, we're both going to suffer for your stubbornness."

She walked her skirt up her long, slender thighs. As much as it killed him to see her and not have her, it bothered him far more to know that she would let herself ache with unfulfilled desire if he didn't do what she asked of him.

"Ellie, come on." He scrubbed his hands through his hair, deciding to be blunt. "I'm about to fuck you half into a coma."

"It's not like your dick was cut off. You don't need that hunk of carbon fiber to make love to me." She dared him to deny it.

Maybe he didn't, but it made him feel less awkward. Less like a freak.

But God it *was* really starting to itch now.

"What if you give yourself blisters or your skin breaks down into open wounds and you can't go with me to the casino?" She bit her lip.

Well, shit. That was all it took. No way would she go alone. But she was right—he could end up unable to wear his leg, and then what? He'd either have to rely on his forearm crutches or a wheelchair. Either one would make it pretty damn obvious for the crooks to figure out who he really was. Then Ellie would pay the price.

Lucas was slipping the strap out of his proximal lock in seconds flat. He would never do that to her. But she didn't know what she was asking for. Backing him into a corner made him feel jagged and rough. He hoped she could handle the result of his raw emotions when they were translated into actions.

As soon as he had his liner and socks stretched out in the sunlight and his leg toweled dry, he rounded on her. "Why are you still wearing clothes?"

"I thought you wanted to take them off me." She smiled softly at him, victorious.

"That was when we were playing nice." He lifted her hand to his mouth then bit her finger enough to sting. She sucked in a breath but didn't run from him. "Now I'm riled up and you're gonna get what you asked for. All of me. Tell me if that's not what you want anymore, E."

"I want you. Exactly how you are. No polish and no cover-ups," she said.

"Fine." He commanded her, "Take your dress off so I can watch; then I want you facing that tree, bent over at the waist. Put your hands on it to brace yourself. You're going to need something to hold on to."

If she'd shown a moment's hesitation, he would have changed their course.

She didn't.

Before he had finished his instructions, she climbed to her feet and dragged her dress over her head, letting it fall to the grass, forgotten. Completely bare beneath, her perky tits bounced enough to have him rearranging his cock in his shorts before scanning down her svelte stomach to her trimmed mound.

"Did I tell you to stop?" he asked.

"Ah...no"—she pivoted, showing him her ass and the colorful tattoo on her shoulder instead—"but you looked like you were enjoying the view."

"True. Not as much as I'm going to like being inside you again, though." He groaned just thinking about it. "You were so fucking hot. So tight and so wet."

Lucas couldn't say what inspired his dirty talk, but she moaned and wiggled as she settled into place, so he went with it. He reclined on the blanket only long enough to strip his shorts and briefs off then rolled to his knees.

Thankfully, he hadn't been wearing a shirt. Saved time.

The light breeze couldn't do anything to cool him off as it caressed his fully nude body. Out here, in the broad sunlight, he didn't care who or what saw him as he was, so long as they also noticed how he fit with Ellie. They belonged together. She had been made for him, and he for her.

He crawled between Ellie's legs like the animal she turned him into. She didn't seem to care how he got to her when he spread her pussy lips from behind then sampled the arousal he could already see making her glisten.

When her knees threatened to buckle, he wrapped his hands around her waist and suspended her above his head in midair until she could regain her balance. To know that he could impact her like that was potent.

Steady once more, she resumed her position, thrusting her perfect ass at him as if she offered him a present.

And she was.

Her trust and faith being the two most important of them.

Her indiscriminating affection being another.

And her body being the last.

Though it wasn't the most important of the treasures she shared with him, it was one he prized. And planned to take care of to the satisfaction of them both.

Lucas gripped her ass cheeks in either hand and spread her apart so that he could bury his face in her folds and drink deeply, flooding his mouth with her taste.

His cock pulsed, begging him to skip the warm-up, but he'd done that yesterday and he had something entirely different on the menu for this afternoon.

When she began to chant his name and rock so that she met his strokes, he paused, shifting his attention to her breasts, which hung beneath her, swaying in time to the flexing of her body.

Ellie cried out his name and begged him to give her relief.

"Oh, I will," he promised her. "Soon."

Lucas scooted back until he could suckle her breasts. He remembered how sensitive they were and how she'd unraveled for him a couple of days ago when he'd feasted on them. So he decided to start there.

When he took her nipple into his mouth and began to tease it with his tongue, he complemented the sensation by reaching between her legs. A few flicks of his fingers across her clit had her knees turning to jello. He grinned as he steadied her before doing his best to melt her bones.

Without removing her hands from the tree bark, she peered down at him, watching him play her body like some fine instrument. Focusing the skittering of his fingers over her clit into a gentle circular massage while increasing the suction on her breast made her moan.

Good thing he didn't have any neighbors or they would probably be outside jacking off as they watched how beautiful she was when she came.

Because there was no way she could hold back when he took his free hand and used it to pinch her other nipple.

Above him, Ellie quaked. She called out his name and rained her pleasure on his fingers. Before she'd even finished shattering, he took his drenched hand and moved it to her mouth, feeding her the result of their passion.

Ellie opened her mouth without hesitation. She drew his digits between her lips and sucked them clean as if she could read his mind. Or maybe their desires were simply so in tune they both wanted the same things.

"That's right," he whispered as he watched her draw on his fingers, her eyes slightly closed. "You're in sync with me. It hardly takes anything for you to come with me, does it?"

She moaned, already fidgeting as the arousal raging through her returned more fiercely than before. This time Lucas went farther, returning his hand to her pussy, though not only to toy with her clit. He used the combination of her slickness and spit to tunnel inside her with three fingers at once.

Unprepared for the invasion, she jerked.

He would swear she came on him again before he'd even fully embedded himself within her sheath.

221

Wet, velvety heat distracted him momentarily. It felt so good to slide his fingers through it—feel her massaging his hand and know that soon it would be his cock—that he got a little carried away and gave her a couple more orgasms in a row.

It didn't matter, though—she still needed more.

Finally, he was starting to believe that she might just need *him* as badly as he needed her. Not because he was some random means to sate her Sex Offender-induced cravings, but because they had this impact on each other. Fuck, he knew for a fact his cock had never been as hard or eager to impale a soft pussy as it was when the cunt in question was hers.

Still, he refused to allow himself the indulgence.

Not until she was as desperate as he was.

If he was going to give in and show her all of him, she had to be ready to accept it. Better if she joined him in being fully naked to the soul. For her that meant embracing this new, incredibly sexy, wild side of her sensuality. And if it took making her mindless with delirious pleasure to get her there, he'd do it.

Gladly.

Every day for the rest of his life.

Lucas abandoned her breasts with a groan of regret, raking his teeth over her nipples one last time before edging toward her pussy. By now, he was supporting most of her weight, though he didn't mind in the least. And still she stayed where he'd put her, never once letting him down.

Maybe he'd have to talk to JRad and Lily about booking a session at their club to explore this side of her further, once they'd put this cops-and-robbers bullshit behind them.

This time, Lucas changed direction, sitting facing her body from behind her so that he could peek at her expression from time to time. She was so engrossed in the rapture assaulting her that she had closed her eyes and seemed to be drifting far away from where her body rested in his capable hands.

That was fine with him. Whatever she needed to do to maximize her experience, that was what he wished for her.

So he got back to work.

This time he allowed himself to lick her from clit to ass, swirling his tongue around her tight back passage a few times for the hell of it.

Ellie groaned and shoved against him, inspiring more wicked thoughts for another time when he was better prepared. That didn't stop him from lashing her with his tongue as he began to ram his fingers inside her, taking his cues on how hard and fast to set his pace by the rate at which she rocked back.

It felt savage at first, until he monitored her escalating cries and the orgasms that began to roll through her, one after the other, with no distinct end before her body surrendered to another.

Only when she shouted his name and begged did he consider allowing his stiff, leaking cock to finally take what it wanted.

"Please, Lucas," she cried. "I need you inside me. Give me your cock. Please fuck me, please."

How could he resist a plea like that?

When he shifted, she began to sink to the blanket, maybe expecting to ride him or somehow help him fight gravity while he fucked her. "Hell no, E."

He smacked her ass a bit harder than he'd intended, though her resulting howl made him think the pleasurable pain had tipped off yet another climax.

"Did I tell you to move?" he asked.

"N-no." She bit her lip as if it required special concentration to think through the sensations bombarding her.

"Then stay right there if you want my dick," he snarled, letting her have what she'd asked for...his passion, fully unleashed.

Lucas could only hope that she liked the man he was beneath the polite coverings as much as she had thought she might. If not, it would crush him. He was fully exposed, completely vulnerable and prepared to give her every bit of him there was.

In every way.

Ellie stayed stock-still. She could have been bound to some of the bondage equipment at Black Lily for how flawlessly she maintained the position he'd set her in.

"That's good, E. Perfect. You're so fucking hot," he growled as he put his hands around her waist and used her to anchor himself as he stood. Balancing on his left foot, he leaned slightly to one side, cantilevering himself so that his center of gravity adjusted. With her fuckable ass on display, and making a perfect handhold, he found it was actually pretty easy—and surprisingly comfortable—to enter her this way.

So he did.

He took his throbbing cock in hand and pumped it a few times, afraid to get carried away, but needing a little relief at least before he pummeled her harder than she would enjoy.

With her head down, she could observe him.

Ellie must have had a great view because she cried, "Yes, Lucas. Put it in me. Come on, quit playing with my prize."

"You *have* been awfully good, haven't you?" He smiled savagely as he leaned forward and kissed along her spine as well as he could in their positions.

She shivered in his grip.

"Damn straight," she replied, making him laugh even in the midst of the hottest, most desperate sexual encounter of his life.

And that was when he knew, without a doubt, that he loved her.

Not that he planned to share that tidbit at the moment.

Not when they were both fanatical with lust.

He had other things to attend to first. Primarily, her.

"Then I think I have something for you." He took his cock and slapped it against her pussy, loving the moist smacks that resulted, filling the afternoon air with the undeniable sounds of their joint arousal.

"Yes!" she shouted when he notched the tip of his dick to her opening and leaned toward her, allowing his weight to drive him inexorably inside her.

"E!" He would never tire of this moment, the one when their flesh entwined as closely as their hearts and minds seemed to be most times. There was magic in that first contact, their bodies becoming one.

She felt it too, gasping and rocking back to aid his advance. When she bumped her ass into his pelvis, she inadvertently knocked him slightly off-balance.

He hopped to keep himself upright, causing his cock to slip from her pussy. He didn't let that deter him. Instead of wasting time being embarrassed, he simply followed his instincts, which insisted that he get the hell back inside the paradise between her legs as soon as fucking possible.

Ellie sighed when he fitted himself to her and glided to the hilt in a single stroke.

For a couple of seconds, he stayed there. Still. Allowing himself to simply revel in the clasp of her body. Her pussy clenched and released, making him certain that if he lingered there long enough, he could shoot from that sensation alone.

But she needed more.

"Lucas, please." Her fingers clenched on the tree steadying them both.

He gave her what she desired. Himself too.

Using her waist to guide them, he shoved himself inside her. He withdrew before yanking her onto his dick then repeating the motion over and over.

When she came on his cock, slathering him in fresh lubrication, he gritted his teeth and threw his head back, staring at the blinding light in the sky to keep from joining her.

It still wasn't half as bright as looking at her as she found her ecstasy.

So he redoubled his efforts, fucking her nearly as madly as he loved her.

It felt a little weird to have his stump swinging free as he pounded her, but it acted as kind of a pendulum, helping him to return to position before starting another circuit within her.

If she minded it bumping into her from behind, she sure was a phenomenal actress.

Lucas bent at the waist. He slid his hands up her torso, from her hips to her breasts, squeezing them as he humped her harder, faster and more furiously than ever.

Almost immediately, she was crying out his name in the unique tone she used when she was surrendering to her pleasure. He couldn't get enough of her and her bliss.

He bit her shoulder, above her tattoo, hoping she wouldn't mind if he left a mark. He wanted to be represented there, in her depiction of her ideal self. It was egotistical, but honest.

This time when she shattered, she went limp, unable to stand any longer.

Together, they tumbled to the blanket. Lucas kept them locked together and cushioned their fall.

They'd barely hit the ground when he blanketed her prone body, drilling into her harder now that he had both knees to use for leverage.

He reached beneath her and cupped her shoulders in his hands, yanking her to him as he filled her savagely. Her face was turned sideways as she surrendered to his ultimate possession. He couldn't wait for next time they were intimate so that he could let her ride him and return the favor.

He wanted to belong to her every bit as much.

Hell, he already did. He'd given her every ounce of himself, even if she didn't know it yet.

Lucas leaned forward so that he could growl in her ear. Stopping now would be impossible. He'd pushed himself beyond even his restraint. Taking her like this, so that she had to know he was staking a claim, threatened to burst his heart right in his chest.

"Next time, I'm coming with you," he promised.

"Please. Need it. Feels so good when you come in me. Makes it stop." Ellie's speech was fragmented, spoken in spurts as he rocked her body against the blanket.

He didn't quite understand what she meant, but he figured there'd be time for clarification later. As if the promise alone of his release was enough to inspire her final orgasm, she went stiff beneath him. Her entire body gathered, froze and then seized.

She screamed his name so loudly it echoed off the lake, shattering the stillness of the afternoon.

Before she'd finished spasming, he withdrew his cock.

Lucas couldn't say what made him do it, except maybe the possessive streak he didn't know he had, which reared its head right then. He rolled Ellie onto her back then pumped his cock, his fist flying over the impossibly engorged length of his shaft.

She rose onto her elbows and smiled at him then cupped her breasts, making the perfect canvas.

Lucas roared as his climax hit. He jacked himself as his balls gathered then launched streams of semen from his cock. He used the opalescent fluid to paint himself all over her front from her mound to her chest and even rained a few drops on her swollen mouth.

And that was when he saw it.

The instant his come decorated her skin with the proof of how she affected him, the animalistic hunger in her eyes faded to something manageable, though no less steamy. She looked up at him with a combination of fulfillment and gratitude.

The final surges of come dripped from him onto her skin and he suddenly needed to kiss her. To show her that the fierce loving he'd given her had come from a place deeper than lust.

Lucas settled over her, staring into her eyes for a moment before pressing his lips to hers for the sweetest, most tender kiss he'd ever had the pleasure of giving or receiving in his life.

While they sipped from each other, he kept rocking softly over her, as if the motion were burned into his motor memory. Hell, it probably was.

His softening cock rested between them and the mess he'd made of her, which mingled with their sweat to help him glide lightly across her entire front.

It took a while for him to wind down from the incredible peak she'd lifted him to. When he did, he flopped to his back, gathering her to his chest, wondering if she could hear his heart speaking so deafeningly to hers that he could hardly hear anything but the three words it dared him to utter.

Lucas might have.

If the first of Ellie's tears hadn't fallen on his skin, making everything inside him freeze.

"E?" He lifted her face so he could read her expression. "Are you okay? Did I hurt you? Shit, I'm sorry—"

He couldn't even say that he didn't mean to be so rough with her, because he had.

"I'm happy"—she sniffled then put her fingers over his mouth, silencing him—"so don't ruin it with your big mouth."

When she took her hand away, he grinned. "Didn't hear you complaining about that earlier."

She smacked his abs, reminding him to thank his trainer for torturing him with endless crunches. He'd used the hell out of those muscles today.

Then she opened up to him, spilling her guts as surely as he had done in a more physical way with her minutes ago. "I feel like you're finally being honest with me. Not holding back. Giving me your true self. And I'm so, so grateful. Thank you."

"E, that's not necessary—"

"It is." She beamed up at him, a tear running down her cheek. "You're the first person to treat me like I'm not broken. And maybe, after a while, it will be true."

The affection in her stare made him nervous. Could he live up to her expectations? All he'd done was give her what had been inside him for her from the start. Was that the same thing?

He needed to think when he wasn't riding on endorphins.

As he mulled it over, she kept talking, shocking the shit out of him.

"Lucas?"

"Yeah?" He ran his fingers through her hair, loving the feel of the silky strands between his fingers.

"I'm different than before."

She hesitated as if she didn't know how to say what she meant. So he gave her a moment to collect herself while amusing himself by stroking her.

"I like things I never tried before that time. Today...was amazing. Everything. Do you think we could experiment more later?"

"With what, E?" He paused, lifting his head to look more closely at her.

"I like when you're in control," she admitted. "Knowing that I can trust you to take care of me and satisfy my needs, even when I'm completely at your mercy...it's freeing. I want to do more. Will you tie me up sometime? Stuff like that?"

It was eerie how her thoughts ran along the same lines his had while he was buried balls deep in her body. But now that they were back to reality, he wasn't sure it was such a good idea.

"I don't know," he hedged.

Her face fell and she nipped her bottom lip. "Is it weird that I would like that, considering..."

"No." He hugged her tight. "I just want to make sure we know what we're doing. Would you mind if we talked to JRad and Lily about it? They're experts.

Not only in how to do it safely, but in the emotional aspects too."

She grinned. "Professionals, even. No, I don't mind at all."

"We'll do that then, E. Just know this. Whatever you need, I'm going to be the one to give it to you." He curled his arms around her tighter, refusing to let her go.

"In that case…can I ask one more thing? It's fine if you don't want to, though."

Her indecision made him sure he would say yes, simply because he wanted to deserve the trust she put in him even to ask.

"Of course." He brushed his lips over her forehead.

"If we're going to keep doing this"—she wiggled a finger between them—"would you mind coming to some of my sessions with my therapist, kind of as a couple?"

"Is being physical with me upsetting you?" He frowned, hoping he'd gauged things correctly.

"No, but I want to make sure we're being responsible, you know? I don't want any misunderstandings to sneak up on us when things are so new. It's complicated between us. Confusing sometimes. I don't want either of us to get unintentionally hurt. And I definitely think we should try to avoid either of us coping by putting distance between us again."

"It's probably not a bad idea." He shrugged, willing to do whatever it took to make their relationship viable long-term, even if they weren't committing to that aloud just yet. He knew what she was really asking, and he planned to be there for her. "Sure, E. I'll go with you."

"Thank you." She kissed him so gently, for agreeing to something simple and decent, he thought he might shed a tear of his own.

"No, thank *you*." He felt it was only fair to be as open as she was. "For taking me as I am, I mean."

"You're finally listening, Lucas." She tossed him a sassy wink as she patted his chest then sat up, hugging her knees to her chest and resting her cheek on her knees so she could keep him in sight.

Though he was sad to lose her heat, a sudden urge came over him.

He dug through his shorts until he found his pocketknife. Fisting it, he said, "I'm going to open my knife. Are you okay with that?"

Without tensing even a bit, she nodded.

Maybe seeing him use the blade for something positive would help lessen her fear.

He opened it then crawled to the tree trunk. While she watched, he carved a heart into the bark, putting their initials and the date inside it.

He knew this was the moment he had irrevocably given his to her and prayed she kept it safe.

Soon, when their lives had settled and they'd had enough time to adjust to what was happening between them, he would make sure she knew it too.

CHAPTER FOURTEEN

Ellie hummed as she flipped an omelet in the skillet she'd unearthed from Lucas's cabinet. She hoped he liked ham, cheese and mushrooms with his eggs. As she cooked, she reflected on the past half of a week. How could it only be Thursday?

This was her fourth morning at Casa Lucas. In some ways, it seemed like she'd just arrived, and in others she felt like she'd been here forever. In no way did she feel like she wanted to leave anytime soon, though.

She smiled to herself, wondering if shacking up with him was a possibility. As long as her brother didn't find out about it, anyway. Ryan might object, though maybe not if he saw how happy being here made her.

Ellie danced around the kitchen island to pop some bread in the toaster. It would go along with the glass of orange juice and the folded paper napkin with her ridiculous good-morning doodle on it. She began to arrange everything on a wooden tray that had been a receptacle for clutter on Lucas's counter, holding things like his keys, some random bullet casings, spare change and an assortment of device chargers.

She'd swiped it with the intent of serving her man breakfast in bed.

After the quality time they'd spent making love the past two days, she figured his energy stores could use some replenishing. And he deserved to be pampered some, even if he would hate for her to think that way about him.

When she'd gotten everything just so and slid the steaming omelet onto the white plate with navy edging, she tapped her lips, looking for one finishing touch.

Outside the door, a clump of daisies swayed in the breeze.

With a grin, she slipped out to pick a few.

By the time she'd selected the prettiest ones and come back inside, Lucas was flying into the kitchen. He had his leg on and a pair of loose gym shorts, but nothing else.

"Are you all right? Who's out there?"

He shoved her behind his back and began surveying the yard through the windows, even as he reached into a drawer she'd thought was full of junk. Nope. He pulled out a handgun. The other fist held bullets and he began to load it with rapid, deadly precision.

"Holy crap." She shook her head. "Lucas, calm down. There's no one there. It was me. I went out to get a flower for your breakfast tray."

He turned around and stared at her with such a weird look on his face she had to laugh.

"What?" His head tipped to one side as he studied her handiwork.

"Would you mind putting the gun down?" she asked in a voice too high-pitched to be as casual as she was aiming for.

"Oh, fuck. Sorry." He made sure it was unloaded, then tucked it back into its hiding spot. "I should have warned you about the alarms. I'm not used to guests."

Or being so domesticated, she imagined. For the better part of his life, he'd been surrounded by deception and violence. More than ever, she wanted to give him a normal day or longer. As much as she could manage before they either were torn apart or went their separate ways.

Because sometimes she found it hard to believe that their lives—so drastically different—could actually mesh. That's not to say that she didn't *hope* for the impossible, like she had those times in Morselli's dungeon. It just meant that she wasn't betting on it.

Lucas must have sensed her melancholy. He put his arms around her and kissed her "good morning" properly.

His warm chest encouraged her to snuggle against it. Her hands wandered down his back to his perfect ass and rested there as she took another taste of him.

Finally he pulled away, wincing. "It looks like I may have ruined a surprise in progress."

"Oh crap. Yeah. Your breakfast is getting cold." She picked up the plate and carried it to the table, patting the chair beside the setting where she'd left her coffee.

"Would you hate me if I wanted something else instead?" He was staring at her with enough hunger in his gaze to guess that he might rather eat her.

"Save that for later. Come on. It's not every day I go to this kind of trouble for a dude." She grinned, knowing she'd gladly cook for him anytime.

"Oh, so I'm a *dude* now, huh?" He grabbed her around the waist and lifted her, spinning her around until she was dizzy and laughing.

She sighed as he lowered her, letting their bodies glide across one another so perfectly that she might have surrendered to his pleas for alternate nourishment if he'd been even just a bit taller, extending the contact.

As it was, her body betrayed her, her stomach rumbling just when they grew quiet.

"Didn't you make yourself anything?" he asked.

"I was going to share with you." She smiled. "Unless you really plan to put all that away."

It was a mountain of food by her standards, but he burned a hell of a lot of calories each day. Maybe she should have made more. Ellie took a mental note for tomorrow, assuming she'd still be there. With him.

"That sounds even better." He sat, so she did too.

For a while, they ate quietly, enjoying the meal she'd prepared for them. He fed her from his fork, making sure she had her fill before devouring the remainder.

"Is that my music playing or yours?" he asked with a mouthful. She was just glad he'd enjoyed her cooking.

"Oh, I hope you don't mind. I swapped my phone for your iPod in the speaker thingy. I kept the Internet and location stuff switched off like you showed me. Just the incoming calls and the music player are enabled." She wrung her napkin in her fingers. "Is that okay?"

"Yup. Not to freak you out, E, but it's less important to hide since those crooks who broke into your house probably aren't still hunting us. It's been too long. By now, they know the money has slipped between their fingers. If they're smart, they're laying low so that the people who were expecting the cash don't realize it's missing. And once we meet with the guys they were trying to impress, those assholes are going to run me. They'll know where you've been hiding, but hopefully then they'll think of us as their partners. Assets anyway, which will protect us until the true heist." He shrugged. "Don't worry about that shit."

"It's hard not to. I know you're used to this kind of drama, but I'm not." She frowned. "And I'm still not happy that I'm putting you in jeopardy."

"*You* didn't do anything. We're in this together. And you're doing great, E," he promised. "This is the worst part of a mission. The waiting. Distraction is key. So let's go back to other things. Like how I think your choice of music is pretty funny."

"Why?" She scowled at him even though she realized he was probably trying to get a reaction out of her. It worked. Was it a sin to listen to music while doing chores?

"It seems like we have all the same stuff. The last four songs have been ones I have on my playlist too."

"Really?" She grinned.

"Uh-huh. I knew you had good taste." He kissed the tip of her nose, transferring some cinnamon sugar from his toast onto it. Laughing, he reached for his napkin to wipe it off. And that was when he noticed her drawing.

"Wow, E."

He set down the glass in his other hand and took extra time examining the hasty sketch she'd done. Of the tree, the heart he'd carved in it, their blanket beneath it and the lake in the background. She'd run out of room to really do the landscape justice, though.

"You drew this?"

"No one else here." She shrugged, kind of nervous for him to judge her newfound talent.

"It's great. I can't believe this didn't take you like...weeks."

He seemed in awe as he ran his fingers over the grooves a simple ballpoint pen had etched in the paper. Still chewing his food, he stood up and crossed to his fridge, hanging her drawing on it with one of those magnet-backed bottle openers.

"Hey, that's your napkin." She laughed.

"I'll wipe my hands on my shorts. No way am I going to get that greasy or crumple it." He grinned at her. "I'm going to find a frame for this. You're really talented, you know."

"Thanks. It's just something I picked up. You know, to calm myself," she explained.

"Hang on, you mean to say you weren't already an artist before..."

"Nope." She shook her head.

He blinked at her a couple of times, then let it go at that.

"What kind of stuff did Shari bring for you the other day?" he wondered. And she knew he wasn't talking about her vibrator, because they'd already played with that the night before.

"Paper, some small canvases, paints, a whole rainbow of markers—"

"Like permanent ones?" he asked.

"Yeah, why?"

"Remember those tattoo designs you showed me last night? I wasn't shitting you when I said I really loved them. Could you copy one of those, E? Maybe put one on my prosthesis?"

"I thought you realized...um...I drew those too. They were original art, Lucas."

He marveled at her. "No shit?"

"No shit." She beamed. Since it had been for herself, really, she hadn't shown anyone her projects. "I can't believe you like them enough that you'd want to wear them all the time."

"You know how I don't really like to show people this thing?" He rapped his knuckles on his prosthesis.

"I might have noticed." She nodded.

"Part of the reason is because it looks so...fake, you know?" He glared at the dull-peach carbon fiber that didn't match his skin tone in any way, shape or form. It was blatantly *not* him.

"Is that the only option? Aesthetically, I mean?"

"No. They have cooler-looking ones that are black, and some custom options, but they're pretty expensive. I get my stuff through the VA. They're not always concerned about factors beyond the functional. With so many people in need, they can't be, really. I get that. I've been fortunate. The hardware itself is good. My prosthetist is pretty fantastic too, which makes all the difference in how things fit and feel. Sadly, he has a lot of practice, considering how many guys are getting torn up overseas lately."

Ellie put her hand on Lucas's, glad he was finally sharing some of this with her. "A prosthetist is a person who makes these, right?"

"Yep. They're custom jobs. Every one. Have to be to mold precisely to each person's stump. Or stumps." He winced. "Anyway, they assigned me to K-level 4, which is the highest. I guess that means I'm eligible for parts that will help me be most active, you know? My foot is actually kind of sweet—it bends and adjusts in a lot of ways to mimic a real one, instead of just being a blob on the end of a stick. Plus, just last week I got a running blade, which is cool. I can push my road workouts a lot farther now with that. I'm thankful, I am. You know, that I can do pretty much everything I did before, with some practice. It just means that my stuff isn't always very attractive. I guess that's a pretty vain thing to worry about."

"Nah." Ellie stopped him. He was obviously a man who took a lot of pride in his body. And his self-expression. Otherwise, he wouldn't be so boldly decorated. His skin was his canvas. That peach socket was like a giant ink-blot stain on a magnificent painting. "I completely understand. It should feel like part of you."

"So...would you decorate it for me? In kind of a tattoo style?"

"What?" She was shocked. He'd trust her with something that important? "I...Lucas, I don't have any training or anything. I just do this for the hell of it. What if I fuck it up?"

"First, it couldn't be any fuglier than this. Second, I'm even more impressed that you've taught yourself how to do this." He leaned in for a lingering kiss. "You're a natural, E. I believe in you. How about you just stare at it for a while and see what you come up with? If it speaks to you, do it. If not, that's okay too."

"Actually, it's kind of a weird thing." She shrugged one shoulder. "That *is* how it happens for me. It's like I can sense things in a different way than I used to and once I have that enhanced representation in my mind, I can copy it down on paper just the way I see it. I know that's bizarre—"

"More like incredible, E. In the best sense of the word." Lucas studied her as if she might have some other random superpowers. "Do your doctors have any idea why that happened to you?"

"Obviously, nothing concrete. A few theories, though. The one that makes the most sense to me?"

"Yeah?"

"I used to do a lot of things to put my mind somewhere else. You know, during..." She swallowed hard and his arms came around her immediately.

"You don't have to talk about it if you don't want. I was just curious."

"There isn't much more to say. Just that I think I might have unlocked part of my brain I never used before. It became my safe place. Where everything around me seemed as enticing as my reality was repulsive."

"I guess we can sometimes be a lot stronger than we ever suspected we were capable of, when we're challenged by life." He sighed.

"You're right about that." She thought of how he'd coped. Sure, they were both working on shit, but they'd done pretty damn well, considering.

"Well, I think it's a phenomenal gift, E. I'd really love if you'd use it on me. Please?"

He surprised and thrilled her by reaching down and doffing his prosthesis all on his own. As if he finally was sure it didn't bother her and wouldn't change what she thought of him to see him as he was and would always be from now on.

That kind of courage alone deserved to be recognized.

And if it would make things easier for him...

"Okay. Let me see what comes to mind. Or do you have a design you're thinking of?" she asked.

"I'm open. Do whatever you like."

Lucas sat there and watched her spin his foot around in her hand, cataloging the unique curves and bumps. She didn't know how long she'd been there, letting inspiration strike when he stood.

To her surprise, he hopped into the sunroom and retrieved her supplies, bringing them back without even flinching as she smiled up at him. "Thank you."

She hoped he realized she meant for trusting her more than for his fetching.

"I'm gonna leave you alone so you can work." He kissed her quickly so neither of them could get out of hand.

"Wait..." She hated to admit she liked having him near.

"I'm not going far." He pointed to the air beneath his shin.

A laugh bubbled up from the region of her heart. They really were a hot mess. One she was beginning to appreciate. Fucked up, yet perfectly so.

"Just going to exercise some while you're doing your thing. I've been slacking on my routines since you've been here." He grinned at her. "Wouldn't want to go all flabby on you."

"As if." She snorted. "Besides, you've been working out plenty, just in different ways."

"Hmm, that's true." His smile warmed her entire body. "Maybe we'll have to get some more of that cardio in later."

"I'm not opposed."

"Wench, stop distracting me." He put his hands up and gripped the top of the doorframe. Then he bent his knees to keep his full leg from touching the ground. She ogled his rippling muscles as he began to pull himself up then lower his entire body in a controlled descent before reversing and doing it again.

Who the hell could do that? So many times in a row?

She probably had enough upper-arm strength to do half of one. *If* he held her so she started at the top then fell straight down and that somehow counted. His abilities were as impressive to her as hers had seemed to him.

"Go on, do your thing and I'll do mine," he said between motions.

She kind of liked the idea of that. Being together, yet independent. So she concentrated as hard as she could on the colors and shapes swirling through her mind when she studied his socket from every angle.

A while later, a thought occurred to her.

"Hey, Lucas," she called to him without pausing her drawing.

"Yeah, E?" He paused midcrunch to look at her.

Lord, that man. Glistening muscles, killer smile and a never-quit attitude—he was about to make her drop his leg and go get him sweaty the old-fashioned way instead.

"What do you need?" he asked again.

"When you're done showing off over there, would you mind doing the laundry? I only bought a few things at the mall and they're mostly dirty now. Pretty soon I'm going to be wandering around here naked."

"In that case...hell no. I won't do it." Lucas grinned at her as he rose and went back to his pull-ups, which he'd been rotating in between other exercises. He kept raising and lowering his entire body as if he were lifting a bottle of beer on a lazy summer afternoon. No wonder he was so damn solid. He counted down ten more repetitions then dropped to the floor on his good leg with a slight crouch that reminded her of a jungle cat on the prowl.

But then he glanced over at his prosthesis in her hands, the initial ink from her markers damp and very smudgeable at this stage.

"Oh no. No way." She shook her head. "You're not messing this up. I think it might not totally suck."

From the other side of the room he smiled at her. "I like that you never pull your punches."

"You're not a baby. You're a very grown-ass man." She appraised his sweaty body. "I'm sure you'll think of something. Didn't I see some forearm crutches upstairs?"

"Yes, but I hate them. I'd rather just do it my way."

"Okie dokie." She smiled over her shoulder at him. "I don't care how you do it. I'd just like some clean panties, please."

"Fine, fine. If you insist. I'm running low on stump socks anyway." Lucas grunted then spun around. He did his hopping thing over to the stairs, grumbling the whole way. "It's all fun and games until my shorts fall down. I think I need some fucking suspenders."

She was as adamantly opposed to that idea as he'd been to providing her with clean clothes to cover up. Let his shorts drop. Why put all that effort into a body you weren't going to show off?

Then again, she liked that she was the only woman who got to enjoy it.

At least for now.

She didn't have anything against her polyamorous friends who'd elected to live in a committed ménage. Or the nontraditional people she'd met through Lily's club, who found their peace in any number of consensual sexual arrangements.

Hell, she'd half expected her brother to tell her he was hoping for something unconventional with Shari *and* Ben, though he never did. At least, he hadn't yet.

Still, she found herself possessive.

Maybe because of the things that had happened to her. Or maybe simply because that's the way *she* was wired. Either way, she hoped to keep Lucas exclusively hers for a while longer yet.

Daydreaming about what might develop between them, she let her mind wander. Her hands flashed, selecting different markers, picking up on a variety of his things surrounding them to guide her. The indigo wine bottle holding the flower she'd picked earlier. His forest-green hand towels. The deep chocolate of his eyes.

She tried to take the essence of him and infuse it into the design.

If she added a bird here or there to ride the currents of him—lifted up on his spirit—well, that sure was a coincidence, wasn't it?

Ellie grinned as she thought of her own tattoo and hoped he appreciated the art she'd made representing them.

The laundry had been done, dried and folded by the time she raised her head.

The sun had advanced well beyond the zenith for the day. How had so much time gone by?

"Lucas?" she called.

"Right here, E." He waved at her from the sunroom, where he was reading something on his tablet. "Finished?"

"I think so."

She rubbed her eyes then looked for the first time at what she'd created, really seeing what she'd produced.

Huh.

Lucas hurried to her side, clearly curious. When he saw what she'd made for him to wear, he was speechless. The first time she could say that about him.

He picked up his prosthesis and admired it from every angle.

She might have been nervous if it weren't for the absolute joy shining in his eyes.

It would blend well with the rest of his tattoos.

And there was no way he could mistake her intent.

"I love it, E." He put it down carefully then reached out to frame her face in his hands. Bringing them together, he bestowed the absolute richest kiss she'd ever shared with a man. He infused every bit of his appreciation, attraction and awe for her into that one interaction. "I love—"

The shrill beeping of her phone made them jump, breaking apart. He'd set it to the most obnoxious ringtone possible so that they wouldn't miss it when the crooks made contact.

Ellie's heart raced then turned to stone in her chest.

"We don't have to do this," he said.

They both knew that was a lie. They were in too deep already to make it out unscathed.

"I'm going to answer it on speakerphone." She repeated the steps they'd drilled over and over until she knew them by heart.

"Go ahead." Lucas's smile had already been erased.

Those fuckers.

They would pay for ruining his moment.

"Good afternoon, Ms. Ellie." It was Yankees guy.

"I was starting to think you'd forgotten us," she said, terser than she'd planned to be.

"Not likely." He huffed. "You're my new best friend. In fact, I like you so much I'm sending a limo for you and your boyfriend. Tomorrow—8:00 p.m. sharp. At the end of the night, we'll all catch a ride back together. Sound fun?"

The getaway car! He was going to make them ride in it.

No. She shook herself. The Men in Blue were going to squash the operation long before then.

Well, that was fine by her. They'd put away the criminals in style. She was determined to do nothing less. Hopefully, as quickly and painlessly as the Men in Blue forecasted, so that she could get back to figuring things out with Lucas.

Except, when the job was done, where would that leave them?

Ellie finished making arrangements with the Yankees fan then disconnected. It'd only taken a few seconds, but she felt like those moments had changed her life irrevocably.

Either Lucas could sense her frazzled nerves or he felt it too.

"Come on." He held her close, rocking her back and forth before kissing the top of her head. "Give me a couple minutes to relay the details to the guys and then I want to go check out my new hammock with you. Sound good?"

When she nodded, he collected her masterpiece, put it back on and then called the Men in Blue.

Afterward, he used some spray sealant from his boathouse to lock in her design before anything could damage it. She wished he could slather them in the same protective coating.

They spent the rest of the day cuddled together, being blasted by the sun that cured his prosthesis, so that neither of them could regress into darkness.

Swaying gently lulled her, but nothing could replace the easiness of the morning they'd shared together. It had been a glimpse of what their life could be like if the world would stop intruding. Lucas's utter stillness and the fact that he was content to clutch her to him for hours, instead of making a move on her, made her fairly sure that his second thoughts were screaming at least as loudly as hers.

Unfortunately, they'd given their word. And neither of them was the type of person to go back on that. They'd simply have to survive. At least their odds were better together than apart.

CHAPTER FIFTEEN

Ellie paced the length of the front porch in her sapphire evening gown. If they hadn't been about to do something incredibly dangerous, she might have been more appreciative of the beautiful dress Lily had snuck her. It was some cunning contraption made of nude fabric beneath a layer of rhinestone-studded navy lace.

It almost made her look naked beneath the sparkles, which were clumped over her important bits, supposedly to protect her modesty.

The illusion seemed to work when Lucas joined her outside and hissed a curse beneath his breath.

"Is that a good thing?" She peeked up at him from under the fake lashes she'd added to the rest of her extravagant makeup. Though she never went to these extremes, her goal tonight was to be as distracting as possible. The bad guys thought she was misdirecting the casino workers, but hopefully she was going to keep the goons from catching on to their imminent demise instead.

"Fuck yes. You look gorgeous." He strode to her, pressing her against the railing when he kissed her, smudging some of her lipstick onto his own mouth.

She smiled as she wiped it off with her thumb.

"Thanks." She admired his suit—cut to hug his narrow waist and flare out to the broad expanse of his shoulders. He would make women drool as he strode past. "You look pretty sexy yourself."

He grinned at her. "You know, normally I would have been cool with this getup. Now, I'm actually bummed I can't show off my leg. It looks so kick-ass."

There wasn't anything he could have said to make her happier than that. Finally, he was becoming comfortable in his own skin. The customization was only the final step.

Lucas kept staring at her, so she shimmied to allow the reflections of the porch lights to twinkle in the dusk.

"Seriously, E. This color. *Damn.* It reminds me of your eyes when I'm buried inside you."

"You mean my crazy eyes?"

"Don't. Don't do that. They're part of you. One I adore." He took her and held her close. "In fact, I can't wait until we're home, safe, and I can see them again."

"So you're planning on me coming back here, even when we're through with this?" She couldn't believe she'd opened that can of worms right before they had to do this. *Focus!*

"You weren't?" He frowned.

Before she could tell him that she wanted to but hadn't been sure about her extended welcome, a piercing alarm cut through the evening, followed by a double blink of the porch lights.

"What was that?" She looked around as if there'd be a faulty wire jutting from the wall.

"A car. They just pulled through the gate."

"And you're sure they're not going to know who you are?" She didn't mean to question him. It was more that she was so afraid something terrible would happen to him because she'd agreed to this.

"They'll know Lucas Barnes lives here. I'm sure they'll also have uncovered my official military history. The completely ordinary one that's a cover for where I was all those years. They have no idea about who I really am, my codename or the agency I worked for. No one does. That's why I've hidden my leg from them. I don't want them to have the one clue that could link you and I and my undercover work. Right now they probably think you're with me since we're sort of neighbors, and I'm ex-military. It's entirely plausible that we could have bumped into each other—out jogging or at the local grocery store, whatever—become friends, and that you would have come to me when you needed help because I'm a soldier. Or used to be, anyway."

"Okay." She swallowed hard, her palms sweating instantly.

"You've got this, E." He came near to her and braced his palms on her shoulders, giving her a gentle shake. "All you've got to do is climb in the car, look beautiful—which isn't a problem—and get out at the casino. We'll head for the table games, hang out for an hour or two while the cops finish up their business, then bum a ride home off one of them. I mean, have them take you to your house if that's what you want. But you're welcome here. Always."

"Lucas—"

"You don't have to make your decision now. See how the night goes and you can choose then. It would be normal to be exhausted after the adrenaline wears off." He smiled as he presented an out for her. This time it didn't quite reach his eyes. She hadn't meant to inspire misgivings.

The opportunity to set things right vanished when headlights shone directly on her as a limo pulled into the gravel lot at the top of the driveway. In the spotlight, every tiny move was highlighted. And her dress probably blinded the driver.

Oops.

"Come on, E." He held out his arm to her as if they were really off to some luxurious formal event.

She couldn't help but grin as she threaded her hand through the gap between his elbow and his ribs. When they got to the stairs, he stepped down then acted as though their careful descent was due to her shoes or the restrictive skirt of her dress, instead of masking his slightly uneven gait.

In reality, she was wearing flats. Ellie had learned that lesson the hard way, thanks. And her dress was extremely comfortable since the entire thing stretched and flowed. Probably not an accident either, just in case she had to run or duck for cover.

Both of them were wearing GPS locators, microphones and cameras. She worried about the criminals busting them for that, but Lucas insisted they wouldn't know.

He led her to the waiting limo. Instead of handing her into it then rounding to his side of the car, he let the chauffeur take that role.

Earlier, Lucas had prepared her for that, saying there was no way he'd let her get in the car and shut the door before he was in there with her. Simply as a precaution. Apparently there was a lot of protocol he had developed for these kinds of situations in his military days. Things she never would have considered.

Ellie trusted him completely.

So when she met his eyes over the roof of the car and he gave a barely perceptible nod, she ducked down and got in simultaneously with him. They linked hands immediately, scooting next to each other on the bench seat. From her place in the middle, she could see there was another man in the passenger seat.

The only thing she could make out was the back of his head and he didn't speak. Not once.

For that matter, neither did the driver. The whole thing set off her creeptastic sensors.

She shivered. Lucas put his arm around her shoulder and tucked her against his side.

It took quite a while for them to wind their way down the mountainside via Lucas's intentionally absurd driveway. When they passed through the gate, it automatically swung closed behind them.

Ellie barely restrained herself from kneeling on the seat to look out the rear window at the place that had become her safe haven. She wanted nothing more than to be back on the other side of that wrought iron, in bed with the man beside her. Soon, she promised herself.

His hand squeezed hers twice in a row, the signal for *calm down*.

Ellie tried to relax, bringing her bouncing knee to a standstill.

It wasn't easy. Something about the interior of the car made her feel like she was trapped again. With no way out. Suddenly, opening the door to tuck and roll didn't seem like a bad plan.

Lucas rubbed his thumb over her knuckles in a steady pattern intended to soothe. It wasn't quite working.

She took deep breaths to keep from hyperventilating. They'd pulled onto the highway when she finally managed to get her heart rate under control.

Unfortunately, that was when Lucas's thigh tensed against hers.

"You're going the wrong direction," he said to the driver. "We need to be heading north, not south."

A grunt was the only response.

Ellie looked at Lucas, but he remained calm, at least on the outside. Where his hands rested in his lap, he did the most terrifying thing she could imagine.

He made a ring out of the fingers of one hand then poked his middle finger through it.

That was as loud as a scream of terror from him. She read his intent loud and clear. *FUCK!*

A rushing in Ellie's ears made her think she might be blacking out, scared shitless. But then she realized what it really was. Water over a dam. The limo sped across a bridge that led into the industrial sector of the city. Definitely not on the way to the casino.

Oh God, where were these guys taking them?

Lucas gripped her hand tight. He squeezed in the code they'd set up to mean *abort* followed by the one for *run.*

Very funny. Where was there to go now?

Ellie knew what he wanted. She prepared herself.

The instant her car door opened, she would fly out of it. How could she, though, and leave Lucas behind? How would she know he was right behind her?

She steeled herself to do what needed to be done. Survival mode descended on her like it had all those months ago when she'd forced herself to march out of Morselli's lair to freedom.

It was dangerous, because she was afraid of cracking, but she looked over at Lucas. His eyes flew everywhere as if cataloging their surroundings and trying to formulate a plan. Hell, that's probably exactly what he was doing. At the same time, she could see that he'd put one hand in his right pocket, where she knew he had a weapon of some sort. Not a gun, he couldn't have managed that, but she knew he had tricks up his sleeve.

She prayed they were enough to see them safely home.

Both of them. To his house in the mountains.

Why the fuck hadn't she told him that's what she wanted when she had the chance?

He'd been very stern that once they were in the car they shouldn't talk and she assumed that went doubly now.

It wasn't long before they rumbled over some railroad tracks and turned into a crumbling lot. At the far side of it was a run-down warehouse. Windows busted out, it seemed that grime was the only thing holding the structure together. It looked as if it had been abandoned for years.

Apparently, some parts of it were still in use. By these thugs.

They rolled to a stop and Lucas gave her the *run* signal again. She prepared herself, coiling her muscles to spring the moment the door was open.

However, she didn't expect the passenger to turn toward them at the last instant.

He smiled at her, staring directly into her eyes as he lifted out his knife and flipped it open. "It's good to see you again, Pretty. When I spotted you at Lucky's Bar and realized who would be joining us tonight, I could hardly believe it. You always were one to get in trouble, though."

Ellie clutched her chest. She thought she might be having a heart attack. The driver got out and opened her door, but her legs were frozen. It *couldn't* be him!

255

"RUN!" Lucas screamed at her. He opened his door and kicked it hard enough to take out one of the men who were standing nearby to assist in their intake to this nightmare facility. She knew whatever waited for them inside would not be good.

But the moment of hesitation had cost her their only chance.

The terror freezing her insides and sending her back in her mind to those horrible days kept her from escaping.

Lucas went immediately to Plan B. He snatched her right hand in his and tugged her out his door. Or would have if the driver hadn't grabbed ahold of her left hand. The men played tug of war with her, making her fear she was going to snap like a wishbone.

She hoped Lucas got the bigger piece of her, at least.

Ellie let some of the animal they'd turned her into last time surface. She leaned down and bit the man keeping her from Lucas. She felt her teeth break the surface of his skin before he instinctively jerked his hand back, freeing her.

Lucas nearly tumbled when the pressure released in an instant. It helped him yank her from the car. By the time she'd cleared the vehicle, he was already taking people out with some version of martial arts. He used the car door as a shield, limiting the angle of attack for the oncoming goons.

The world seemed to turn more slowly or something because she watched in sick fascination as he elbowed a guy in the face, dropping him like a sack of potatoes before reaching for the man's gun.

He had it out and aimed before she could even see through the blur.

Still, there were too many to be dissuaded by a single weapon. So as he fired the first shot, taking a man down, he also kicked out, slamming another in the chest. The impact knocked both the man he'd kicked and the person behind him, whom the sucker crashed into, back.

Ellie watched Lucas's flurry of motion, so well ingrained that it made him look like an ass-kicking machine. He kept her blocked from the encroaching danger, easily dispatching four men before one got a blow in to the side of Lucas's face. He spat blood and kept going—shooting, punching, kicking and otherwise impressing the hell out of her.

Or at least he would have if it were some generic demonstration filled with dummies and targets instead of living, breathing—mostly, though some had stopped—angry humans.

One of Lucas's kicks resulted in his pants getting stuck over his prosthesis.

With a weakness to aim for, the thugs grew more vicious. One approached carrying a baseball bat. He snuck up from behind the car, out of Lucas's field of vision.

"Look out!" she screamed, but it was too late.

The man swung right for Lucas's knee on his residual limb.

He buckled.

It took a second well-placed strike to take him down.

Even then, he fought from the ground. He fired his gun until it ran out of ammo. Then he threw it at the next man who tried to attack, hitting him square between the eyes with a sickening *thud*.

Despite his best efforts, Lucas had to admit they were outnumbered. No man was able to win in odds of twenty or better to one.

When people started to beat on him, Ellie threw herself into the fray. No way would she stand by while they maimed him—or worse.

Unfortunately, if he wasn't able to take them on, she had no chance. Still, she would go down swinging. It only took a minute for her to be subdued, squashed to the chest of a man she would know anywhere. His vile odor, like black licorice and cheap alcohol, washed over her, making her want to retch.

Lucas groaned and got to his hands and knees, crawling toward her.

Someone kneed him in the face, but he kept charging. It was the most determined and completely impossible thing she'd ever witnessed.

"Let him go," she begged her old guard. "Do whatever you want with me, but let him go."

"I'm gonna do whatever I want with you anyway, Pretty. Look how you're all dressed up for me too." He sniffed her hair, making her shudder.

"No!" Lucas roared, somehow finding the strength to surge to his feet once more.

It didn't matter.

The guard passed Ellie to the limo driver, who got blood all over her gown. He was rough as he snarled in response to the injury she'd inflicted. They would make her pay for that. She knew it. And still she fought.

Pointlessly.

She watched in horror as the guard took out his knife and stabbed Lucas. He dodged at the last second, taking the blade to his upper arm instead of his chest.

Still, he howled, making everything inside Ellie shrivel and die.

This couldn't happen.

Not to him. Not to her. Not again.

More reinforcements spewed from the warehouse like ants on a dropped piece of candy. Blood soaked the ripped sleeve of Lucas's suit. When he couldn't stay upright any longer, they let him drop in the dirt.

Ellie sobbed.

"You like this piece of shit?" The guard kicked Lucas hard in the ribs for effect.

He didn't grunt or move except from the force of the blow.

"Oh God!" she screamed.

Was he dead?

"Say goodbye, Pretty. Better hurry before he's gone."

The guard leaned down and said something to Lucas, low enough that she couldn't hear. It must have been something horrible, though, because he twitched, trying to get up again.

The guard punched him in the jaw. Lucas's entire body went limp. Out cold.

Please let him only be unconscious.

Stay down, Lucas, she begged in her mind. *Stay down.*

And then he didn't have a choice. The guard jammed his thumb on the proximal lock of Lucas's prosthesis and yanked it off. He put it under his arm and said, "A trophy for my collection. Saves me from cutting out his eyes."

He admired the drawing Ellie had done for a moment before turning to the limo driver and ordering, "Leave him here to bleed out. It should take a good, long while. Be very painful. Make sure he suffers."

With that, he snatched Ellie and dragged her kicking and screaming toward the warehouse.

She didn't care what he subjected her to from then on. He'd already done the most painful thing possible. Sobbing, she watched Lucas's still body until he was out of sight. Lost to her.

"You're in for a treat, boys. This one's a sex fiend. The rougher you are, the better she likes it." He grinned at her. "Isn't that right, Pretty?"

"Fuck you!" she snarled.

"Yes, you will. We have a lot of time to make up for."

CHAPTER SIXTEEN

Lucas almost pitied the dumb fuck who'd left him there less wounded than he appeared. When he'd seen the sheer number of enemies approaching, he knew he needed a different tactic if he was going to get Ellie out of here unharmed.

Hopefully he wasn't too late for that.

Her screams had blistered his soul.

Leaving her in the hands of the man who starred in her nightmares was one of the hardest decisions he'd ever had to make. It was only temporary.

Very *temporary,* he promised them both silently.

The Men in Blue had to be close. He and Ellie were wearing enough tracking gear to be found from halfway across the galaxy, after all. But even the seven or eight minutes it might take for the guys to devise and execute an infiltration strategy might be more than Ellie had.

She would fight that bastard.

Lucas wouldn't love her quite so much if it weren't in her to rage, as he knew she would.

And if they got out of this shitstorm in one piece, relatively, he planned to make sure she knew how he felt.

He lay still, tracking the boot clomps of the men moving indoors, with the exception of the poor sucker assigned to Lucas-watch. When they'd disappeared inside the warehouse, the steel doors clanging shut behind them, he still refused to budge.

Lucas waited as patiently as he could, concentrating on the pain in his shoulder from the gash there, to keep alert and grounded while appearing anything but that.

It was only thirty seconds or so before the guy came near, clearly half-assing his responsibilities. He used the toe of his shoe to nudge Lucas's stump.

When there was no response, he spun away.

"Fucking gimp—who would've guessed?" he mumbled to himself.

Just for that, Lucas added some extra power to his grip when he lunged upward and put his uncut arm around the fucker's neck. He didn't need fancy weapons to dispatch the man. He just needed his superior strength and determination to finish the job.

They fell to the ground, rolling around as the man thrashed, gurgled, then finally went limp.

To make sure there was no chance he made the same mistake as his captors, Lucas snapped the man's neck. He took the guy's gun, jammed it in his waistband then stood, balancing on his one foot.

It was kind of a long way to the warehouse from where they'd left him, but what choice did he have but to hop or crawl?

Well, there *was* the car.

Lucas peeked in the limo. Keys still in the ignition.

Grinning, he got in and drove himself right up to these assholes' front door, using his left foot to operate the gas and brakes for his short journey. He surveyed the outside of the building. No hint of cameras. Perfect.

Without much to go on but absolute desperation, he carefully opened a side door to the warehouse and peeked around. Loading docks led to a large, empty cement floor. Way down at the other end, there was an enormous window overlooking what once was probably a factory or logistics operation. A nasty orange light glowed from the area where the crooks probably had their headquarters.

Nearby was a shabby office. He hopped into it and searched for any tools he could appropriate.

A rolling desk chair? He could work with that.

Lucas plopped into it, put his back to the illuminated sector of the warehouse and began to push himself in that direction. On the smooth surface, it was an extremely effective mode of transportation. Until he heard a noise off to his right.

Shit, some dudes were still hanging around up here. And hiding wasn't even an option as he scooted across the wide-open area. He was going to have to cowboy this thing. His least favorite way of operating. He much preferred stealth and intelligent attacks.

It wasn't in the cards today.

Sure enough, they spotted him soon after he noticed them. Concrete flew as their bullets made divots in the floor too close to him for comfort.

Lucas used the arm of the chair to brace his elbow and steadied the gun as best he could, given his injured arm, which was growing numb. Thankfully, he'd done so much range work that this was nothing.

He didn't pause his trajectory across the factory, rolling and shooting as he went.

The men fell one by one, a single bullet for each.

Never say he didn't do his homework.

He would pay for this later. Killing was one of the things he was not sad to leave behind when he had been forced to retire, but he would do anything for Ellie and these scumbags had brought it on themselves. If there were any other way, he would have taken it. There simply wasn't.

The back of his chair bumped into the wall sooner than he would have thought. He'd made quick work of that distance. Ellie would have been proud to see him doing things his way and not giving a fuck about it.

No, she *would be*, when he told her about it later.

He had a moment of doubt when he stood from the chair, rising just enough to peek over the edge of the window, which started at about hip height. The firefight above had sent another wave of attackers in his direction, leaving their forces divided. In fact, only two guys had stayed behind with the guard who had Ellie.

Sirens in the distance told him the Men in Blue were closing in. Would that evil fucker, who even now held his gleaming knife to Ellie's throat, let her live if he knew his game was up?

Lucas didn't think so.

His best chance was to act. Right then.

He peered around and saw a pulley on the other side of the glass. It was hooked to the wall, probably used to raise and lower things to the level below. He had to hope his mental math was right and that the rope was just short enough to stay suspended when fully extended.

Otherwise, this was going to be a rough landing.

He gauged the distance, fairly sure he could reach it if he got a good enough push off the ledge.

But he didn't have time to be 100 percent sure as boots clomped up the metal stairs to his right. Any moment they were going to burst through.

Lucas roared, releasing a battle cry. He shot out the window, which shattered into a billion pieces, raining glass shards onto the level below like some kind of extreme waterfall. He didn't stop to be impressed with his handiwork.

Instead, he climbed onto the busted-out window frame, stood on his good leg, bent his knee and swung his arms once...twice...

"Lucas, no!" Ellie screamed from below.

He wasn't going to stop now.

On the third swing he had enough momentum— he hoped. Recalling what Ellie had told him about hope and how she had used it to stay alive, he figured that was the best he could do given the situation. He leapt, shoving off hard with his foot.

The rope flew toward him, and for a moment he thought he might have overshot it. Then it was in his hands and the impact of his full weight broke it loose from its hook in the wall.

His guts lifted up to flop around somewhere in the vicinity of his throat as he rode the pulley in an arc down to the second level like some insane version of a bungee jump crossed with a zip line. And when he skimmed the floor below, he dropped off, tucked and rolled.

Good thing too since his reception wasn't very warm with the two henchmen below.

His inertia took him straight toward one, bowling him over. Lucas kept his momentum going, landing on top of the stunned man. He took advantage of that hesitation to punch the man in the face a few times until he could wrestle the guy's gun away.

Seeing as the limo driver's had fallen out of Lucas's pants somewhere around the time he did his Tarzan routine, he was grateful to be armed again. Lucas shot the man between the eyes then came to his knees, blowing away the second gunman before the bewildered guy had even processed what happened.

That only left Ellie and her guard.

Lucas edged closer to them on his knees.

"I can see why you like this freak." The guard laughed as if they were best friends. "He's as nuts as you are, Pretty. Too bad he's still not going to be able to save you."

Ellie gasped when the guard pricked her neck, drawing blood.

"Put the gun down or I'll slice her open." The guard grinned. "You don't know how many times I dreamed about that."

The guard wasn't alone. He was the bastard who haunted Ellie. Lucas had known their limo passenger was her old guard the instant he'd called her Pretty. And he wanted to make the man pay.

But the knifepoint was sinking into her a sliver deeper with every instant.

So he tossed the gun away.

"This is the OSPD," someone—Mason, it sounded like—blared through a bullhorn. The commotion from the upper level increased as the cops rounded up the majority of their opponents.

The guard snarled. He glanced up to the first level as if he could see the raiding cops.

Lucas couldn't believe what happened next. He wasn't prepared when Ellie took her chance. She picked up her foot and kicked blindly between the guard's legs, catching him directly in the balls with her heel. *Thatta girl!*

The guy went down. His knife skittered away.

Ellie dove for it and the guard chased her.

Lucas looked around, but the only thing within easy reach was his prosthesis, which the guard had displayed beside where he was holding Ellie, presumably to upset her. That would do. Carbon fiber was strong shit.

He rose to his good foot, snatched the socket and bashed the guard over the head with it, imagining the birds Ellie had drawn on it were pecking him to death as he made a second impact on the man's skull.

It was enough to slow him down but not stop him entirely.

At least it diverted the guard from Ellie and the knife. He changed directions, taking Lucas down by swiping his leg out from beneath him.

They grappled with each other. Wrestling. Rolling over and over.

Ellie screamed for help, begging for the Men in Blue to make it to them in time.

Lucas didn't think there was a chance of that. They were on their own.

The guard landed a particularly painful jab directly to Lucas's gashed arm. It went completely numb and hung by his side. It probably would have recovered fairly quickly, but there simply wasn't time.

The guy scrambled to his feet then hauled Lucas up, with his hands around Lucas's neck.

Lucas couldn't breathe and the furious thrashing he did was making darkness encroach on the fringes of his vision pretty damn quickly.

If he was going to die like this, he wanted to see Ellie one last time.

When he peeked over at her, she was staring at something on the floor. Her fist unclenched and she leaned forward to take it.

Ellie picked up the guard's knife—likely the one that he had used to torture her so often in Morselli's dungeon—and while Lucas watched, with huge eyes she charged, stopping only when she'd plunged it into the man's neck from behind and slightly to the side, just enough to miss his spine. The tip of the blade emerged clean on the other side, nearly severing his head in the process.

Blood gushed from the guard and he gurgled out his final breaths. His hands fell from around Lucas's neck, allowing him to suck in huge lungfuls of air. At the same time the guard collapsed, Lucas set his prosthesis down, jammed his leg in the socket and ratcheted the proximal lock tight before jogging to his discarded gun.

Even Lucas wasn't cruel enough to leave someone to suffer like that.

He returned, putting the gun point-blank against the man's temple.

The guard surrendered a wet whisper. "Please."

"Close your eyes, E," Lucas ordered.

She fell to the floor and put her hands over her face.

He pulled the trigger.

When the body quit flopping, Lucas toppled over then dragged himself to Ellie with his unhurt elbow. He wrapped her in his arms and held her tight, cocooning her in whatever comfort he could muster.

He shouldn't have been surprised when she looked after him before herself.

She tugged on his tie, loosening the knot then using the silk to put pressure on his wound. If he'd expected her to unravel into hysterics, he would have been mistaken.

They sat there, propping each other up, until Matt and Clint burst through the stairwell door, guns drawn. When they took in the human wreckage around them and the two survivors sitting relatively calmly at the center of it, Matt cursed.

"I always knew you were a badass, Lucas," Clint said in awe. "But...*damn*."

"Thank God you two are okay." Matt used his radio to alert the team to their status. "We had no idea that guy was part of this organization."

"I don't care," Lucas practically growled. "It's over now. You hear me? She's done. For good. This will *never* happen again."

"Roger that." Matt put his hand on Lucas's shoulder.

Thirty seconds later, paramedics hit the scene in response to Clint's call for help. They began fussing over Lucas's arm and Ellie's shock, wrapping her in a warm blanket. Still she plastered herself against Lucas and he was happy to have her there.

"Lucas?"

"Yeah, E?" he asked, his lips set in a flat line.

"I decided," she said, sounding drained.

"What's that?"

"When we go home, I want to go with you. To yours."

Lucas couldn't help it. With all the lights and noise and blood and gore, he laughed, remembering that he'd told her to wait and see how the night went before committing to their future.

Even in the darkest of times, she brightened his world.

CHAPTER SEVENTEEN

Two days later

I t took a while for Ellie to get her wish. Turned out they had to file a zillion reports, do paperwork out the ass and then talk to a bunch of doctors. Both the physical kind, so Lucas could get stitched up, and psychologists, who helped her deal with her PTSD following the incident.

They'd spent the first night in the hospital under observation.

No one had bothered suggesting that they be kept in separate rooms. Hell, different beds were even out of the question.

Lucas had stayed with her the entire time, and she had returned the favor. She'd listened to him talk about the burden of taking a life and wondered again at how much he'd sacrificed for her.

By the time they made it to his house late the next day, they then endured a parade of well-intentioned visitors—Ryan first, of course, then the rest of their friends—and officials who dropped by to ask questions, snap pictures, record statements or even just to see if they were okay.

After nearly two full days had passed, Ellie and Lucas respectfully asked for some breathing room.

Finally, *finally*, they were alone.

Ellie had taken a shower and pulled one of Lucas's faded T-shirts over her head. She toweled off her hair as she wandered downstairs then into the sunroom, where he was lying on one of the couches, staring at the painting she'd started before they'd left the house on the night of the thwarted heist.

"How are you doing?" she asked quietly.

"Okay." He patted the space beside him and she accepted the invitation without question, stretching out next to him with her head on his chest and their legs entwined.

Lucas no longer flinched when she touched his residual limb.

"You sound about as talked out as I am." She smiled softly as she traced the ridges of his muscles with the tip of her finger. It distracted her from the sight of the fat bandage wrapped around his upper arm. The terror she'd felt when she thought she'd lost him... She shivered.

"Everything's all right now, E," he promised, completely in sync with her.

"But it almost wasn't." She had tried not to think about it but, honestly, she couldn't get her mind off what might have been. How unfair it would have been. "I just found you, Lucas. I don't want to lose you."

"Not gonna happen." He rubbed her shoulder then down her back. The motion, intended to be soothing, did something entirely different to her instead.

Something about their near miss made her need to reconnect with him on a carnal level.

Ellie hummed and rocked against him.

A thought occurred to her and she shared it without reservation. He wouldn't judge her. "You know, this is the longest I've gone without an orgasm since I got free from Morselli and the Scientist."

272

"Shit, E. With the chaos, I didn't even think about that. You should have told me what you needed." His hand wandered to her ass and squeezed. She liked the possessive flair to his touch. She wanted to belong to him. In all ways.

"Honestly, it didn't occur to me. And even now it feels kind of different. I want you, Lucas. But...it's more like because *I just do* than because I need relief."

"I noticed you didn't have any nightmares last night either." He tipped her chin up so he could stare into her eyes.

"I feel like, maybe, they might start to fade, now that I know the guard isn't out there anymore. And because he got what he deserved." She swallowed hard. "I'm sorry if that makes me a horrible person."

"It makes you honest." He sat up and hauled her onto his lap.

Ellie straddled him, laying her face on his chest, her forehead touching his neck. She could see his pulse pounding there and it made her want to celebrate. They were still alive. Survivors.

"Lucas, I need you," she whispered.

"Thank God. I didn't want to pressure you after everything, but I'm dying for you, E." He stripped the shirt over her head and dropped it on the couch beside them. "For some confirmation that we're both still here, and that we're in this together. Long term."

"You can't get rid of me now," she confirmed.

Putting her hands on his cheeks, she cupped his face as they kissed. This time their interaction was slow and gentle, long and lingering.

As if they both realized they had all the time in the world together.

Ellie knew nothing was powerful enough to separate them now.

She lifted up on her knees, giving him room to slide his athletic shorts down and off his legs. He wasn't wearing his prosthesis since it tended to tear up the furniture, though it was nearby. It had come through their ordeal unscathed, and the irony of her bird design having helped to free them wasn't lost on her.

"What's that smile for?" Lucas asked.

"I'm not scared anymore." And it was true. Despite any additional trauma they'd endured, she'd quit looking over her shoulder so much. "Everyone kept telling me how strong I was to have survived what I went through, but now...with you...I actually feel like I am. We can make it through anything, Lucas, as long as we stick together."

"I like the way you think." He buried his fingers in her hair and let her grind her bare pussy over his hard shaft, which rested against his abs.

For the first time with him, she didn't feel frantic. Something had shifted in her to sublime and she hoped he noticed it too.

Lucas reached between them and tipped his cock up. "Ride me, E. Nice and slow, huh?"

"Yes." That was exactly what she craved.

So she aligned their bodies then sank onto him, letting gravity do the work for her. After sliding down his entire length, she sighed, holding him entirely within her.

Only when they began to kiss, their mouths savoring more than devouring, did she allow herself to move in time to the rhythm they set. They maintained that pace for longer than she could imagine, watching each other enjoy being connected so tightly.

But, eventually, even Lucas couldn't hold out. His abs began to tighten beneath her, giving her something to stroke her clit on as she swung her hips over him.

"E, I want to try something," he groaned.

"I hope you have lots of lube if you're planning on"—she made their ridiculous sign for fucking—"me in the ass right now. I'm relaxed, but..."

Despite his obvious intense arousal, he laughed. Though it kind of sounded like a launt—a mix between a laugh and a grunt. "Not that. Though for how often you bring it up, maybe that will be fun for next time."

Ellie kissed him. "Whatever you want. I'm sure you'll make anything you do to me pleasurable for us both. I trust you."

"Good. Because I'm about to come in you."

"Yes." She loved feeling his liquid heat inside her.

"But then I'm going to keep fucking you," he proclaimed.

"What?" She blinked a few times, trying to make sense of his words despite the Sex Offender-induced lust that hazed her logic.

"You've noticed it too. Right?" he asked, though he didn't stop thrusting up into her. Neither did she pause the rocking action of her hips in his lap. "That when I come in or on you, it fades. The SO effect."

"I noticed." She didn't give a shit right now, though. All she wanted was to come with him. Once was plenty when it was a solid twelve out of ten on the fuck-of-a-lifetime scale.

"Well, this time I want to see what it's like to make love to you. The regular you, not the enhanced you, which I also adore, by the way. Please don't think I have a problem with that."

She understood perfectly. "You want to see that, drug or no drug, I still want you beyond reasoning?"

275

"Yeah." The idea alone must have been blissful to him. He closed his eyes and said, "Just thinking about it is going to make me come, E."

"Go ahead."

The tempo of her riding increased, using her channel to lure him into giving them both what they wanted. She used her muscles to squeeze him, hold him and grant him ultimate pleasure while she kissed him reverently and brushed his hair off his forehead with every scrap of tenderness she could muster.

Then she whispered in his ear, "I want to feel you flooding my pussy, Lucas. Come on; do it. Give me your come."

"Fuck!" He stared directly into her eyes as he gave himself permission to do as she'd asked. He surrendered to his release and pumped her full of his semen.

Like ice on a sprained ankle, it soothed her. Taking away the fiery edge of her passion.

And though she'd been too focused on him to climax simultaneously, her need receded. It didn't hurt when he paused to resituate them. Or at least that's what she thought he was doing.

So she flung her arms around him and squeaked when he tipped them forward and brought her to the floor instead.

Something crinkled beneath her. She realized he'd spread her out on the tarp she used beneath her easel to make sure she didn't ruin the carpet.

"How do you feel?"

"So far, so good," she assured him. "Other than kind of frustrated. The normal sort. I was close, Lucas."

He chuckled at that, a completely self-satisfied, male sort of sound that had her toes curling. "I'm getting to that, E. But, first, I thought I'd make a little art of my own. I need a couple minutes to recover, you know."

"I thought you were a superstud. Isn't that one of the skills they teach you in spy school? Like James Bond 101 or something?" She loved teasing him.

"Do you think it's smart to sass me when you want to come and I have this?" He stuck his tongue out at her and pointed to it.

"Mercy," she said then laughed.

"Oh no, not yet." He grinned up at her. "Your eyes are so lovely right now. Bright like the sky. I'm sure I'm not going to hurt you if I take my time here."

"You jerk!" She wasn't really upset and he knew it.

In fact, it sounded sweet to be able to lie back and enjoy the ecstasy he gave her, without having to rush to an orgasm or a dozen just to keep her system in check. Though, honestly, that could be fun too, this time she wanted something different.

Expecting his mouth to seal over her pussy and for him to use his very talented mouth to massage her, she let her eyes drift closed. So she was surprised when something cool and squishy draped across her left breast.

Ellie levered up onto her elbows. She looked at what he was doing—painting her, in a way. Another squirt of acrylic from one of the tubes nearby decorated her collarbone. Various hues of blue and green splattered across her body as he dipped his fingers in the mess he'd made and began to use it to adorn her skin.

"What are you doing?" She couldn't help but crack up. "Have you lost your mind?"

"I think you're a masterpiece, and you should look like one." He shrugged. "Besides, it seemed like it would feel interesting."

She could vouch for that.

His fingers glided all over her, leaving a dab on the tip of one nipple before wandering off to draw a heart around her belly button.

As his hands twisted and played in the goop, he settled in between her legs and nudged her thighs wider to accommodate his broad shoulders. He ate her with the same enthusiasm he showed for his newfound artistic skills.

His lazy swipes drew out her pleasure and she appreciated every extended moment, since she was so used to rushing for the summit. Eventually, though, he proved too good.

And this time, when she rose toward orgasm, he made sure that he didn't stop short.

It was almost odd for her to feel the rush of climax without the feral urging from Sex Offender for her to take more. If he had stopped there, she would have been fulfilled.

But he didn't.

Lucas rose above her. He winced. "E, will you give me a hand here?"

He held his palms out to her, showing her the streaks and blended colors he'd dyed himself with as he embellished her. Glad to help, she reached between them, took his cock in hand and guided him to her body, where he belonged.

They moaned together as he slid home. And when he leaned forward and applied his torso to hers, the paint suddenly seemed genius. It enhanced the slide of their bodies, swirling the colors he'd applied earlier.

She loved the vibrancy he brought to her life. In every aspect.

This was no different.

Ellie hugged him to her in every way she knew how. Her legs locked around him, her hands scratching gently up and down his back and her pussy clenching on his cock as he thrust into her, slightly less evenly as he began to really enjoy himself.

"Will you let me see you come, Ellie? The real you?" he practically begged. "Show me that you love this as much as I do."

Well, that was an easy request to honor.

Ellie left herself open to him all the way to her soul. She hoped he could read the absolute rapture in her eyes. This was special. Unique. Something only they could elicit from the other. It wouldn't matter if she'd never taken Sex Offender.

They would spark brightly every time they collided like this.

Instead of ramping up his pistoning, Lucas slowed, torturing them both with long, languid glides that were no less pleasurable for being intimate and thorough, instead of frenzied. Both were amazing in different ways.

This, she knew, was a part of their healing. There was nothing to hide behind when they were together like this.

Ellie felt her toes curl, and her spine arched.

"Lucas!" she cried out.

"I'm with you, E," he promised. "Let's let go together."

"Ready?" she asked.

He grunted as he pushed in as deep as possible before retreating in that maddeningly steady cadence.

"I've been waiting for this my whole life. I just didn't believe it was possible."

"With you, anything is possible." She looked up at him. The next time he plowed into her fully, she was gone. Flying. With him by her side.

They came together, calling each other's names.

It was spectacular even if it didn't have that extra edge she'd learned to love too. Either way was amazing, as long as she got to share it with him.

They stayed like that, locked together, until his flesh softened and he slipped from her, allowing a trickle of his come to escape along with his retreating cock.

Lucas lifted up high enough to look at their bodies, smeared in his favorite colors of the rainbow. He took one of her canvases from where it leaned against the easel leg and pressed it to her chest and belly. Her paint-splattered skin made an interesting impression.

Satisfied with the results, he collected another blank and smooshed it against his torso. The result was two mirrored modern art paintings. Maybe it was only because she knew how he'd made them, but she actually thought they were kind of brilliant.

They could capture her attention for hours.

"Hey, E?"

"Mmm." She couldn't manage more than that.

"Remember when you told me I should ask you to be my girlfriend?"

"I think I was joking at the time, but yes."

"What if I ask you to move in with me instead?" he wondered. "Permanently. I love you, Ellie. I want to be your partner and share my life with you. You're the only one who gets me."

"Lucas..."

"Hmm?"

"You haven't asked yet." She stared up at him, smiling like crazy as her fingers brushed his cheek.

"Ellie, will you make my house our home?"

"Absolutely. Because I love you too. And I always will. We may have a lot of healing left to do, but I know our chances of erasing these scars are better if we work on it together." She leaned up to kiss him gently. "I do have one condition, though." Ellie winked at him.

He laughed then said, "I'll give you anything in my power, E."

"I want to hang these paintings in the living room." She pointed at the oddly pleasing mixture of colors, textures and bold splatters that was the visual representation of their sexual perfection.

Lucas high-fived her. "Deal."

Then he kissed the shit out of her and they churned out a whole series of paintings. Enough for a lascivious gallery show if they wanted one. They could probably make millions with them. At least in her eyes, they were beautiful in their natural imperfection.

Just like Lucas.

Maybe even just like her.

EPILOGUE

Ryan sat on a wicker love seat in Lucas's sunroom. Lucas and Ellie's, he corrected himself mentally, since his sister had taken up permanent residence there about a month and a half ago. Bathed in sunlight, she'd just flashed her engagement ring, practically blinding him and the rest of their friends. The brilliant oval diamond was surrounded by a halo of blue and green stones that somehow suited her perfectly.

He was happy the furniture in this room was a tad undersized because that meant that Ben and Shari, who sandwiched him, had to sit extra close. Having them nearby made it easier to focus on how thrilled he was for his sister—who'd finally found the happiness she deserved, with a man who cherished her—instead of wondering what purpose he had in life now that she was well and truly out on her own.

As much as the gathering of Men in Blue, their spouses, girlfriends, boyfriends, kids and friends oohed and aahed over her bling, they totally lost their shit when Lucas and Ellie turned around, lifted the backs of their shirts to their necks and revealed their coordinating tattoos. They were portraits...sort of.

Ellie had designed them. Ryan recognized her style of drawing immediately, even translated onto skin. Hers was a bust in the likeness of Lucas. It had been shattered. Pieces scattered on the ground around it. But a female hand, one sporting his sister's engagement ring, held a bottle of glue, the other one picked up the shards, cementing the bust back together. In the lower corner there was even a little foot that looked like it had broken off the statue.

On the bottle, where the infamous cow would normally be, was a stunning miniature of Ellie. She was Lucas's brand of glue.

Lucas's tattoo was the same but opposite. It was Ellie's shattered bust he held together.

Ah, fuck.

Ryan tried to hide his sniffle by turning his head. Except Ben was staring right back at him. The guy reached out, like he might hug Ry, but he froze with his hand awkwardly in the air between them. This was not the time for them to hash stuff out. Ben was straight. Or had been before their stint in Morselli's dungeon. Since then...well, the guy had been *confused*...and Ryan was tired of his heart getting stomped on when Ben's fickle dick changed its mind.

Concentrating on Ellie once more, Ryan pushed thoughts of his disastrous relationship with Ben from his mind. His sister was saying something as she gestured to her art supplies. Not about the tattoos. No, she'd moved on to even more good news.

"I really can't believe it." She beamed at Lucas. "The drawing I did on his prosthesis was just...for us...something I enjoyed doing. I didn't even know if he'd really like it."

"Are you kidding?" Lucas nuzzled the side of her face and then kissed her with enough heat and promise to make Ryan uncomfortable.

"Hey now, save that for when I'm gone," he teased, sort of.

284

Lucas grinned then saluted him. "So anyway, I realized there were probably a lot of people out there like me who had standard beige sockets. That's what you get at places like the VA or if you have older equipment or no insurance."

Ellie winced.

So Lucas kept explaining, "I posted a picture of the custom artwork she created. It's totally badass, right?"

Julie hopped off Ben's lap to go check it out when Lucas waved to it, beneath his shorts. It was still odd getting used to seeing him in them again. Not because of his prosthesis, but because he'd insisted on pants only in public for so long after his accident.

Ryan knew Ellie was responsible for some, if not most, of his desensitization about that.

Julie looked up close, trailing her fingers around the swirls of black-outlined colors. The whole thing looked a lot like the sleeves of ink Lucas wore more permanently. It really did make his leg look like part of him—his style, his way—instead of some generic attachment.

"You're really good at drawing, Aunt Ellie." Julie asked, "Will you teach me how to make a doggie later?"

"Sure." Ellie scooped Julie up and hugged her tight.

When she wriggled, Ellie set her down and Julie skipped over to Lily and JRad, who were listening intently, as were the rest of their friends.

"So what happened then?" Razor wanted to know.

"Oh, well"—Ellie tried not to grin, but failed miserably—"by the end of the day, we had over a hundred requests placed from people asking to hire me for custom work. I'm booked solid for the rest of the year. We're looking at doing a couple dozen generic designs that can be sort of heat wrapped over a socket, like those sleeves you put on Easter eggs. Those will be really affordable and removable. Plus, people who don't want to wait a long time for me to be free or who want something in the interim can get it."

"And when JRad built her a website and we mentioned that we were donating a portion of the proceeds to survivor charities, those places started promoting us in return." Lucas beamed at his future wife. "It's blowing up. It's going to be a big freaking deal."

Jambrea broke out of Matt's lap to hug her friends. "I'm so proud of you two."

Ryan couldn't believe it. He laughed at how much good fortune his sister was finally raking in. She deserved every bit of it and more, as far as he was concerned. Hell, she hadn't even heard their contribution yet. The whole reason they'd called this impromptu party in the first place.

"Well, since you're about to be rolling in it and doing something you love while helping others too, I suppose you don't need these big, fat reward checks we came to deliver." Mason pulled them from his pocket.

"What?" Lucas looked stunned, something that didn't happen very often.

"Did you see his face?" Tyler asked before he and Clint fist-bumped each other.

Ellie clung to her man, supporting him even as she drew strength from him. "Are you joking?"

"No, ma'am. We're cops. Very serious officers of the law who definitely do not jest." Razor couldn't even finish that whole sentence without cracking himself up.

JRad, closest to the couple, nudged them. "Go ahead, take them. You earned them."

When Lucas accepted his paper and read it, his eyes widened even farther. "That's a lot of zeroes."

Ellie squeaked when she looked at hers. "Holy shit!"

"S-h-i-t is a bad word, Aunt Ellie." Julie wagged her finger at them. "You gotta watch your mouth in front of baby Ezra."

Ryan laughed, seeing as that sounded an awful lot like what he and Shari were always telling Ben.

Mason kept going despite the adorable interruption. "Yeah, well. It turns out that the felons you busted were wanted for several other jobs. When we raided their headquarters, we found about three dozen missing artifacts, paintings and a crap ton of stolen money. There were several rewards posted for the return of those items."

Lacey added to her husband's explanation, "Plus, the casino kicked in your original winnings and a hefty sum for keeping their name out of the papers when they're first getting started. Reports of your attack would have been very bad press for them. Besides, you helped them pin down the mole, the teller, who was making the heist possible."

"Whoa," Ellie said as she looked from her check to Lucas and then back.

"I guess we know where we're going to get our start-up capital." He grinned. "If you handle the artwork, I'll head up production on the stock designs like we talked about. The business end of things too."

"Are you sure you want to live with me *and* work with me?" Ellie asked.

Everyone in the room groaned. Was that girl blind?

"Positive," Lucas confirmed.

"Then I guess it's time to bust out this champagne I brought." Izzy hoisted a bottle over her head. "Though I'm thinking we could have used a case or two more, with all this good news."

Jambrea grinned at her friend, then at her guys. They nodded and squeezed her hands. "I'll help you out, Iz. None for me."

"What? Don't be silly. You love—" Izzy broke off as she put her hands over her mouth then let out an ear-piercing squeal.

Matt and Clint sat there with dopey grins on their faces as they stared at their woman, whose hand had drifted to her still-flat belly.

"Seriously?" Lacey shrieked as she started bouncing up and down then trotted over to Jambrea. Soon Shari, Izzy, Lily and Ellie were there too, fused into one giant, girly group hug.

"What's happening?" Julie looked mildly alarmed at the chaos around them.

Ben picked her up and set her on his knee. "Aunt Jambi is going to be a mommy."

"Really? She's going to have a girl, right?" And like that she was off again, shoving her way to Jambrea.

"Me and your daughter can be best friends, Aunt Jambi. She's going to like purple and we'll share a pony. We can braid each other's hair. And I think Rachel is a pretty name, don't you?"

Ben shot Ryan a horrified look. "Where does she come up with this stuff?"

The best part of all, though, was when Matt caught the trail of Julie's rambling, then paled.

"Wait, what? A girl?" He shook his head as if he hadn't considered the idea. "No, no. Razor got a boy. I can handle that."

Baby Ezra clapped his hands as if he seconded the idea.

"Means it's time for a girl next." Razor grinned.

Clint, Tyler, Mason, JRad, Ben, Ryan and Lucas all cracked up as their friend squirmed uncomfortably at the thought.

"Go ahead and laugh." Matt glared at them. "I'll remember this when it's your turns."

Wouldn't that be nice? Now all Ryan needed was for a little of that luck to rub off on him.

Maybe Shari and Ben too.

Yeah, right.

As if she could read his thoughts, Shari looked over at him. She smiled softly before taking in Ben too. Which is precisely when Ben got up and left the room.

Fucking idiot.

When Shari hugged Ryan, he wondered if he was being equally as stupid. Maybe it was time he took things more seriously with her. She, at least, seemed to care for him.

Impulsively, he leaned over and kissed her cheek.

She didn't smack him, which was a start.

Instead, she looked up at him with questions in her eyes that he planned to answer as soon as he could get her alone.

WHAT HAPPENS TO BEN, RYAN, AND SHARI?

BOUND for YOU

MEN IN BLUE

JAYNE RYLON

Ben has lived through hell. He only survived captivity and torture by the brutes who'd been attempting to develop Sex Offender, a potent aphrodisiac used as a date rape drug, because of the guy he met—and fell in lust with—in the drug lord's dungeons.

Ryan became Ben's roommate after they escaped. His nearness is constantly tempting Ben to force Ryan to submit to his dark desires. Disgusted by how similar that makes him to their captors, he's managed to hold off so far. How long can he keep his cravings for Ryan's sexy body at bay?

On top of that, they both seem to be falling for the same woman. If Ben has reservations about unleashing his sexual appetites on Ryan then that goes double for Shari, who is entirely too sweet and inexperienced for either of them. Or so Ben thinks.

When Shari teams up with Ryan to change Ben's mind, it seems like Ben might consider turning their three-way fling into something serious. Until a threat to Ben's niece reminds them that it's not always possible to keep those you love safe. After losing his sister in the Sex Offender scandal, Ben might never be ready to take that risk again.

None of them could have realized they were bound for something greater than a traditional partner in life, but Shari and Ryan are sure the three of them will benefit from the love of not one, but two, strong, giving soul mates who can help them leave the darkness of their past behind.

Will they be able to convince Ben that living fully is better than living cautiously?

AN EXCERPT FROM BOUND FOR

YOU, MEN IN BLUE, BOOK 6

Clank. Huff. Clank. Huff.

Ryan admitted it. The sound of his roommate working out in the spare bedroom across the hall acted like the world's most potent aphrodisiac on him. His cock hardened, as if Ben was pumping iron into it instead of his own already magazine-worthy build.

Sprawled in bed, Ryan had been paying half-attention to some late-night comedy host, unable to muster a single chuckle. Against his better judgment, he muted the TV, then dropped the remote. It bounced, utterly forgotten, on the mattress. He glanced at the screen of the baby monitor on his nightstand to double-check that Ben's eight-year-old niece Julie was knocked out in her room at the other end of the second floor in the better-days Victorian they rented, as she had been for hours. If one of her periodic nightmares roused her, he'd know long before she ventured this way.

Clank. Huff. Clank. Huff.

Ben now had his full attention.

Nothing new about that, though the other man would probably grimace—or maybe deck him—if he could read Ryan's thoughts.

From where he leaned his shoulders against his padded leather headboard, Ryan could make out the curve of sweaty muscles in the spare bedroom directly across the hall. A sheen highlighted them in the mirror propped against the wall of their makeshift gym. They flexed and bunched as Ben did about a million reps with his fully loaded weights. In between sets he rotated some CrossFit shit, pulling himself up on whatever handy contraption he could find, inadvertently flaunting his spectacular body and the amazing things it was capable of doing.

There was a reason Ryan swore his room had the best view in their shared apartment. Fascinated, he could hardly stand to blink.

Though he had plenty of ideas about more enjoyable ab exercises Ben could try, Ryan knew better than to suggest them. Instead, he settled for taking enough mental snapshots to get him through another lonely night.

As he had in the past, enough times to diagnose his Ben-infatuation for what it really was—obsession—Ryan spread his legs. His fingers unfurled from the fist they'd unconsciously made as they mustered weak resistance to the inevitable. Then they wandered toward the growing bulge in his cotton shorts as if they had a will of their own. Ignoring the diminishing protests of his mind, which called him a perv for stealth-jacking to the sight of his unsuspecting roommate's glory, he slipped his hand beneath his waistband and cupped his hard-on.

Despite his best attempt to remain silent, he couldn't repress a soft gasp at the first contact of his hand on his cock. In his mind, he imagined Ben commanding him to be silent. He would do anything to please the other guy, especially if Ben was the one in control of Ryan's pleasure.

He allowed his thoughts to wander, only for a moment, to the times they'd spent in captivity together. Of course the entire situation had been fucked up beyond belief. Chock full of danger, extreme emotions, and a very unhealthy heaping of terror. But he'd thought some of the ecstasy they'd indulged in had been real rather than forced.

The times they'd served Mistress Lily in tandem sprang to the front of his memory.

His dick twitched and thickened in his trembling grasp.

Lost in his remembrance, Ryan wasn't sure if the hesitation he'd imagined in the steady rhythm of Ben's workout was real. Had he heard? Was he affected? Had he ever truly been?

Ryan paused and grew still, though he knew the shadowed interior of his private space would make it nearly impossible for his roommate to discern what was happening inside.

Disaster averted. Ben kept on lifting, as if his cut frame wasn't already irresistible.

It was foolish to think anything had changed between them, anyway.

Hell, he was lucky the other guy hadn't kicked his ass or tossed him into the street with all his shit by now. It wasn't as if he bothered to hide his unrequited lust.

Ryan gritted his teeth and worked his temporarily wilted shaft back to full hardness, refusing to let his doubts or regrets steal what crumbs of relief he could scavenge. It might have been wrong, but he didn't care. If he didn't find something to soothe the anxiety shaking him to the core soon, he might not survive.

Sure, it sounded melodramatic, especially considering the true jeopardy they had endured. Others hadn't been lucky enough to escape and go on to pout over an unreciprocated crush—Ben's sister April included. Ryan prided himself on the fact that despite his sexual preferences as a submissive bisexual man, he hadn't depended on anyone to make it this far in life. To thrive against all odds. To do what had needed to be done in those dark moments he refused to dwell on. Lately, though, the foundation of his confidence had developed a network of widening cracks.

Not the least of which was due to the man across the hall and what felt like one hell of a rejection, even if it had never been voiced aloud.

Ryan groaned, then lifted his head and dropped it onto his pillow a few times in a lame attempt to smash thoughts of anything except Ben's utter hotness from his cluttered mind. If he couldn't even focus on that long enough to rub one out, he was definitely in trouble.

He relied on his training, enabling his psyche to play more pleasant tricks.

After drawing in a series of deep breaths, he locked away his negative thoughts. Compartmentalization had ensured that even in captivity he'd been able to perform on demand. That skill had saved others who weren't so...let's say, willing, from being violated in those dungeons. More than once, he'd gladly served men high on a vicious sexual stimulant—Sex Offender—in Ben's place, protecting the other man from crossing his own boundaries. On their first night free, after downing enough alcohol to supply a frat house on a rowdy Friday night, Ben had tearfully admitted that Ryan had saved his soul.

So he didn't think his friend would mind returning the favor now.

Ryan stuffed reality into some far corner of his brain. In its place, he imagined himself bound to the sturdy metal frame of Ben's home gym. Not with silk ties or soft restraints. No, in his mind he pictured coarse rope. Tied tight around his wrists, it would chafe, leaving lingering red marks he could smile over for days to come. He'd press them and savor the burn, knowing Ben's show of possession hadn't been some dumbass fantasy.

Ben would stalk closer so that Ryan could smell the effort his best friend had made in honing his body into the most perfect version of his already phenomenal self that his striking Turkish genes would allow. Dark stubble would rasp over Ryan's face as Ben rubbed against him, snarling and biting his lip so that he was forced to peer deep into those nearly golden eyes, which had the power to mesmerize him.

"I figured I'd give you a close up view of the action, since you seemed so intent on spying on me," Ben would goad with a gloating half-smirk that proved he knew just how impossible it would be for Ryan to look away from a sight as magnificent as him.

His arrogance would heighten Ryan's need, making his cock throb in his shorts.

Though Ryan was tall, Ben was even more so. The crick in his neck from looking up would enhance his arousal. He shivered at the thought alone.

His bare toes curled into the sheets as he shifted, placing his ankles at the corners of his mattress, envisioning himself spread for his roommate's wicked pleasure. No matter what that might entail, he was game. Any way in which he could thrill the other man, and probably a couple extra Ben would never dare think of himself, would be just fine by him.

Maybe Ben would leave him there, strung up on the equipment as he did endless crunches, push-ups, and squats. Oh God, squats. Taunting him with that perfect ass.

Ryan swallowed hard.

Only when Ben was good and ready—plenty sweaty, too—would he return. With his trademark grin, which lifted the left half of his sinful lips slightly higher than the right, he'd ask, "If I'm the one doing all the work here, why are you breathing so damn hard?"

Because the hammering of Ryan's heart demanded extra oxygen, that's why. Even in his dreams, he didn't dare admit that aloud, though.

Instead, he'd yank at his bonds, impatient and riled.

If the tugs resulted in additional abrasions to his wrists, well, wasn't that a shame?

In real life, one of his hands choked his cock hard enough to edge into discomfort. The other reached down and wrapped around his wrist, squeezing until he could drown himself in his bondage fantasy. If only he could swipe the length of rope he kept in his nightstand. Even he wasn't bold enough to push that far with Ben so close. So he pressed harder. It would feel just like that.

Fuck, yes.

Immersed in his mental movie, he shifted, allowing his palms to roam so that one cupped his balls while the other began to stroke.

Just a little. It wouldn't take much to set him off with such vivid desires burning through his imagination, and he'd prefer to savor the waves of rapture, which finally reached into the cold spaces inside him and brought him alive.

When Ben began to towel off in the room next door, Ryan bit his lip to keep from moaning at the sight. What if he had free rein to run his hands over that taut, glowing skin?

To lick and bite and savor.

He'd certainly make the most of it.

Ryan remembered falling asleep next to Ben as members of the temporary harem Lily had constructed within Morselli's dungeon. She'd protected them, sheltered them, as much as possible. Which was why he'd read more into Ben's clean scent and the slightly awkward way they'd woken up cuddled together in their shared bed than had obviously been there.

Especially in those circumstances, Ryan couldn't fault his roommate for needing to form a simple human connection with anyone who happened to be handy. That was part of the reason he'd never called Ben out on mornings where he had pretended to sleep after he'd clearly awoken, as reluctant to break their connection as Ryan had been. Or maybe Ben had endured those blissful moments to give Ryan the only comfort he could in their captivity.

Shit. Shit. Shit.

Ryan shook his head, refocusing on the apparition of fictional post-workout Ben instead of the ghosts of dungeons past.

Right. Right. Tied to the home gym. Ogling Ben's package and wishing like hell he could taste it.

"Something interesting down there?" Ben would ask when he caught Ryan's gaze locked on the front of his jersey shorts. His fingers would spear into Ryan's slightly shaggy blond hair, gripping tight enough to have him panting all over again.

"May I—?" he'd ask, his throat too dry at the mere thought to finish his request.

"Are you asking for permission to speak, or permission to suck?" Ben cocked his head, then grinned, as if there were any true doubt.

"That." Ryan nodded, increasing the sting Ben's grip imparted to his scalp, too fervent to be more specific.

Ben chuckled, then cut him loose with the bone-handled pocketknife he always had handy. If the blade pricked Ryan's skin, he wouldn't complain one bit.

Without wasting a single second, Ryan would drop to his knees and paw at Ben's shorts, tugging them to the tops of his thighs. More than that was unnecessary for his purpose.

In his fantasy, he nuzzled Ben's heavy balls, licking them with the flat of his tongue a few times before swallowing his best friend's cock inch by inch. His fingers dug into Ben's ass, drawing him closer. So close Ryan choked, but he didn't give a fuck.

A hum of approval and the tightening of the glutes in his hand were reward enough for the minor inconvenience. Who needed air anyway, when he could have this?

What could be better?

As they sometimes did, his waking dream shifted. Shari appeared, perched on the balance ball in the corner. Their mutual friend radiated approval as she beamed at the two of them, witnessing the power of the raw energy surging between them. In her most prim voice, she would ask, "Have I ever mentioned how much it turns me on to watch a man sucking another man's dick?"

Oh, fuck.

Back in his bedroom, Ryan's hips began to rock, jabbing upward to meet his hand when it plunged toward his body. His cock jabbed through his fist, long and proud.

"Do you want me to fuck you while she watches?" Ben asked. "Show her how you take me so deep inside your tight ass? I bet she'll like that show even more."

"Yes. Yes, please." Ryan would have done a better job of begging if he could have sucked more oxygen into his lungs at the thought.

"Fine. But no coming yet." Ben reached down and pinched Ryan's nipple, making his cock pulse. "When I'm finished with you, you're going to take care of her. However she likes. And if you do a good job, maybe then we'll reward you, you hear?"

"Yes, thank you." He meant it sincerely. The chance to please these two would bring him as much joy and delight as he imparted, maybe more. In fact, the idea alone was enough to nudge him toward climax. He tried to slow down. To muster some self-control, but it was no use.

Ryan hovered on the edge, desperate for his daydream to continue. Refusing to go over until his balls ached from holding back. Until even rapture became a special brand of torture.

Only then did he allow himself to imagine the impossible, though the seductive thoughts tumbled through his brain in fast-forward.

Ben would mount him, face-to-face, so there couldn't be any mistaking the lust in his stare. For Ryan. Without apology.

That was Ryan's greatest desire.

Sure, Ben's big fat cock would feel amazing plowing into him with enough force to shake the home gym and clank various metal parts together in a furiously escalating tempo. The pressure of his dickhead on Ryan's prostate would be divine. The eventual liquid heat of his come filling Ryan's ass when he lost control would grant some affirmation of their compatibility both in and out of bed. But unflinching acceptance of their attraction—hell, their bond—despite the fact that Ben identified as straight(ish) and Ryan was most definitely not a woman...

Well, that was what he craved above all else.

"Ben..." he whisper-gasped into the night.

To his horror, a soft grunt came in response.

Ryan's eyes flew open, yet his hand didn't stop its furious shuttling along his length.

Flesh and blood Ben turned and stared into the mirror, indirectly meeting Ryan's gaze. He had to know it was a monster erection clutched in Ryan's fist. The motion of his masturbation was unmistakable.

The dominant flare in those molten eyes was irresistible. Close enough to Ryan's vision.

He surrendered. Shattered, pumping his release from so deep in his balls he'd swear they were in danger of flipping inside out.

He hoped his roommate could see every bit of the longing, desire, and pure need etched onto his face as he allowed his orgasm to overtake him, possessing every molecule of his being. Ryan grunted as the first blast of his thick come shot from his dick and decorated his chest.

Ben inched closer, as if drawn by the pull of so much naked arousal. He approached until his toes teetered on the threshold to Ryan's room.

ABOUT THE AUTHOR

Jayne Rylon is a *New York Times* and *USA Today* bestselling author. She received the 2011 RomanticTimes Reviewers' Choice Award for Best Indie Erotic Romance.

Her stories used to begin as daydreams in seemingly endless business meetings, but now she is a full-time author, who employs the skills she learned from her straight-laced corporate existence in the business of writing. She lives in Ohio with two cats and her husband, the infamous Mr. Rylon.

When she can escape her purple office, Jayne loves to travel the world, SCUBA dive, take pictures, avoid speeding tickets in her beloved Sky and—of course—read.

48199800R00174

Made in the USA
San Bernardino, CA
19 April 2017